AMULET BOOKS
NEW YORK

A NOVEL BY

A. G. HOWARD

UNT

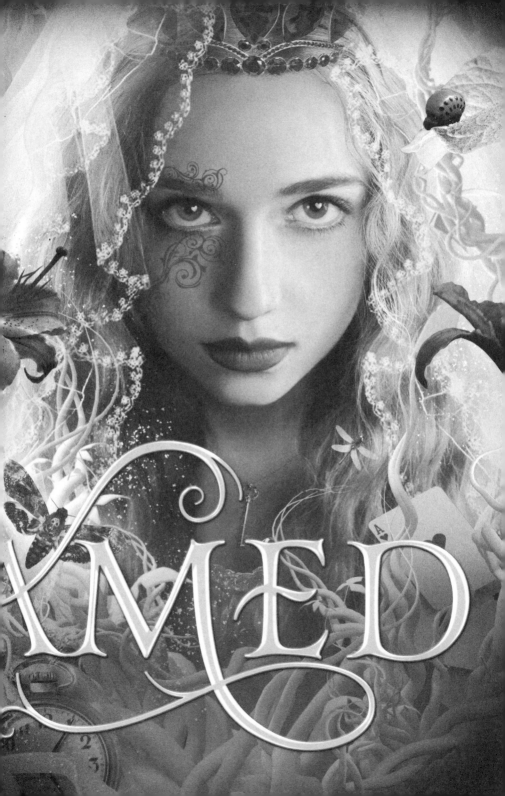

Cataloging-in-Publication Data has been applied for and may be obtained from the Library of Congress.

ISBN: 978-1-4197-1869-4

Printed and bound in U.S.A.
10 9 8 7 6 5 4 3 2 1

Amulet Books are available at special discounts when purchased in quantity for premiums and promotions as well as fundraising or educational use. Special editions can also be created to specification. For details, contact specialsales@abramsbooks.com or the address below.

ABRAMS
THE ART OF BOOKS SINCE 1949
115 West 18th Street
New York, NY 10011
www.abramsbooks.com

❊⋅⋅CONTENTS⋅⋅❊

THE BOY
IN THE WEB

LUNGE & PARRY

"If we're going to survive this, Alison, you have to go for the jugular. *No. Mercy.*"

Thomas's deep, commanding voice warms my ear as he helps me stand up, then molds my fingers around the sword's metal handle that had slipped from my gloved hand. A mixture of his sweat and the citrusy scent of his bath soap lingers in the air, muted by the perfume of flowers and greenery surrounding us.

I rub my hip where it still throbs from my fall, then resume my stance and stare across the bloodstained grass at our opponents: mine, with the beautiful, otherworldly glow to her skin ... Thomas's, with his muscled build and fearless green eyes. Their silver swords flash beneath the autumn sun and reflect light off of faces that give nothing away, until, in a sweep as slow as a storm cloud, curiosity crosses their features as they try to predict our strategy.

My heart pounds out a steady pulse of anticipation. I wipe some sweat from my brow. They're younger, faster—but Thomas and I have wisdom on our side, and an incomparable connection. We've been a team for twenty-two years. These amateurs have nothing on us.

Ignoring how hot and itchy my skin is beneath the layers of clothes, I coax my body to relax, yet hold position, sword raised and ready, before snapping my mask over my face.

My husband often offers cues, gestures that only I can decipher: a nod of the head for a parry, a squint of the eyes for a block. But I don't need his instructions this time. I know my opponent. I've watched her long enough to learn her strengths and weaknesses. She'll lunge at my left, and I'll defend with a parry of six. Unless this time she decides to mix it up.

As if thinking she's figured me out, she glares with piercing blue eyes and then smiles, overly confident, before dropping her mask into place. Her stance tightens and mine does the same, inviting her to make the first move.

With stealth and grace, she shifts her feet and thrusts, attacking on my right in a surprise tactic. I strike her blade with a beat to compromise her rhythm. She totters off balance and overcompensates, executing a messy parry. Her hasty reaction creates an opening at her chest.

Growling, I aim my sword's tip at her heart, feeling the burst as I puncture her white jacket. She drops her blade and grips her sternum. Her eyes grow round behind her mask. Blood spurts across the grass and spatters my white tennis shoes.

"Mom?" she mutters in shock, then folds to the ground.

I snap up my mask, shuck my gloves, and drop to my knees beside her, poking her ribs relentlessly. "Say it!" I shout. "Say I'm the queen!"

Jebediah and Thomas laugh from the sidelines as Alyssa giggles hysterically, rocking on her back like a turtle turned over on its shell, trying to catch her breath and escape my tickle torture. Her mask pops off in her efforts, revealing flushed cheeks.

"Say it!" I insist again.

"Never!" she screeches and captures my hands, wrestling me to the ground beside her.

Soon my own ribs ache from her relentless fingers and we're hugging and laughing so much tears stream from our eyes.

"All right." Thomas regains enough composure to call a ceasefire. "The elders won, fair and square."

"Foiled again," Alyssa quips, referencing our flexible practice swords. Her pun coaxes a deep chuckle out of Jebediah as he reaches down for her blood-smeared hand.

Thomas helps me up and I pat the wet, red streaks on my fencing jacket and pants, the stickiness clumping between my fingers.

My husband offers towels for us to clean the mess. I use mine to blot my face and brow.

"I still think the Halloween blood packets were overkill," Jenara says from her place on the porch swing where she and Corbin are waiting to challenge the winning team. They're sipping lemonade the same shade of pink as her hair. She wrinkles her nose. "That's a pretty gruesome scene."

"You're kidding, right?" Alyssa says with an eager grin, appraising the thousands of red splotches across our clothes and the lilies, honeysuckle, and silver licorice plants in the garden. "It's beautiful. Like any window dressing, it just needs to be shaped into something new."

The long, blond braid down her back swishes and sways as if coming alive. She uses her magic to lift the shiny droplets from the plants and flowers, then reanimates the spatters on our clothes to join them. The fake blood floats into the air in bead-size balls and hovers in place, melding together like raindrops on a windowpane until they've formed a virtual latticework—a shimmery red archway that looks like stained, spun glass. Alyssa grabs Jebediah's hand and pulls him to her. He grins, taking the lead as they dance beneath her makeshift gazebo. Their movements are graceful and synchronized, their bodies never once disrupting Alyssa's display.

Thomas tilts his head in a scolding gesture, although the pride in his expression would be impossible to miss. If not for the nine-foot-tall wooden fence he recently installed to protect us from prying eyes, he probably wouldn't be taking Alyssa's showmanship so lightly.

Then again, she's always had him wrapped around her finger.

Our daughter glances at him, beaming, more at peace and more comfortable in her own skin than I've ever seen her in all of her seventeen years.

As a result of her magical training with Morpheus in her dreams, she's becoming flawless in her execution—able to unleash her powers with just a thought. It's moments like this when I see it: the netherling queen simmering below the surface. A predisposition toward blood and chaos. How she thrives in flames and ravaging storms. How her magic can both inspire and tame pandemonium. How she finds beauty in the morbid and bizarre.

It's ironic. I tried for so long to hone those same qualities in myself, but my humanity was too strong to be swayed. I was never meant to be queen. I had the desire, but I didn't have the heart.

The dance ends, and with a flick of Alyssa's wrist, the droplets of blood fall in slow motion—like a macabre flutter of crimson snow—and nestle again on our clothes, the leaves, and the petals where they originated.

Jenara slurps down the rest of her lemonade, the ice in her cup rattling. "That's going to be one big mess to clean."

Alyssa shrugs and laughs. "Nothing that a bottle of bleach and a garden hose won't fix."

"Nope. I won't be using bleach on this masterpiece." Jenara holds out her arms to showcase the hot-pink fencing jacket covering her petite frame. She dyed it a few weeks ago and added delicate lace trim to the sleeves and neckline. Setting her cup of ice on the ground next to Corbin's foot, she slides off the swing. "If we're going to insist on blood and gore, I'm changing into my black one."

Corbin grabs her around the waist and pulls her back into his lap. "Aw, come on, punk princess. We'll take down the oldsters before you can even break a nail. Jeb and Al, they just don't have the right moves."

Jenara smirks. "Good point."

"Oh, ha!" In one smooth motion, Alyssa taps her toe against her fallen sword so it rises perpendicular from the ground and slaps the handle into her waiting palm. "Come over here and say that to my face, *Cor-bin-ara.*"

I exchange glances with my husband and laugh.

"Nice maneuver, skater girl." Jebediah grins, brandishing his foil. "Want to spar under the willow tree?" He lifts a brow.

"You won't last two seconds." She flashes a smile, her engagement ring sparkling in the light as she tosses her sword from one hand to the other in a single, smooth stroke.

"Oh, yeah?" he scoffs, then, without warning, scoops her up and tosses her over his shoulder. Her sword hits the ground with a clang and she giggles as he carries her to the tree and tumbles them both into the low-hanging leaves.

She could easily use her powers and break free. But that's the point. She doesn't want to break free of him. She never has. He's her human match, in every way.

She and I have discussed what her immortality means . . . how hard it's going to be when he's gone and she remains. She's assured me she can survive—even though her eyes grow distant when she imagines it, and her face clouds with torment at the thought. But I believe her devotion to Wonderland and Morpheus is strong enough to help her overcome that loss. And I know that when the day comes, her forever will be dazzling. Morpheus will cherish her. He'll treat her like royalty. He would even if she weren't a queen because he admires her bravery.

She's a warrior, and I'm the coward. My fear of losing Thomas overpowers any loyalty I once had for the nether-realm. I can't live without him for an eternity. For this reason, among many others, I'm glad my spirit doesn't harbor crown magic and I'm mortal still. Even if I outlive my husband, it won't be by very long. And I'm secure in that inevitability.

Watching Jeb and Alyssa wrestling and laughing prompts a smile of my own. They're so like Thomas and myself at that age—filled with hope. The difference is, they have a real chance at getting everything they've dreamed of, because there are no lies between them. Wonderland is an open book they've both read and lived. They've even brought Jenara and Corbin into the circle of trust.

Thomas and I didn't have the truth to bridge us, until recently. And I have my daughter to thank for giving us this second chance, and for giving me back my sanity. I close my eyes, listening. All I hear is the gurgling water in our fountain, and Jebediah and Alyssa's horseplay. No bugs chatting. No flowers whispering.

At my request, three months ago when Thomas, Alyssa, her fiancé, and I returned from our final sojourn to Wonderland, Alyssa used her royal powers to put a stop to the endless nattering in my ears, and she's made sure that her descendants will hear only silence. She alone has a direct line to the insects and plants now. Just as she's the only one who still makes regular visits to the nether-realm in her dreams.

Although I still have my wing buds and eye markings, my netherling attributes will make an appearance only if I allow it. So for the first time since I was sixteen, I feel normal. And for the first time since I was twelve, I remember silence.

I thought I might miss the tiny whispering voices that carried me through my adolescence, that became my confidants when no one else would listen, but I don't need them as a crutch anymore. I have a family now, and a husband who knows and shares my Wonderland history.

I'll never be alone again.

My eyes open as I feel Thomas's strong fingers weave through mine as if he's reading my thoughts. Nothing anchors me like the feel of his hand in mine.

"You kids have fun," he says. "We're calling it a day." He turns his coffee-rich brown eyes on me and kisses my knuckles, prompting a thrill that races all the way from my arm to my heart. "I promised my blushing bride I'd take her out for our twentieth anniversary. We'll pick up again tomorrow." He squints toward Corbin and Jenara. "Unless you two are ready to forfeit now. We all know how this is going to end. Age and wisdom always trump youth and reckless-ness." His teasing Elvis sneer is met with guffaws and huffs by the younger set.

"*As if*, Mr. G." Jenara snorts. "Tomorrow . . . same time, same place. I'll be the one in the black fencing gear. And remember: The loser has to wear a short, frilly dress in public. Prepare for the makeover of your life."

❈ · I · ❈

While Thomas showers, I study myself in the mirror over the bathroom sink. A mundane task to most people, but one I had avoided since the day I first met my husband.

At last, after all these years, I don't have to hide from mirrors anymore. I no longer have to worry about seeing Morpheus's judgmental frown behind me in my reflection.

My dress is simple and elegant: ivory lace with a low V-back and cap sleeves. A strip of contrasting lace—the color of a cappuc-cino—slims my waist and complements the sun-kissed glow of my freshly scrubbed skin. The bodice hugs my breasts and the skirt my hips—the hem swishing at midcalf. Alyssa and Jenara helped me pick it out at the thrift store, swearing it was sexy enough to make Thomas's eyes bug out. I'm eager to test that theory.

We were apart, needlessly, for too long. Maybe that's why he makes me feel like a young girl in love, because each moment spent together is like learning everything—his sweet words, his kisses, his laughter, and his goodness—anew.

With a sweep of rouge at my cheeks and a blot of burgundy on my lips, I'm ready. Energy and vitality pulse through me and trigger little sparks of magic beneath my skin. My shoulder-length platinum hair twines seductively around my face, so I begin the task of pinning it up in ringlets at the base of my neck with glittery, jeweled clips to imprison it.

A woman about to go on a date with her husband of twenty years . . . this is what I see. But there was a time when it wasn't just me looking back, when any reflective surface would conjure the doorway to a mad and chaotic Wonderland that I once craved to rule. I saved the boy in the web from that world, then did my best to turn my back on it by breaking every mirror in sight.

It was wrong to abandon it all without an explanation. I can see that now.

I reneged on my responsibility, on a deal with the devil himself. So Morpheus found another way to make me pay by crashing into my daughter's dreams—using me as an unwitting conduit. He spent time with her every night for the first five years of her life, making himself young—to the point he became a child in both form and mind—so he could be her playmate and win her trust and affection. When I found out, I tried to counter his mental attack with a physical parry, to protect her by doing the only thing I could: *leave.*

I blink, and for an instant, my lacy dress in the mirror transforms into the straitjacket that became my weapon of choice.

How could I have thought there wouldn't be consequences for hiding away in the asylum? I had hoped he'd find another sparring partner . . . another Liddell to exploit, one who would save his spirit from his curse of spending eternity trapped in Sister Two's lair. To escape his fate, he had to fulfill Red's Deathspeak by crowning a queen of her lineage with the ruby tiara while Red possessed her body. I mistakenly assumed, when I failed him, he would move on and find another victim in a distant relative, out of respect for my choice.

But there was a chink in my armor, and my adversary broke through. I should've seen it coming. For as long as I've known Morpheus, he has never moved on. Not when his goal is in sight. He's the most brilliant and patient strategist I've ever encountered.

The steam from Thomas's shower blurs my reflection, and behind the fog I see myself as I was when I first discovered Morpheus's plans for Alyssa: that naive young mother, terrified for her toddler's future. Guilt-stricken for putting her child in danger in the first place. My little girl was never meant to be my substitute, but through my betrayal, that's exactly what she became.

I chose not to tell Alyssa about my choices, about the repercussions, because I thought I had managed to spare her. But all that time in the asylum away from my husband and child didn't matter. Neither did the vow Morpheus made not to contact Alyssa again. Because he'd already planted memories of their moments together in her mind, counting on her inherited Liddell curiosity to lure her into seeking him out. At the age of sixteen, she found the rabbit hole on her own, just as he planned.

My hand jerks involuntarily at the memory, and I pull a strand of hair too tight. It pinches my scalp, causing me to wince. Repositioning the curl, I pin it in place.

Morpheus tricked my daughter into winning the crown I once craved and had come to despise. He saved himself in the process. It was a responsibility Alyssa hadn't asked for, although she came to accept and even embrace it. But still . . . he'd lured her into becoming queen without offering her all the facts.

The one thing that gives me satisfaction is that he didn't go unscathed. He paid a price. One he never anticipated.

While "growing up" with Alyssa in her childhood dreams, while watching her meet every challenge he laid at her feet as a young woman in Wonderland, Morpheus—the solitary and selfish fae once incapable of love—fell head over heels for her. I wouldn't have believed it, had I not seen it myself. He proved the depth of his devotion when he gave up his chance to have her at his side in the nether-realm. When he opted instead to wait, so the human half of her heart could heal until she'd be strong enough to reign over the Red kingdom eternally.

Because of this sacrifice, I'm starting to suspect that maybe he's not the devil after all. That maybe, after all these years, I'm seeing a side to him bordering on vulnerable and caring. A side he kept locked away from me, other than a glimpse or two I might've forgotten over the years.

Still, I'm not ready to forgive him for using my daughter quite yet. Because to do that, I'd have to forgive myself for making her responsible for my messes to begin with. And as much as Thomas wants me to . . . I'm not sure I can.

Alyssa's life will always be split down the middle because of me. She's taken it in stride. No one could see her with her netherling subjects and deny that she was meant to be their queen. She loves the very world that I came to hate.

And because I love my daughter, somehow I have to learn to embrace that world again. Otherwise, I can never move past letting

Morpheus and all of Wonderland's lunacy into our lives in the first place.

My filmy reflection reels me back into the here and now. I spritz my favorite perfume across my collarbone and wrists—swimming in notes of passion fruit and blood orange—then blot my nose with powder, stepping out of the bathroom before the steam from Thomas's shower can smear my makeup.

I slip pearl earrings and a matching necklace and bracelet into place, then sit on the bed's edge and wiggle my toes, concentrating on our closed bedroom door. The sounds of cabinet doors and clanging pans drift in from the other side. The kids are in the kitchen, putting something together for dinner. I debate helping them while I wait for Thomas, but I'm not ready to force my feet into the pair of pewter heels on the floor next to me. The carpet feels too nice . . . plush and luxurious. Instead, I lie back on the fluffy comforter, spread out my arms, and close my eyes, relaxing muscles that still ache from our bout of fencing earlier.

Attuned to the rhythmic patter of water against the shower door, I allow myself to fall back into another day and hour, when I was thirteen, staring out at a rain-drenched world. When I embraced the nether-call during one of the bleakest and loneliest times of my life.

It was the day Morpheus came to me and offered power and vengeance in the palm of his manipulative hand. The day that would change who I was going to be, forever.

BOXED IN

Twenty-six years earlier . . .

Rain pounded the empty refrigerator box atop my head. I had turned it on its side and climbed in just minutes before the storm hit. The Dumpster beside me reeked of dead fish and decaying fruit, overpowering the fresh scents of wet asphalt and dirt. Puddles filled the uneven gravel street and water gushed out of the gutters that hung from the back of my eight-story apartment building on the other side of the alley.

A damp gust of wind blustered through my makeshift shelter. I hunkered down against the box's back, tucking my canvas tote bag behind my neck like a pillow and holding the pages of *Alice's Adventures in Wonderland* so I wouldn't lose my place. A few weeks before, I'd crossed out *"Alice's"* in the title and replaced it with *"Alison's."* It was partly to make sure everyone knew the book belonged to me. But there was more . . . a part of me wished I could live those same adventures . . . that I could somehow be Alice and escape into a rabbit hole where a new world awaited—one where maybe someone as peculiar and mismatched as me might find a fit. A place to belong.

I'd never been good at understanding other people. Mostly because I moved around so much. At least that's what I told myself. It had nothing to do with how hard it was to trust people, or my inability to relate to them on a daily basis.

Reading offered me friends enough, and my Lewis Carroll books were my favorite, being one of the few things my mother had left behind when she died right after giving birth to me. The stories made me feel closer to her, even though I never knew her. Maybe because I secretly understood how real the Wonderland tales were to her heart, considering our distant relation to the London Liddells.

Once, when I was staying at an orphanage while waiting for a new foster family, I broke into the office and read my records. It was the only way I could find out about my background. Alice Liddell, the real-life girl who inspired Carroll's fictional tales, had a son who was involved with a woman before he went off to war and died on the battlefield. His lover ended up pregnant and came to America to raise their illegitimate child. That boy grew up and had a daughter: my mother, Alicia.

Somehow, all of this made my mom go crazy. My records stated she spent time in an asylum as a teenager after painting Wonderland characters on every wall of her home and insisting they talked to her in dreams. The day I was born, she jumped out of her second-story hospital room window to test the "fairy wings" the voices told her she had. She landed in a rosebush and broke her neck.

The doctor claimed she committed suicide—postpartum depression and grief over losing my dad months earlier in a factory accident. Whatever it was, one thing was never explained . . . the dime-size welts on her shoulder blades, too big and perfectly spaced to have been caused by getting pricked by thorns.

My opinion? She did have wings. Ones that never sprouted. If it made me crazy like her to think that, I could live with it. Because if I was off my rocker, it meant we had a bond. Something in common. As long as no one else ever knew.

My mother had also left behind a Polaroid camera—the kind that spits out completed pictures at the push of a button. I'd known how to use it since the age of five.

I snuggled deeper into the nest of photographs I'd dumped from my tote. It was something I'd become good at: hiding behind trees on playgrounds or parked cars at the mall to capture stolen moments of other people's families and friends. I liked to surround myself with them—to cushion me from the absence of my own.

I lifted my denim jacket's cuff to scan my watch. Only ten more minutes and school would be out. Then I could go to my apartment and pretend I'd been where I was supposed to be all day. I'd shown up at the beginning of my last class, long enough to be counted present, before "taking a trip to the bathroom" and never returning. With any luck, Mrs. Bunsby, my latest foster caregiver, would never know I'd skipped. I'd only been living with her for a month. I didn't want to upset her and get thrown away again. Other than her being a forty-something-year-old vegetarian widow, she was the best keeper I'd had since I could remember.

I peered up at the sixth floor of the building. Our apartment was the farthest on the left, where the fire escape had rusted through and left a jagged black skeleton hanging askew and useless. I was aces at climbing, and had tried a few weeks ago to descend the railing and sneak out at night for a session with my camera. I had slipped and fallen.

Six stories was a long drop. I should've died, or at least broken multiple bones. But I lapsed into a dream state on the way down and somehow, when I woke up, didn't have a bruise on me anywhere. I didn't even ache. All I had was a strange memory of giant, flapping black wings.

Sorting through my pictures, I found one at the bottom of the pile: a sparrow-size moth with a blue body and black wings, splayed on a flower between a slant of sun and shade. I remember the day I saw it in the park, as if it was sitting between two worlds. I took the shot not only for the symbolism, but because I'd seen the bug before. My mother had sketched one that looked just like it on a slip of paper that she kept in her Alice books. The strangest thing was she'd also made a rough sketch of Alice from the Wonderland illustrations right next to it. Somehow—in her mind—they were connected. I'd lost the drawing during one of my many moves. So when I saw that identical moth, live and in person, I had to immortalize it with my camera.

Sighing, I tucked the picture into my *Alice* book to hold my spot. That shot was Mrs. Bunsby's favorite. She said I had a gift, that if I kept improving, she would give me her late husband's camera—a Yashica 44—along with his books on developing your own film.

She was one of the few adults who'd ever believed in me without being judgmental. But if Mrs. Bunsby knew that I thought this very moth had played a role in my mother's Wonderland fantasies, she would think my imagination was too vivid, like my teachers and caregivers always said. I'd done research at the library. Moths have a life span of months, certainly not decades.

Thinking about it even kind of gave *me* the creeps. But it also made me feel special, like my mom and I mattered to someone somewhere—enough to warrant watching. It wasn't the first time I'd felt like bugs and plants were reaching out to me in a way they didn't to other people. I'd been hearing their voices ever since I hit puberty close to my twelfth birthday a year ago. Still, I knew better than to share that tidbit with anyone for risk of ending up in a psych ward like my mom.

My stomach growled. I shoved a fist beneath my ribs. Mrs. Bunsby would be serving pickled beet and tofu casserole tonight. Just the thought made my taste buds want to run for cover. I had to stretch out my snack as long as possible. The package of peanut butter crackers I'd saved from lunch lay open next to me. I slid one out and munched on it. Crumbs gathered on the illustration of Alice fleeing from some card guards in hopes of keeping her head, and I shook the cracker remnants off so they fell on my thigh.

A roach skittered out from under one of the box's flaps and climbed onto my pants to gobble up the residue without so much as a please or thank-you. In my opinion, they were the rudest of all the insects. I'd had conversations with houseflies and mealworm beetles that were civil and interesting. But roaches never had much to say, other than to grumble about the lack of trash piles and dirt now that humans populated their world, claiming garbage bags and vacuum cleaners were the bane of their existence.

I waved my hand, shooing the bug away. It skittered back into the folds of the box and scolded my bad manners.

"I'm trying to help you, moron. You want to get squished?" I gathered up my canvas tote, shoving my pictures and books inside, then bounded into the storm, making a run for the skinny space between my apartment building and the run-down barbershop next door.

The only way in was from the front. Our landlord, Wally Harcus, kept the back door to the building locked for "safety reasons." Or so he claimed. He just wanted to gawk at all the single moms and young girls who lived in his low-rent building. His door was the first one down the hall from the entrance, meaning he had the ideal situation from any perv's perspective.

Shards of rain, laced with ice, pelted me. The denim of my jacket and jeans absorbed every droplet, and I felt ten pounds heavier and twenty degrees colder by the time I pushed inside the building.

My hands were too wet to hold on to the knob, and the door slammed shut. I cringed at the sound.

I'd barely skirted by Wally's room when his door flung open. I backed slowly down the hall toward the stairway, keeping him in my sights.

His sweaty face appeared first, then the rest of him, rolls of flab barely contained within a tight blue T-shirt and grease-stained khaki pants. I could smell his distinctive odor even with my eyes— the scent of rotting cabbage and meat. Pools of perspiration formed uneven circles beneath his armpits, darkening the blue to navy.

He'd always reminded me of a walrus—bald head, deep folds of skin over his brow, double chin, and a handlebar mustache that looked like a half-chewed kielbasa dangling over his sausage-fat lips. The wheezes and clicking sounds he emitted with each breath only added to the illusion of a beached sea mammal.

"Hey there, Alison. Get a little wet, did ya?" His gaze glittered—watery and dark like liquid charcoal—as he took a bite of an overripe apricot. The juices drizzled down his chin and he offered a sleazy smirk. His incisors—two sizes too big for his mouth—hung low like underdeveloped ivory tusks.

My stomach twisted with disgust as he stepped full into the hallway and made an obvious appraisal of my chest where my shirt clung to me. He looked famished, as if he wanted to gobble me up. I snapped my jacket closed and shoved ringlets of dripping blond hair off my face.

"I've got some hot chocolate on the stove. Wanna cup?" he asked.

I'd caught him staring plenty of times, but he'd never had the guts to ask me in. I swallowed and held tighter to my bag's straps. "Nah. Mrs. Bunsby's waiting."

"Nope, she's not. Had to make a run to the grocery store." He flashed a note at me.

I only had time to see a tiny triangle torn from the top, right above the words *I'll be back in an hour*, before he shoved it into his pocket.

"In fact," Wally wheezed, "she told me to keep you company. Says you're too young to be on your own and stay out of trouble. I can come to your room instead, if ya like." He jangled the keys that hung on one of his belt loops and smirked bigger.

Idiot.

I hated him, and hated myself more for being scared. I'd faced monsters like him before. Two foster families ago, I had a fourteen-year-old foster brother who trapped me in the basement and stuck his tongue down my throat while his hands found their way up my shirt. Yet I was the one who got sent back to the children's home for biting off the tip of his tongue and breaking his thumb. *I* was the one with issues.

Unfortunately for me, Wally Harcus wouldn't be as easy to fend off as a skinny teenage boy.

The bottom step hit the back of my heels, stalling me. It was fight or flight. One thing I knew: Mrs. Bunsby wouldn't have asked the walrus to keep me company. He probably saw her leave and decided it was the perfect chance to make a move. So there he stood between me and the only way out. And even if I locked myself inside our apartment, he had the keys to get in.

I could prop something against the door and buy myself time to clamber down the broken fire escape. I'd probably fall to my death, but that had to be better than the alternative.

I spun around and hightailed it up the four flights of stairs. The sound of his footsteps followed, slow and plodding. He was in no hurry. Everyone minded their own business here. No one would stop him, which made the chase about as challenging as a fly already stuck in a spider's web.

Tears blurred my vision as I made it to our door. A piece of Scotch tape dangled the missing puzzle piece from Mrs. Bunsby's note where she'd stuck it next to the peephole. Wally had taken the letter she left for me.

Gulping back bile, I struggled to fit my key in the lock. Adrenaline used my heart like a punching bag, slamming it until it quivered uncontrollably in my chest. I'd just managed to get inside, shut the door, and lock it when Wally cleared the final step onto our floor.

Straining every muscle, I wedged Mrs. Bunsby's favorite wing-backed chair into place under the knob and raced for my bedroom, dropping my bag just inside the threshold after I shut myself in.

The overcast afternoon hazed the light to a gray fog, and with my heavy curtains covering the window, shadows cloaked the room and painted eerie shapes along the bare walls.

Keys jangled outside our apartment, loud enough I could hear them through my closed door. Sobbing, I stumbled over to the window, shoved the curtains apart, and opened the pane. A rain-drenched gust caught my hair and slapped it around my face. Tears burned trails down my cheeks as I flung one leg over the sill, about to throw myself out.

"Tsk, tsk. Now, that would be a tragic waste." A deep cockney accent froze me in place there, straddling life and death. "Surely your existence is worth more than that oily rat's."

I snapped my head toward the voice. In the left corner of my room, the shadows moved and took on the indistinct silhouette of a man.

A gasp broke through my lips. "Wh-who's there?"

"Introductions aren't necessary amongst friends." My intruder leaned into the dim light, revealing a face both beautiful and terrifying. He wasn't human. No, he was far too perfect and mystical for that. Markings, resembling tattoos, flashed with jeweled colors beneath his dark, fathomless eyes. His blue hair swayed, out of sync with the wind gushing through my window. "I believe I've merited the title of friend, don't you? Considering the last time you almost cracked your skull clambering around on that fire escape." Giant wings splayed out from behind his shoulders, glistening like black satin in the grayish light.

Adrift somewhere between terror, disbelief, and hope, I eased my leg back into my room and leaned against the juncture of the window frame and the wall. "You . . . you were the one. You saved me."

He smoothed the wrinkles from some red gloves on his hands. "Not quite, Alison. You saved yourself by daring to defy the natural laws in the first place. The fact that you even tried to make that climb merited a second chance at life, yes? Courage paired with folly becomes abandon, which is an honorable trait where I'm from, and should always be rewarded."

I squinted at him. "You were rewarding me for my folly?"

He held a top hat in front of him and stroked it as if it were a cat. "Your *abandon*." A deep chuckle rumbled in his chest. "You're an odd duck, aren't you? You haven't balked at me yet, nor have you questioned if I'm real. Or even how I know your name. It doesn't matter to you one way or the other, does it?"

I clenched my hands into fists at my sides. "It doesn't matter if I'm crazy, as long the madness helps me survive."

He raised an eyebrow, obviously pleased and surprised by my answer. "Ah, spoken like a true netherling. Madness, like any other facet of irrationality, can be used as a tool and a weapon, in the right hands."

I didn't have the chance to ask what a netherling was because in the other room, the wing-backed chair's wooden feet scraped across the tile floor and clawed through my nerves like talons. Wally was in the apartment.

My throat dried. I glanced outside at the slippery rails, then back toward the man with wings, now standing in full view next to my door. He was tall and graceful, around the age of nineteen or twenty, and dressed in lace and velvet, like a gentleman from another time and place.

"Are you . . . are you my guardian angel?" I'd heard of such creatures but had never believed they might be real. Yet in that moment, I was willing to believe anything if it would save me from my landlord or a broken neck.

My visitor flashed his teeth in a stunning smile that transformed his face to the devil's playground—malice concealed within a veneer of lovely persuasion. "I'm the furthest thing from an angel, little ducky. But I *am* here to watch you dole out some righteous retribution upon a sinner most foul." He placed the top hat on his head. A string of dead moths trembled at the brim in morbid tribute to the gusts fluttering my curtains. "Now, let's have us a bit of fun with old Wally, aye?"

THE LONG LEG OF
THE LAW

Wally the Walrus's footsteps scuffled toward my door.

"You won't let him in, right?" I asked the demon . . . angel . . . savior . . . whatever. He stood still as a statue, the gems on his face blinking through different shades of gold. You're going to help me like last time?" My pulse pounded hard in my neck, and my vocal cords shuddered like a snare drum.

The creature's wings spanned wide. "Oh, no, little ducky. You're going to help yourself. After all, you're the one with a direct line to the most ancient and heavily populated inhabitants on earth. They're adept at more than conversation, Alison. They have skills. All you need do is ask for a hand." He gestured toward a daddy longlegs creeping across the wall behind him, casting a spindly shadow on the white plaster. "Or eight feet. Whatever fits the bill."

Before I could make sense of his riddle, my mystical guest vanished in a poof of sparkling blue dust, only to be replaced by a bird-size moth that dove back into the shadows.

The moth from my picture . . . from Mom's sketch.

My gaze fell to the Polaroids that had spewed out from the opening of my tote bag. Before I could focus on them, the door crashed open, sweeping a pathway through the stolen memories.

My stomach turned as Wally stepped in. Glistening apricot pulp was tangled in his mustache. He used the back of his pudgy hand to swipe it off and almost tripped over my *Alice's Adventures in Wonderland* book.

He picked it up and snorted. "*Alison's* adventures in Wonderland? What's wrong with you, girl? Are you crazy, or just stupid?" The moth picture slipped out of the book as he shook it. He watched it drift to the floor. "Wait, I've seen that bug. I was tryin' to get it out of the building earlier. It's what led me to your door—" Wally stopped himself, as if he'd said too much. "Come away from that window. That ain't no rabbit hole. You're gonna trip and I'll have to scrape your scrawny ass up off the pavement."

I clenched my jaw, unmoving.

He tossed the book down. "Look, I can make you sigh, or I can make you cry. But either way this is gonna happen."

My attention flickered from his leering gaze to the tiny space of wall over the door. Behind him and the parade of spiders skittering free from a hole in the doorframe covering the wall and ceiling. There had to be thirty daddy longlegs now, and still more were pushing through. Had the storm driven them out?

Ask for a hand, or eight feet . . .

Maybe I was hallucinating. Maybe I had finally teetered over the edge like my mom. But whatever was happening, I had to use it to my advantage. I couldn't move, and I'd missed my chance to dive to my death.

"Help me," I pleaded—not sure exactly what I meant or to whom I was talking.

"Oh, I'm gonna help you." In a matter of seconds Wally had me pinned to the wall with his clammy palm at my neck. I gripped his wrist with both hands and dug my nails in hard. He laughed, his sour-fruit breath hot on my face. "Yeah, I'm gonna help you real good. See, I'm the white rabbit, and I'm takin' you on an adventure you'll never forget, *Alice*."

He lifted me by my neck until only my toes touched the floor. The pressure constricted my throat, and black fuzz began swimming in my gaze's periphery. I kicked at him, but he sidestepped my feet and, with his free hand, started to work at my belt buckle.

My abdominal muscles clenched in revulsion. The dark fuzz grew, but not from lack of oxygen. I turned my eyes and saw a sweep of daddy longlegs along the walls and ceiling—hundreds of them.

"Help me *now*," I commanded this time. My only hope was to drive Wally out of this apartment and back down the stairs on an avalanche of arachnids.

Their response was instantaneous and violent. Wally yelped and dropped me to the floor as the swarm began to clamber over him, creeping up his shoes, then along his legs. I moved away from the window and gasped for air as the insects continued their march, overtaking his chest. His horrified screams were drowned out by the spiders' angry whispers as he swatted at them. More arachnids came to replace the ones that fell. They found their way to Wally's neck and face, then filled his gaping mouth, muffling his bloodcurdling cries. He clutched at his throat, his bare arms covered with sleeves of spindly legs and throbbing thoraxes.

His nose and eyes disappeared under the ever-growing infestation. He lost his footing, and tried to catch himself against the wall, but his aim was off. He fell through the opened window, choking on the way down.

Numb, I backed up to my bedroom door, gagging when I heard the sick, heavy splat of his body on the wet asphalt.

Sudden movement in the left corner of the room distracted me. The moth fluttered out from the shadows, then landed on the windowsill, observing the mess below. A rush of nausea burned my gut.

"It was an accident," I whimpered to the insect, as if he was my confessor. "I—I didn't mean for it to happen!"

"Oh, but I did." That cockney accent stirred inside my head. The voice belonged to both the moth and the man. Somehow, they were one and the same, and somehow they were also tied to the Wonderland tales. My mom had figured that out. Which meant he'd been watching us for years. Not only that, he had led Wally to my apartment earlier. It was his fault the landlord found Mrs. Bunsby's note before I did. This whole thing had been a setup.

I couldn't speak, dragged into a vortex of confusion, shock, and regret.

"Do not concern yourself with that drowned rat, Alison," the British voice scolded me in my mind. *"There are countless young girls he*

damaged. It was up to you to set things to rights. Imbalance brings balance. Chaos is the great equalizer. But there will be repercussions. You'll ne'er belong here now. It's better that way. You are meant for so much more than this paltry world has to offer." The moth flapped over to me, hovering in front of my face. *"Take things into your own hands. Power is the only path to happiness, and I can help you acquire it. My name is Morpheus. Find a looking glass and call on me when you are ready to claim your destiny."*

With that, the huge bug turned and flew out the window.

"Wait!" I shouted. Tears scalding my lashes, I stumbled over to the sill and gazed down. Two teen boys on bicycles stared up at me from beside Wally's corpse. Just moments ago the man had been overpowering me . . . now he looked like a broken doll whose arms and legs had been twisted in unnatural poses until they'd popped out of their sockets. The rain puddles beside him were tinged red with the blood seeping from the back of his skull.

Dogs barked and people screamed as more spectators emerged from our apartment building. Slowly, each one turned to my window. Several pointed at me; some shook their heads.

I wanted to run but couldn't release my white-knuckled grip on the sill. The spiders were gone, having slipped within the thousands of hiding places accessible only to insects, leaving me to wish I was their size, so I could disappear and never have to face the accusations and questions about to come my way.

❧ · I · ☙

Morpheus was right. I didn't belong anywhere after that. And I suspected that's why he arranged for Wally to find that note and prey on me in the first place.

Child welfare services accused Mrs. Bunsby of negligence, stating someone with my "violent tendencies" shouldn't have been left to my own devices while she ran errands. They also pointed out that I'd been skipping classes, which only made her look more inept. They took me out of her care that very evening.

While the police and my child care advocates interviewed Mrs. Bunsby in the living room, I packed up my sparse belongings, trying to avoid looking at the window. Mrs. Bunsby had left a brown grocery sack on the bed. Funny, how she thought she'd failed me. I could see it reflected in her teary hazel eyes when she came home to the mess I'd made. Too bad I couldn't tell her the truth. That she wasn't to blame for me being an accomplice to murder . . . that the responsibility fell on Wally himself, along with a mystical moth and a swarm of daddy longlegs.

Inside the grocery sack, she'd tucked her husband's camera, film, and a book on picture developing. There was also a packet of peanut butter crackers, an apple, and a bottle of water. My heart twisted tight, because I knew I could've been happy with her, if only Morpheus hadn't had other plans for me. But as much as my chest hurt, I refused to cry. I was done crying.

And I would never be a victim again.

As I left the apartment, Mrs. Bunsby promised to try to visit sometime. I knew better.

A month passed, filled with psych evaluations and doctor exams, to make sure I wasn't traumatized. Hard as they tried, the doctors couldn't pin any crazy on me, because I refused to give details about the event. All I said was that the landlord had tried to force himself on me, we wrestled, and he fell out the window. Simple as that.

When the psychiatrist held up the cards for the inkblot tests, I never confessed what each one really looked like. I didn't tell them that I saw rabbit holes, hookah-smoking caterpillars, little girls in aprons with knives in their hands, winged men, sparrow-size moths, or armies of spiders. I also never let anyone catch me talking to the flowers and bugs that kept me company. I knew how to *appear* sane.

I did such a great job, I was released from any more evaluations after only six weeks. The problem was child care services wouldn't be able to place me with a foster family considering all the baggage I carried. So the children's home became my permanent residence.

Or so they thought. I didn't intend to stay. I planned to go some-place where their laws and watchful eyes could never find me again. And I knew just who would aid me on my escape.

All those weeks in therapy, I'd procrastinated reaching out to Morpheus. I needed that time to think things through. And I'd come to three realizations. One, my family really was somehow tied to the Lewis Carroll tales, which meant Wonderland had to exist on some level. Two, Morpheus was also tied to Wonderland, and he needed me for something, because no one helps anyone without wanting a favor in return. And three, before I was going to help him, he was going to give me a couple of things: a way out of the children's home, and answers to all my questions.

Solitude was hard to come by. The grayish brick building had multiple levels with bedrooms on each floor. They were like dorms, three to four girls per room . . . or boys, depending on the floor. The place was surrounded by a tall wrought-iron fence to keep strangers out and to keep the occupants in. There was only one gate, and it remained locked.

The laundry house—a flat-roofed building with hopper windows located just beneath the eaves—was abandoned except on weekends when we took turns washing our clothes by dorm number. I decided it would be the best place for a Wednesday night meeting.

I snuck out of my room, flashlight in tow, about two hours after lights-out.

I'd found a handheld vanity mirror in one of my roommates' drawers and carried it over in a pillowcase, along with my mom's Lewis Carroll books, a spiral notebook, and a pen. I still wasn't sure how a "looking glass" figured in, but Morpheus had insisted I use one to call for him. Since the laundry house was locked, I climbed a tree beside it, lowered myself onto the roof from the branches, opened a hopper window, and slid in feet first. A dryer met my boot soles, so I didn't have far to drop.

I slashed the darkness with my flashlight, revealing a cement floor, dinged and dented washers and dryers, and four vinyl laundry baskets. A mix of dust and detergent made me sneeze. A few night crawlers offered hissed greetings before going about their business.

Moonlight seeped through the hopper windows and cloaked the room in a creamy, silver film. I scouted out a spot next to the door to set my things down. My body would be a barricade, in case anyone found out I wasn't in bed and came looking for me. If I blocked the way in, it would buy me extra time to think up an excuse.

After spreading my jacket on the floor for a cushion, I propped the flashlight against the wall so it gave off a halo of light, then sat down and held up the mirror.

"Morpheus," I whispered, and that was all it took.

TWENTY QUESTIONS

A blue flash skated across the glassy surface of the mirror and pulsed. But the pulse wasn't just visual, it was tactile. I could *feel* it vibrate through the handle. Cautiously, I set the mirror on the floor. Alight with an icy cerulean glow, the now-familiar moth climbed out from the glass, as if it had been waiting inside the whole time.

It took flight and perched in a puddle of moonlight. Its wings folded over its thorax, then expanded to the span of an angel's, swooping open to reveal flawless skin and masquerade-style patches lit with jewels beneath inky eyes. A mass of blue, shoulder-length hair, messy from the magical static emanating across his humanoid form and extravagant clothes, moved about his head.

Morpheus loomed tall over me—re-situating his hat on his head to a cocky slant.

"Alison," he said simply, and the sweet scent of licorice drifted my direction. "Ready to strike a bargain?"

I held up my forefinger. The last time we were together, I was distracted by the danger around me and mesmerized by his magic. All of which led to the murder of a man. Tonight, I would take the lead.

"Have you ever played the game Twenty Questions?" I asked him.

He tilted his head and grinned, pulling one of his wing tips over his shoulder to preen it. "Let me see . . . is it anything like Riddle Me This?"

I squinted. "Huh?"

He stretched out his wings and took a seat in the middle of the floor, his complexion aglow with the soft blue light radiating from his hair and the gems under his eyes. "Riddle me this: I belong to no one, yet am used by everyone. To some, I am money, to others I can fly. I make up space, yet don't *take* it up. To those who never change, I hold no sway. But to those who do, I carry the weight of desert sands. *What am I?*"

I bit my lip. It wasn't easy to ignore the intense craving to compete—to prove to him I could figure out his puzzle. But I sensed that would be exactly what he wanted, and I needed to stay focused on *my* goals. "Ball's in my court, Morpheus. Twenty questions. I ask them, and you respond. I'm not striking any bargains with you until my curiosity is satisfied. No chasing rabbits."

He snorted. "Not even white ones?"

Frowning, I opened my bag and took out the pen and spiral notebook. "No getting off track. Straight answers. You want something from me. If you're going to get it, *I'm* calling the shots from here on out."

"My, my. So tyrannical for one so young. I like that in an accomplice." Legs crossed and folded in front of him, he steepled his hands under his chin and narrowed his eyes. "By all means, little ducky. You have the floor."

Blue lightning branched out from his shadow along the cement beneath us, racing across the room in all directions. The washers and dryers activated and began to rumble and swish.

I ground my teeth. "I'm not *ducky*. Do you see any feathers on me? I'm Alison. Nothing more, nothing less. Got it?"

The jewels under his eyes blinked a warm orange hue. "Oh, I *got* it. But you don't. Because you're so much more than just a name."

I frowned. "What does that mean?"

"Everyone is more. We're each formed of life forces, then blood, bones, and spirit. And your blood is more precious than most."

I couldn't think of a response, too distracted by the motorized disturbances echoing off the walls. "Stop the machines. I need to be able to hear if someone's coming."

"Afraid not. My mind works better with a stir of chaos in the background. And yours needs to learn to do the same. As for our privacy, I have that all taken care of. Sneak a peek in the looking glass, *peaches*."

Gritting my teeth at the new nickname—which was ten times as annoying as the first one—I lifted the mirror. The dim reflection of my face blurred, shifting to a portal that showcased the grounds around the laundry building. Tiny dots of light floated and bounced through the trees and grass. Looking closer, I could make out the shapes of miniature women with glittering scales and dragonfly wings.

A strange prickle raised the hairs on my skin—an awareness of the magic all around us that I never knew I had. "What are they?"

"Sprites. Though they may be small, they can stop anyone in their tracks should they try to interrupt us. Just pay heed where you're walking when you leave. Otherwise, you might trip over a body or two."

I gasped and set the mirror down. "They'll kill them?" I couldn't let that happen. One dead person on my conscience was enough.

Morpheus chortled. "I should've clarified. *Dozing* bodies. They'll be no worse for wear once they wake, other than being immensely satisfied and confused. Most importantly, they'll be too preoccupied with their own thoughts to know you were here, or to care, for that matter. But, I'm speaking out of turn again. You had some questions to ask me, yes?"

I have so many more now.

I shook off the hunger to know everything at once, determined to stay on task. I dragged my mother's books from the pillowcase and laid them out between us, preparing to write his answers in my spiral notebook.

He clapped. "Oh, goody. I like this game. Show me all your cards, and I'll show you mine. Just wait until you see what I have up my sleeve."

"Would you stop talking already?" I scowled. "So, you and those . . . sprites . . . you live in Wonderland?"

His countenance lit up. He was obviously eager to answer, but he kept his mouth closed tight.

"Come on," I pressed. *"Are you from Wonderland?"*

He remained silent.

"Seriously?"

"You asked me to stop talking."

I dug my fingers into my knees. "Ugh. Answer me!"

"Tut." He peeled off his gloves, one at a time, leisurely and maddeningly calm. "No need to get peevish. Yes . . . I'm from Wonderland, as are my lovely little pets outside."

"Which means," I swallowed, "Wonderland really is real?"

"It is."

"And the rabbit hole, too?" I asked around the knot in my throat.

Studying me in the dim light, Morpheus nodded. "I can provide you with a map. Just say the word."

I gripped the collar of my shirt, trying to cover the rapid pulse at my neck. "What role do you play there? I've never seen you in the stories."

A strand of blue magic leapt from his fingertip to my "*Alison's*" *Adventures in Wonderland* book. The electrified currents flipped the pages, stopping when they arrived at the illustration of the Caterpillar speaking to Alice. "Much like our clever and curious heroine, I wasn't quite myself in the earlier tales."

My gaze fell to the text on the page and Alice's answer to the Caterpillar's question of her identity: *I'm afraid I can't explain myself, sir. Because I am not myself, you see?*

I gulped, the realization hitting me like a slap in the face. "You're the Caterpillar . . . hatched from a cocoon."

Morpheus winced, as if offended. "Moths and butterflies do not hatch. They *transform*. Now, six questions to go. Don't squander them, peaches."

"Wait . . . I've only asked four so far."

"I beg to differ." He held up his hands in a strand of moonlight, wiggling his fingers and making shapes on the wall—startlingly real for shadows. Some looked like teacups, some like mushrooms, others like roses getting splashed with buckets of paint. "You've asked fourteen, albeit most of them were inane and wasteful. First, you asked me if I'd ever played Twenty Questions. Well, that in itself is a question. Then, when I gave the riddle, you said—and I quote—'Huh?' Another question. Next, after you told me not to call you ducky, you asked if you had feathers, and then if I 'got it?' Finally, you queried what I meant about you being more than merely a name. Honestly, can you even think of a reason any of those were necessary? Of course, when you asked about the sprites—what they were, and if they would be killing your half-witted zookeepers—that bordered on relevant."

My ears grew hot. "I don't live in a zoo!" I snarled.

Morpheus smirked and merged his shadow puppets into a rabbit hopping along the wall. "Add to that the four questions about me and my home—the only ones that actually bore some semblance of importance, mind—and you asked eleven. Unfortunately, you repeated one of them twice after first asking me to stop talking, and then you questioned my seriousness. Which was another three. So, only six remain. Choose your words wisely."

Suppressing a growl, I squeezed the pen in my hand until it bit into my palm. "Okay," I mumbled, preparing to ask the one question I was most afraid to have answered before he could trick me out of any more chances. "You reached out to my mom, didn't you? When she was a teenager."

The washers and dryers grew silent as his magic receded back into his body, just as the mischief drained from his features. He took off his hat and laid it in his lap. "I tried to, Alison. Her mind was . . . more fragile than I anticipated."

I slammed my notebook down and scrambled to my feet. "You told me that *abandon* always merits a second chance at life. So why didn't you catch her? You caught me! You couldn't have done the same for *her*? Her fall was so much shorter! You could've stopped her with your wings!" Tears blazed down my cheeks. I was furious, maybe more at myself than him. I'd promised I'd never cry again.

He stared up at me from his seat on the floor. His jeweled markings blinked a fuzzy periwinkle shade, mirroring the softness of his expression. It was almost as if some small part of him sympathized. "Your mum chose to leap out in the open. There were too many spectators in the parking lot. She made it impossible to be rescued. If only she'd jumped from a little higher, her own wings could've saved her. Those two miscalculations cost her everything."

"No. It was *you* that cost her everything. Why do you keep bugging my family?" I refused to think about the irony in my choice of words, and hoped he would do the same. If he cracked some stupid joke about it, or taunted that I'd squandered four more questions and was now down to two, I would lose every ounce of control I had left. I'd strangle him with my bare hands, electrical magic or not.

Mercifully, he only shook his head and said, "I am not responsible for, nor am I here to make amends for, all the wrongs you've been dealt throughout your life. Instead, I am offering a way for you to honor your mum's death. To make peace with it."

I slapped the hot wetness from my face. "I don't want to make peace with it! All I've ever wanted was to know her. And the only things I have to remember her by are these stupid stories! The stories that killed her." I kicked the books toward him. They slid along the floor a few inches but didn't go far enough. I glared at them, wishing they would leap into the air, dive down on him like birds of prey . . .

grow beaks and peck out those beautiful, endless black eyes so filled with cryptic riddles and even more cryptic answers.

As if hearing my thoughts, the two books lifted from the floor, pages flapping wildly, like wings. They swooped toward him to attack, but he was ready, safely behind a dome formed of blue lightning.

"Splendid show," he said with something like pride in his voice as he straightened the cravat at his neck. "Do let me know when you're finished with your tantrum."

Wait. *I'd* spurred the books to action? *I* made them fly? My jaw dropped.

Not possible. The books fell to the floor with a clunk, as if my logical reasoning killed them.

"I did that." It was an observation. Even in my state of disbelief, I was aware enough not to frame it as a question. I only had two left now . . . *choose your words wisely.*

I looked from the crashed books to Morpheus, who had reeled in his magic and was unprotected again, waiting in the moonlight, patient and somber.

"My mom, she had the same abilities, didn't she?"

He returned his hat to his head. "Yes, though hers were dormant. I tried to awaken them, to show her in her dreams what she was capable of. Tried to encourage her to animate her paintings on the walls. But before she could . . ." He held up a palm. "Well, never mind that. You enlivened those books almost without trying. Think what you can accomplish with guidance and focus. You see, you *do* know your mum. Because that touch of magic was a part of her. What she left you via the blood you share. What you choose to do with it, that's up to you. All she wanted was freedom and escape. Some might say she got that. But as for you, something tells me such an ending wouldn't be satisfactory for one with your . . . drive and determination. So, what do *you* want, Alison?"

I didn't hesitate. "I want to leave this world." My voice sounded wispy, like a slip of air through a screen window, as I sunk to the floor atop my jacket. I crossed my legs, mimicking Morpheus's pose. "But I also want so much more . . ."

He smiled. "Of course you do. You want it all. The crown, the throne, fearful subjects kneeling prostrate at your feet. And you shall have it. It is your heritage. It was taken from you, and you're going to win it back. I believe it's time to show you *my* ace, little princess." He withdrew a cylinder of paper from inside his jacket's cuff and unrolled it so I could see the beautiful winding letters. The golden ink looked wet, though I knew it wasn't because it hadn't smeared. It was reflecting the flashlight's glow:

Burst through Stone with a Feather; Cross a Forest in One Step; Hold an Ocean in Her Palm; Alter the Future with Her Fingertip; Defeat an Invisible Enemy; Trample an Army beneath Her Feet; Wake the Dead; Harness the Power of a Smile.

"I don't get it . . ."

"They're tests," he answered. "Should you pass each one, you will dethrone the imposter seated in your stead, and be crowned the one, true Red Queen. Half of Wonderland will be yours to reign, and you'll need never return to this zoo again."

I gulped. A slow thrill trickled through my body, warm and sweet, like a tree feeling the sap flow through her limbs at the first breath of spring. It was my enchanted intuition awakening. I had a place where I belonged. Where I was meant to *rule*. There, I would never be lonely again and everyone would be at my mercy. "But how can I accomplish such impossible things?"

Morpheus rolled up the paper again and tucked it away. "That is your twentieth question, and well spent. The answer is in the riddle I gave you earlier. And in case you haven't figured it out, consider this: Any interpretation can be altered simply by looking at things from different, more colorful angles . . . view the words and the world through a kaleidoscope instead of a telescope."

I nodded, because he made perfect sense, in some crafty yet absurd way. After all of his badgering about using my words wisely, I was starting to see everything differently already: connotation versus denotation, instinct versus logic, infinity versus . . .

"Time," I whispered, answering his riddle.

"Indeed." He stood, drawing out a small key on a chain from his lapel. He held it up so it glistened in the moonlight. "Time to train you, time to outsmart the tests, and time to win over your subjects."

"How long will that take? And what's in it for you? You said we'd be striking a bargain."

"Sorry, Alison. You've run out of questions. All you need to know is it's as much to my advantage as yours to see you crowned." He tossed the key to me, and I caught it in midair. "Nothing will get in our way, however long it takes. You give me time, and I'll give you all the tools you need to claim your birthright, to change everything you once thought you were. And then, time will matter no more, for you will don the robes of netherling immortality. Starting tonight, we reshape your destiny."

TRAIN TRACKS

The absence of the shower's lull shatters my nostalgic haze.

I stretch and sit up on the bed, glancing at the half-opened door where steam drifts out in a ghostly dance. Thomas is shaving. Water swishes in the sink, then pauses as he hums softly while passing the razor over his skin. The song is one he used to sing to me when we were dating. The words spin through my memory: a man begging forgiveness for loving his lady too much, telling her he'd want no other but her forever, that it was worth any amount of pain to be with her.

He'd upheld the message from the song, stood by me when any other man would've thrown up his arms and left. I've never once regretted choosing him over my netherling destiny. I only regret hurting him. Just as I regret almost robbing Alyssa of her chance to be immortal.

I thought at the time that I was doing the right thing, keeping silent to save her from Wonderland's barbaric practices. I was only sixteen when I stumbled upon Sister Two's lair and saw what she was using human children for, but even at that age, I couldn't close my eyes to the tragedy, or the similarities: how the grave keeper siphoned away their dreams to feed the restless souls in the cemetery. Similar to what had been done to me by unnameable monsters throughout my life—siphoning away my dreams for their own pleasure and satisfaction. But unlike me, Sister Two's victims never escaped.

Seeing Thomas wrapped inside her webs after having been imprisoned there for ten years—all of his life draining away—changed me. And my betrayal changed Morpheus. It was a tragic chain reaction.

I shudder and turn away from the bathroom, staring down at my bare feet, my mind stalled in that awful place and time.

The mattress sinks as Thomas settles behind me in a pair of gray slacks and a lavender dress shirt hanging from his broad shoulders, loose and unbuttoned.

"Ali-bear. What are you thinking of?" He kisses my neck, surrounding me with the scent of his aftershave. His fingers mold around my abdomen, sending shivers of pleasure through every inch of my skin.

I smile as I melt into his lips, my back snuggling against his bare chest as he kisses the spot beneath my ear.

"You, now," I answer, running my fingers over the slick fabric covering his arms.

"Perfect," he whispers. "Because I'm thinking of you, and how beautiful you are."

"You approve of the dress, then?"

"Not just that . . ." His teasing mouth finds its way to my nape. "You smell good, too."

I giggle and he smiles against me.

"If we're going to go anywhere tonight," I press, trying to concentrate in spite of his soft kisses, "we should leave soon."

He sighs—petals of warm breath blossoming around my left shoulder blade and wing bud. "I guess you're right. Especially since we're not just going out. We're going *away*."

I glance over my shoulder where his mouth makes contact and leaves an imprint of sensation. "Away . . . where?"

"Faraway London." He grins. His damp hair catches the sunset filtering through the blinds—a glossy mess of chocolate waves. When he smiles at me like that, he looks nineteen again.

"You want to go to London, *tonight*." I shift around on the mattress to help him button the shirt. It's one of my favorites, for how the color complements his complexion, and how the silky fabric clings to his form. I skim my fingers along his chest before I close the placket. His daily fencing regimen has refined his muscles to a new level—a sophisticated and seasoned density that only a man his age could acquire. "So . . . I guess this impromptu trip means you've decided to forfeit our sword fight tomorrow. Are you sure that's wise? Don't get me wrong, you're in great shape. I'm just not sure you have the legs for a miniskirt."

He chuckles, causing the dimple in his chin that matches Alyssa's to catch a shadow and appear deeper. "Oh, we'll be back in time to defend our titles. We're going to take a shortcut." He places my key necklace around my neck. "Our royal daughter offered us the use of her mirror."

I force a smile, in spite of the chill that wraps my spine—as if ice-tipped spiders are spinning webs of frost around each bone. Every time I use the looking-glass passages, I feel like I'm falling back into my past, which is why, when we make our visits to the Skeffingtons in London, I always insist we go the traditional route and take a commercial flight.

But tonight, I don't have the heart to put a damper on his plans. I can do this. We'll still be in the human realm, after all.

There was a time I craved stepping through the glass and going down the rabbit hole, just to see the landscapes and creatures again. But after being trapped there a few months ago, spending every day and every night in Ivory's castle, helping Grenadine plug her memory leaks, I'm done. I'm ready to stay here for the rest of my days, with Thomas and Alyssa. I get my fix for netherling companionship at Humphrey's Inn twice a month when we visit Thomas's family. That's enough.

"Okay. Just let me finish dressing." I bend down to gather the strappy sandals, but Thomas beats me to it, falling to his knees at my feet.

"Wait, now," he scolds, low and gentle. "That's a knight's job, princess." He lifts my bare foot, pressing his lips to my ankle before slipping the shoe into place. He does the same with my other foot, then finishes with a kiss at my knee before placing the sole of my shoe gently on the floor.

"My sweet Tommy-toes." I lean forward so our foreheads touch, so I can get lost in his warm, kind eyes.

Grinning that Elvis smirk that I adore, Thomas stands and

helps me up. He grabs a sport jacket and my lacy shawl, then leads me across the hall and into Alyssa's room. Muffled laughter and conversation burst from the kitchen. The scent of melting cheese, spicy pepperoni, and marinara sauce makes my mouth water. The kids must've decided on homemade pizza.

"So, we're going to Humphrey's Inn?" I ask, suddenly craving a plate of spaghetti Bolognese with a side of artichoke-feta garlic bread, my favorite of Hubert's specialties.

"That's on the agenda," Thomas answers. "We'll be spending the night there. But first, we're going to Ironbridge Gorge." He flashes the mushrooms in his jacket pocket—our "tickets" to the memory train—before shrugging into the sleeves.

I frown and help him straighten his lapels, studying our shared reflection in Alyssa's cheval mirror—a French silver-framed antique she found at a thrift store. It was the first thing she bought upon our return from Wonderland, so she could check in with her subjects throughout the day when necessary. "I don't understand. Why would we go to the Iron Bridge? Haven't we seen all there is to see?"

"*You* haven't," Thomas answers, his face glazed with pinkish sunset. "I know you're still wrestling with regrets. I see the pain on your face every day." He traces my frown with his thumb. "It's time to forgive yourself. Time for you to realize the positive impact that letting Morpheus and Wonderland into your life has had on the rest of us, because you've dwelt so long on the negative, you've lost sight of it. I asked Alyssa about lost memories yesterday. She told me that once they're stored as cargo, they become part of the train, even after they're viewed by the one who made them. So, we're going to take one last look at my missing years, but this time, we're doing it together. You need to see what would've become of us all, had you not intervened."

Our trip to the Ironbridge Gorge is simpler than it was the times Alyssa and I came here in the past, each seeking different things. With Jeb's help, she recently installed a tall looking glass in the bridge's tunnel. Transportation here is now as simple as stepping from one mirror to the next. There's no traversing the countryside. It's a straight shoot from her bedroom to the tunnel.

As we step through, moving chandeliers—made of clusters of lightning bugs strung together with harnesses—roll like miniature Ferris wheels across the ceiling. They flash along dingy tiled walls, faded advertising posters dated circa 1956 to 1959, and the pile of old, discarded toys in the tunnel.

In spite of a rash of nerves, I manage enough bites of mushroom to shrink alongside Thomas so we can board the rusted toy train that holds all of Wonderland's forgotten and lost memories.

The fuzzy carpet beetle conductor is expecting us. He opens a door marked *Thomas Gardner* and leads us into a small, windowless room with a tapestry rug under a cream-colored chaise lounge. An ornate floor lamp casts a soft glow on the walls. On the other side, a small stage with velvety curtains waits to showcase Thomas's memories.

"Please, do have a seat and take some refreshments," the beetle offers, more cordial than I remember. Word has spread about Alyssa's bloody rampage in the looking-glass world. She's earned the reputation of a severe yet wise Red Queen, and this warrants us, as her parents, the respect of all the netherlings.

Thomas and I sit side by side on the chaise. There's an end table to the left and a lace doily beneath a plate full of moonbeam cookies. I take one and hold it out for Thomas to sample. He bites off half, brushing away the glimmering moonbeams that fall with the crumbs onto his pant legs, and gestures for me to eat the rest.

Waves of nausea roll over me. I try to attribute the sensation to hunger and nibble on the flaky cookie and delicate almond icing, tensing as the conductor punches a button on the wall with a spindly arm. The stage curtains open, revealing a movie screen.

"Picture your husband's face in your mind whilst staring at the empty screen, and you will experience his past as if it were today." The bug turns a dial that snuffs out the lamp and then closes the door.

I clasp Thomas's hand in mine. The one time I visited this train, I was spying on his past without his knowledge, and the things I saw horrified me so much I wanted to hide them from him forever. Now he's here, encouraging me to look deeper. Even with the comfort of his presence, my trepidation is almost smothering.

I push past it, remembering him as the child I saw that day I came alone—when his name was David Skeffington and he was eight years old. But this time, I imagine him a few months earlier, while he's still living with his mother, father, two sisters, and brother in Oxford.

An image appears on the screen in living color and reaches out for me. It pulls me apart at the seams—every piece of me fraying—until I come together again, on-scene, looking out of little David's eyes and sharing his youthful thoughts, emotions, and senses.

He has a happy childhood, rich with sentimental moments . . . following his father on daily chores at their goat farm, playing with his sisters and brother upon the hills surrounding his home, family excursions and picnics, bedtime stories recited by a mother's gentle and melodic voice. But one night, he's visited by an imperial group of knights dressed in red and white tunics—the same ones who came for his brother two years earlier.

His mother weeps at their arrival, shouting that they've never visited a family more than once, but his father comforts her, assuring her he's had the suspicion all along and called them himself. Then he leads David into a darkened room to be interviewed.

One of the knights, a white-bearded man in a red tunic and chain mail, opens a multi-mirror contraption in the darkness. He flips a switch, igniting the white lights along the frames. Each mirror is set at a precise angle to reflect the other, causing the illusion of infinity.

"Take a walk in the mirror maze, lad," says the knight. "Tell me what you see."

David wanders within and around, at first seeing nothing but a thousand images of himself. Then he catches movement in one of the distant reflections—a silhouette of something inhuman. He turns on his heel to find such distortions in each plane of silver-backed glass. With just the blink of an eye, the shadows resolve to clarity and a strange, terrifying world opens up. Large, ugly birds with two sets of wings, lumbering along an ashy terrain in lieu of flying. Crimson bats twice the size of condors swooping overhead, capturing anything brave enough to share the flaming sky with their long, fanged tongues. He starts to back away, but terror evolves into fascination, and lures him closer as some smaller creatures— puppylike beings, colored and shaped liked snowflakes—drift across the lands. They turn themselves inside out, their innards a ball of snapping teeth that devours anything in its path. Blood splashes everywhere as they feast on the four-winged birds. David winces, half expecting to get splattered by the warm and coppery spray, but the massacre is contained within the reflections. Fear and revulsion clench his throat, but he watches one instant longer, as the smallest creature of all, shaped like a butterfly with a scorpion's tail, flutters down—an elegant angel of death—and turns all the bloody, snarling balls of teeth to statues of stone.

In a dazed euphoria, David winds his way out of the maze and relays all the death he's seen. The knights converse among one another, then turn to his father.

"This is unprecedented: your second son to have the sight," the white-bearded knight says. "He sees the weak points in the barrier between the nether-realm and the human world even more clearly than his brother. You know what this means, Gregor."

David's father nods. He looks both sad and proud as he pats David's head. David isn't sure what to feel. But one thing he does know: He's no longer considered a child. He's a warrior, and will be trained as one.

His father packs his bags, they kiss his sobbing mother and sisters one last time, and then it's off to live with his uncles and cousins in Oxford, England, at Humphrey's Inn. David's searing grief over saying good-bye to his family and old life is stanched only when his older brother, Bernie, comes to greet them at the door.

The scene shakes and shivers as we pass through several months of lessons: studying AnyElsewhere, the looking-glass world where Wonderland's exiles are banished. He learns it's connected to Wonderland by the tulgey wood and to the human realm by infinity mirrors, and that a dome of iron surrounds the prison, warping any incarcerated netherlings into grotesque creatures should they try to use their magic while inside.

During his training, David buries himself in studies of the mutated creatures to earn the honor to be a part of the special faction of knights who guards the two gateways—the one from the human realm and the one into Wonderland. But the violent and gruesome subject matter saturates his nightmares and dreams with vivid and bizarre imagery. Still, he advances, taking self-defense classes and redefining his language—learning how to wield the mind as armor when riddles are the weapon.

The shifting scenes of David's life pause at Hubert's restaurant as his feet skate through ash in the fighting pit while diners watch him learn to fence from above. I feel Thomas's . . . *David's* . . . heart rate climb, feel his eagerness to make his father proud, his competitiveness toward his brother and cousins, and a self-conscious awareness as all eyes fix on him—the youngest and newest candidate. But in time he learns to block everything out but the game. He becomes confident, graceful, and adept, betters all of his opponents—including his own father—and by his ninth birthday, he's ready for his first sojourn to AnyElsewhere, to experience the secrets inside firsthand. Most of the boys are taken in at age thirteen, but he merits an earlier initiation, for not only has he learned to defend himself, but he also has the daring, wisdom, and acumen of someone five years his senior.

A vivid rainbow smears the screen as the memory tilts and turns on David's ride within an ashy white wind tunnel shaped like a tornado. The funnels provide safe transportation across the prison world for the knights, since they're the only ones with the magical medallions that control the winds. Gusts rip through David's hair and clothes as he's carried along with his uncle William to the Wonderland gate, where David will be taught the secrets of his guardian status. Triggered by the medallion at his uncle's neck, the funnel opens up and spits them out, one by one, far above the gate kept locked against the tulgey wood and Wonderland. A giant slide of ash rises up to catch and guide them to the platform, keeping them a safe distance from the glowing vortex of nothingness that separates the gateway from the world's terrain, and holds the prisoners at bay.

David watches it all through illuminated, leather-framed goggles. Being his first time within the domed world, he was determined to miss nothing, even the ride over. His father gave in and let him wear the goggles he and his brother used to keep dust out of their eyes and light the way when they were riding motorbikes at night along dirt trails on the hills of Oxford.

Because of his unhindered vision, he sees—as his uncle is dropped from the funnel behind him—that the chain holding the medallion at the old man's neck breaks and the necklace starts to fall. David reaches up to catch it. Once they're safely beside the gate, he returns the necklace to his uncle. The old man pats him on the back as he tucks it into his chain mail.

"One day, you'll be a bearer of a medallion. I'd stake my life on it." His uncle chortles. David beams at the praise.

Uncle William has always been his favorite . . . He smells like the cinnamon candies Mom used to put in pretty dishes at Christmas, he can outmaneuver anyone in a game of chess, and he always has a jolly good joke to tell. He was the one who took David under his wing when his father had to return to the goat farm. And now he's insisted on being David's guide to all the mysteries of this strange, magical world their family has guarded for centuries.

David moves closer to the solid iron gate, so Uncle William can share the secret to unlocking the way into Wonderland. Embedded within the lower third of the three-story barrier, a hexagonal box appears with five puzzles arranged in a nesting doll structure. David watches as Uncle William solves three, triggering the gate's hinges to open wider at each turn, and revealing glimpses of the dark tunnel behind the gate—a tulgey's throat. A stench seeps in—rotting, moldering wood. Only two puzzles away from fully opening the gate, Uncle William pales and hunches against the iron for support. Then he clutches his chest and collapses to his knees.

Gasping, David drops beside him. "Uncle, what's wrong?" He means to shout the words, but he swallowed too much black mist in the nothingness on the way to the entrance earlier. His vocal cords aren't fully awake, so it comes out a mumble. "Should I call the wind back?" His whisper is indecipherable, even to his own ears.

It doesn't matter. His uncle is beyond answering him. David is too small to drag Uncle William's stocky body to the landing spot. And if he were to take a wind tunnel alone for help, his uncle would be left vulnerable in front of the partly opened gate. David doesn't know how to use the puzzle box to shut the door. He drags out a mechanical messenger pigeon from the old man's bag. It's only to be used in emergencies, and should be sent with a recorded message, but—with his voice asleep—all he can do is send it on its own and hope one of their relatives sees it and figures out something's wrong.

He flips the switch to light its eyes and activate its wings, and sends it into the sky. But he worries that time is waning. Already, his uncle's skin is a translucent blue, like the color of ice over a pond.

David's heartbeat pounds in his chest.

There's one other thing he can do.

Eyes burning behind his goggles, David stares at the partly opened gate. Although the Looking-glass Knighthood has scads of information on AnyElsewhere and its occupants, not many studies have been done of Wonderland. Other than the *Alice* books, they know very little of the beings there. Though rumors abound of fae creatures with healing powers beyond anything comprehensible to humans.

David may not know how to solve the last two puzzles, but the opening—too slight for a grown man to breach—is already the perfect size for his small frame to fit through.

He hesitates. There are other stories, too, about the fairy-kind. That some are tricky and deadly. But how could they possibly be any worse than the monsters on this side of the gate? And he's been taught how to best those. Surely his knowledge can get him in and out of Wonderland unscathed.

Jaw clenched, David leaps to his feet and rushes through the gate before fear or reason can stop him.

ANCHOR

In a chain reaction, the moment David steps through the gate, it slams shut behind him. His uncle would be safe from any stray Wonderland creatures until the mechanism reset itself with the tulgey wood's mouth opening and closing. Only then would the gate allow anyone in from the same entrance again. Even David would have to find a new pathway to it . . . through another tulgey's throat.

A panicked flush burns David's face. He feels alone and scared for all of an instant before remembering that he's been trained as a knight. His plan could work. He just has to find a fae with healing powers to spare and then make a trade of some sort. They're rumored to collect human trinkets.

David removes his gloves, revealing the ring he received after he was anointed: a shiny band of pure gold, inlaid with sparkly diamonds around its circumference and a large glittering ruby setting, with a white cross of jade embedded in the center. To him, it is invaluable, far beyond its monetary worth, but he is willing to give it away if it means saving Uncle William.

The horrible rotting stench stings his eyes even behind his goggles. He turns on the light around the leather frames to illuminate the mossy trail beneath him, and begins running. After what feels like a quarter of a mile, the air seems to thin. He fights for breath in the enclosed, dark space. His goggles fog and he slides them off his face so they hang at his neck, still lighting his steps.

He rounds a bend and an opening comes into view, offering a hazy light to see by and a fresh stream of air. Panting, David turns off his goggles so he won't be conspicuous when stepping from the unhinged jaw onto the ground outside.

He draws his sword as he catapults over the teeth and lands inside a thicket. A loud creaking sound makes him spin to face the tree he just exited. The jaws snap at him. He jumps backward, barely escaping before the teeth retract into the trunk to form what appears to be a benign wooden grain in the bark—though David knows better.

Tall neon grasses feather around his boots as he circles the thicket, looking for a path out.

Some tangled bushes behind him quiver. Clenching his jaw, he centers himself in the middle of a small clearing out of reach of the foliage and trees surrounding him, although there's still a canopy of branches overhead he keeps in his sights.

The bushes shake again, and he holds up his sword, mentally

preparing for one of the netherlings who've been spit back out of the tulgey in strange and horrible forms. Possibly a fire ant with a body made of flames, or a rocking-horsefly, with wooden rockers affixed to its six legs.

Instead, a strained yelp erupts on the other side of the bushes, followed by an outburst of hysterical miniature voices, all the more unsettling for their childlike banter.

"Stupidesses! Stupid, stupid, stupid! She usn't like runner-aways!"

"Atchcay the umanlinghay!"

"Yesses! Or be our necks deadses and stomped."

"Missing stakes happen."

"Mistakens or notses, Twid Two asks usses to tie it up."

"Onay oremay eamsdray!"

"She will hang usses by our necks . . . deadses-deadses-dead are we!"

David picks through his language training. It's like pig latin mixed with nonsensical jargon. Three of the phrases he can make out clearly enough: The miniature-voiced creatures are chasing a runaway humanling, they're concerned about a lack of dreams, and they're about to have nooses around their necks.

The voices grow louder and the bushes rattle again. David ducks behind a large rock to watch. He can't let himself be captured or hurt . . . Uncle William needs him to find help and hurry back. The leaves on the bushes part, and something plunges through.

David gasps to see a naked human boy, maybe six years older than him, stumble into the soft light of the clearing. He's the color of milk, all but the shock of black hair on his head. It's as if the blood has drained from him . . . not just from his face, but his torso and arms and legs, too. Then David realizes the boy's not completely naked after all. His body is coated with something—gossamer, sticky, thick. Silken fibers hang from him in places like threads, as if he's fraying.

Web?

David gulps, louder than intended.

The boy turns toward him, but his glazed eyes look through him. Nothing seems to register on his face. There's no expression other than a blank, somber stare.

A webby rope grows taut on the boy's ankle, dropping him to the ground face-first. He garbles into the grass—a strange, animalistic sound devoid of any sense—as if he's forgotten how to talk.

The chatty little creatures of earlier scurry in—five of them—still arguing among themselves. They look like silvery spider monkeys with hairless hides. Bulbous eyes the color of nickels, with no pupils or irises, glimmer like coins in a wishing well.

Glossy slime oozes from their bald skin. The silver, oily droplets trail their footsteps and long, thin tails. All of them are wearing tiny miner's caps. The lights bob around the clearing, a disorienting display, like glowing bubbles.

As they pass David's rock, a putrid, meaty stench follows in their wake. They surround the fallen boy, hissing. One of them unwinds the web from the victim's ankle and uses it to tie his hands at his back. The boy snaps his teeth in a vicious and feral attempt to break loose, though his face retains that unchanging, empty stare.

The closest creature tumbles back and then laughs—jagged, spiky teeth spreading wide in its primate face. It emits a disturbing sound somewhere between a purr and a growl, then jumps atop the boy, proceeding to stuff his mouth with web. The other silvery monkeys cheer their partner on, driven to glee by the defenseless boy's choking sounds.

Nauseated by the gruesome spectacle, David slings his goggles at the group to distract them, then jumps out from his hiding place.

"En garde!" he shouts, and swipes his sword at the silvery creatures in an attempt to frighten them away.

They screech in unison and squirm into some hedges nearby. Whimpers shake the leaves, followed by flashes of light from their caps.

David sheathes his sword and stoops beside the boy, releasing his binds.

"Yous-es aughtent shouldn't do it, talker," one of the creatures warns in an airy and threatening singsong voice. "The gardener omescay on the ayway." The others snicker in response, causing the shrubs to rattle, but then they grow disturbingly silent, as if listening for something.

Gardener? David keeps an eye trained on them as he continues to untie the boy. Uncle William niggles in the back of his mind. David hopes his other family members have found the old man by now. One thing he knows: Uncle William and his father both would want him to do the right thing. He took an oath to protect all humanity from the magi-kind, and this boy obviously needs protecting.

So intent on his inner battle, he doesn't see the giant hovering shadow until he hears the haunting song:

"The itsy-bitsy spider went up the water spout," an eerie voice croons from above.

His shoulders grow chill in the same instant his eyes snap up— too late. The horrific sight mesmerizes him.

A human-size spider hangs upside down overhead. The top half is female—translucent face with scars and bloody scratches scattered all across her purplish lips, cheeks, chin, and temples. Her silvery hair hangs down in thick coils, nearly reaching David's head. Her bottom half is a black widow's, five times bigger than the size of the medicine balls the knights use to build muscles and stamina. She's balanced on a strand of web affixed to the branches, and it glistens like her hungry blue eyes. Eight shiny spider legs bend around the anchor line, both terrifying and graceful.

David considers drawing his sword, but he's frozen with awe and fear.

She brings her left arm down, and it almost looks human, aside from the garden shears in place of a hand.

Gardener. The word taunts David, biting at him, nudging him back into the moment.

Snip, snip, snip. The whisk of the scissors wakes David completely from his trance. He crab-walks backward, pulse racing as the blades barely miss his face.

The spidery woman alights delicately onto the ground in front of him.

Terror skitters through his nervous system—a thousand icy sparks igniting chill bumps along his skin. Before he can right himself and run, a thick spray of web encases him from his feet to his thighs, catching up his sheath and rendering his sword hidden and useless. David totters off balance and flattens to the ground, right next to the boy he tried to save. The boy stares at him with those numbing, desolate eyes. He pushes the web from his mouth with his tongue and garbles again in that senseless mantra, as if trying to tell David something.

The left side of David's body aches where it hit the ground, and strands of grass tickle inside his ear.

"Well, well," their spidery captor says with a breathy voice that leaves a coppery taste in David's mouth, like flakes of rust and despair. "Did ye two make friends? How precioussss."

The silvery monkey creatures snicker and creep out from their hiding places. In a last-ditch attempt to escape, David claws his hands into the grass and pulls himself along toward the edge of the thicket.

Two of the creatures leap on him and another drags the ring from his finger.

"Sparkly!" it shouts, and holds up its prize.

"Give that back!" David demands, though he has no idea where his courage comes from.

Growling, the spider gardener sweeps the chatty monkeys aside with four spindly legs and then pins David in place, spinning him around and around until he's wrapped in web up to his shoulders.

"This ones-es is a sparkly talker," a silver captor taunts as it jabs at David with a stick.

"A talker he may be, my slave." The spidery woman bends low, her breath rushing across David's face. He coughs, gagging on the scent of decay and damp earth. "But is he a dreamer?" Her right hand, cloaked in a rubbery glove, catches his chin. She looks into his eyes—an intense study that pulls at his insides—like a child worrying at a loose scab. He feels the tug deep within, deeper than his heart, deeper than his bones and blood . . . until it rips free and exposes all of his fears and hopes, all the way to his soul. "Aye. He be a most unique dreamer. And he be *mine*."

At the spidery witch's proclamation, the monkey creatures dance, their oozing silvery slime slinging across David's face.

"Let us go," he pleads, casting a glance to the other boy.

"Oh, nay." Her rubber glove pets his head, tugging his hair at the scalp. "Ye came to Sister Two of yer own free will. Yer a gift for me, ye are. Ye shall be magnificent in me garden. Ye've seen things other humanlings haven't. Ahhh, ye will have the most vivid dreams. And nightmares, oh, the nightmares we will spin together." Drool dribbles from her lower lip and combines with the blood already on her chin. She swipes it away with her scissored hand, slicing her skin once more.

David tenses inside his webby casing, trying to work his hands closer to his sword. But his limbs are plastered in place—immovable.

The fallen boy whimpers across the way, and the spider scrabbles over to him. "It would seem we have a replacement for ye. Wasn't that easy? No more suffering." She inches off her glove, using her teeth to help in the absence of another working hand. The rubber sheath peels away to free five scorpion tails curling and uncurling in place of fingers.

David groans at the sight, repulsed.

Sister Two bows over her captive and rips the web from his chest, exposing pale skin. "Time to join the others." Her venomous hand presses against the boy's sternum and poison wells from the tip of her forefinger; then she punctures through the bone into his heart.

The boy howls and convulses. David cries out and struggles to get to him, but can't move. Within moments, the boy's body has shrunk and transformed to a silvery monkey slave, like the others. At last he stops struggling and closes his pupil-less eyes, his primate face relaxed and a black tongue hanging out of his mouth. Bubbles of slime ooze off what was once human flesh, and a long, thin tail thrashes at his backside.

David clenches his eyes shut, trying not to scream like a little boy. *Be brave*, he tells himself. *You're a knight.* But he's losing courage . . . he's forgetting everything he's been taught. All he remembers is blood and death and snapping teeth and stingers. There's a flash of his mother's soft and gentle hand stroking his head. It's sliced away by a pair of garden shears.

"Be not afraid, little dream boy." Sister Two has returned to lean over him as the slaves pick up their newest member and drag him away. "Ye're home now. Ye have an immortal brotherhood and sisterhood here. One day, when yer dreams dry up, ye'll join them. But first, ye'll feed my wretched, hungry souls."

❖ · I · ❖

"Nooo!" I shout. It's a scream both for David and for the lost boy we'll never know. The lost boy who will never be reunited with his loved ones. Who's now lost forever, even to himself.

I scream louder as the web covers David's face and he's no longer able to cry for himself or anyone else. "Noooo!"

"Alison." Thomas shakes my shoulder, and the scene scrambles and blurs around me, dragging me from his memory and dropping me back onto the chaise lounge, cradled by the dimness surrounding us.

I bury my face in Thomas's arm, seeking his scent and warmth. Reminding myself he's here and will never suffer like that again. "I'm so sorry."

"No, baby. You saved me. You have nothing to be sorry for." He wraps his arm around me and pulls me close, waiting until my heartbeat stops pounding in my ears, until I can breathe without heaving.

"Sister One lied to me," I say, struggling to make sense of things.

"She said the pixies used children's bodies to feed the flowers. But that wasn't it at all."

"No. The pixies were once children themselves." Thomas sighs heavily, his rib cage lifting my head with the effort. "And they can never return to that form again."

My face burns with rage. "I can't watch anymore. Please tell me that's where it ends."

He squeezes me. "It's okay. That's the blessing. Something in the web worked like a sedative. I was in a trance. I have no memories of my time in her lair, because I *made* no memories. All I did was dream. But I do remember stirring when you freed me from her trap and I fell to the ground. I remember you wrapping me in a blanket."

"Yes," I whisper in the darkness. "Sister One let me borrow it. That was all she could offer. She was terrified of her twin's wrath. I used the blanket as a stretcher—to help me drag you out."

"I remember that, too. I saw glimpses of you, glancing behind to make sure I didn't fall off. Your eyes were the color of freedom. Of my future. They were full of so much sorrow, so much determination. And *strength*." Thomas hugs me tighter. "Then as I roused on Morpheus's shoulder when he carried me through the portal, you and your wings flickered in and out of my view. You were transcendent . . . ethereal. Waking up in your bed was like waking from a ten-year coma and seeing an angel. Your face was familiar, I guess from those glimpses of consciousness. For some reason, when Ivory erased my other memories, those moments remained. Maybe because they weren't quite memories yet. They were more . . . awakenings. And with all my other memories gone, you were the only thing I recognized. Later, I convinced myself I'd dreamed of you and those wings, but it didn't matter. Because just looking at you, with or without wings, I was reborn."

I snuggle closer to his chest so I can hear his heartbeat. Shutting my eyes, I replay in my mind that moment we first officially met as if I were viewing it on the screen across the room.

I had sat beside the bed and kept vigil that night, after breaking all my mirrors so Morpheus couldn't find his way back into my room. I knew I'd let him down. I also knew he would be furious. But I didn't care. All I cared about was helping the boy in the web.

Knowing he'd have no identity when he woke, I named him as he slept. He reminded me of a painting I once saw in one of my foster homes. They were religious people, and a portrait of Saint Thomas hung over their fireplace. His hair was brown, his face young but etched with wisdom, and his dark eyes sympathetic and soulful. He was the patron saint of people who struggled with doubt, and I had never believed that I had a place in the human world. So I appointed him my personal saint.

But as I watched the dream boy sleep that night in my bedroom, a boy I'd helped save . . . a boy I'd given a home, I knew I would never doubt my place again.

Nervous and insecure, I watched his brown eyes flicker open the next morning. A peachy dawn danced upon the walls in the room, animated by the tree branches swaying outside my window. I wondered if he would fear me, if he would panic or lash out. But when our gazes connected, I felt—for the first time in all my years—safe. He reached for me as if he'd known me forever. Considering how long he'd been without human contact, I didn't hesitate to reach back. Silently, I took his hand and slid under the eyelet quilt, nestling into his side. Without a word, his fingertip glided over every feature on my face, his breath sugary and sweet across my skin—a residue of the forgetting potion Ivory had poured into him. To me, it was the scent of fresh hope and new life. Then he stopped at my mouth, cupped my chin, and pressed his lips to mine, his touch so tender yet so confident for a nineteen-year-old boy who had never kissed a girl. It was my first reciprocal kiss, the only one that reached into my heart and lit me up like a torch standing strong against the wind. I stayed there in the warmth of his arms and we slept for hours, until the sun peaked in the sky and it was time to give him answers, however false they were.

Thomas couldn't speak for those first few months. He understood the things I said, but he had to relearn words—how to articulate and read them. It was as if Sister Two not only drained away his dreams and imagination, but also stole a lifetime of communication. Though it was frustrating for him, it made it easy for me, to tailor his impairment and amnesia to a car accident and head injury.

I look back now at the lies I told in hopes to keep him sane, and wonder how different things might have been had I brought him here to the train for his truth.

But the past can never be undone. He's forgiven me, and loves me despite it all.

"I only wish I could've saved all those other children along with you," I say, clenching my hands in Thomas's shirt. "Or saved Alyssa from the pain she went through."

"Come on, sweetie. Can't you see how many lives you did save? Not just mine. You and I were both destined to be a part of Wonderland. No matter what paths we might've chosen. We were caught in that web from the moment we were born. Which means it was inevitable that our daughter would be as well, and that her part would be bigger than both of ours."

"I understand that, but—"

"But what you keep forgetting," Thomas interrupts gently, "is that without your role in all of it, our girl would've never been born to begin with, because I would've ended up a pixie, constantly in search of that missing sparkle of inspiration, never knowing exactly what I'd lost. I can't think of a more tragic ending. Can you?"

A new emotion rises inside me. A splash of righteous indignation for all the lost human children and the one I was able to save, hot and overpowering.

"By stepping into Wonderland in the first place," Thomas continues as he takes my hand and presses it to his heart, "you gave our daughter life, and a chance at life to all the children Sister Two would've caught and used up in the future. Morpheus's luring Alyssa into being queen led him to fall in love with her, which in turn gave a selfish, solitary fae the chance to grow and do something honorable . . . She's with us now because of it. Jeb giving up his muse for human children—a boy who didn't have much of a childhood himself—another honorable sacrifice. We're all better people . . . or netherlings in some cases . . . because of *you* being brave and daring enough to seek a better life for yourself. Because of *your* choices as that young, lonely thirteen-year-old girl, and then again as that righteous and caring sixteen-year-old princess, countless lives were saved and improved. And by saving Alyssa's father, you gave her the chance to exist in the first place."

I stave off a sob. "Which gave you the chance to raise her. She's strong and amazing because of *you*." I take his hand in mine, curl his fingers to a fist, and kiss his knuckles. "Thank you for never giving up on me or our girl. You're our hero."

"You're *my* hero, Alison. Literally." He brushes a strand of hair from my face that has fallen from its pin. "How many men can say that about the woman they love? Huh?"

I stop fighting the tears. I let them stream quietly down my face. These are different than the others I've cried. They're pure, healing, and happy. *Blissfully happy.* In spite of the darkness we've all faced, I have my family. I've honored my mother's death by enabling others to live. Just like Morpheus once said . . . he gave me a chance to make peace with her death. And now Thomas has given me a chance to make peace with my life. Everything is as it should be. At long last.

There would be times the dark thoughts would revisit, I was sure. But now . . . now I had a light to shine upon them. A beacon to guide me through.

"No more looking back," I say to my husband, my voice surprisingly strong.

"No more train rides." He strokes my jawline with his knuckles. "Only forward, from this day on. Cherishing each and every moment we have left together in this world. You with me?"

"Until the very end," I answer.

Thomas dries my tears. "Happy anniversary, Ali-bear." He draws me into his lap on the chaise lounge, and kisses me until I'm breathless and blushing like a new bride. After he stands me up to straighten my clothes, he whispers in my ear, "I'm starving. How about some spaghetti Bolognese?"

I laugh. "You read my mind."

As we make our way off the train toward the mirror, he holds my hand. The boy in the web, and the man of my dreams. Always and forever, my anchor.

THE MOTH
IN THE MIRROR

THE MOTH'S
MACHINATIONS

"You're sure about this, Morpheus?"

"I am," Morpheus answered, dragging off his gloves and tucking them into his jacket. "You, however, appear to need convincing." Magic tingled at his fingertips, a pulsing blue light just beneath the skin. Due to the iron bridge outside, his powers were limited to a few benign tricks. But it would be enough to get his point across if necessary.

The carpet beetle—who stood as high as Morpheus's collarbone after Morpheus had consumed a shrinking potion—gulped behind his many clicking mandibles. His carpeted hide quivered. "No, no. Please, you misinterpret my reservations." The insect's twiggy arms trembled as he flipped through the alphabetical tally on his clipboard of all the memories that had been lost in Wonderland. "It looks like a boring way to spend an afternoon, is all . . . spying on a human's forgotten moments."

Morpheus shifted, and his wings cast a shadow over the beetle's face. "Ah, but this particular human has much to teach me."

This particular human had managed to capture something Morpheus desired above all else in the world.

"Have a seat"—the beetle pointed to a white vinyl chair—"and I'll ready the memories for you."

Morpheus swooped his wings aside, sat down, and took a drag from the hookah provided by his host as a courtesy. The sweet, candied tobacco seared his windpipe. He blew puffs of smoke, fashioning them into Alyssa's face. It was easy to picture the way her eyes always frosted to blue ice when she saw him, filled with both dread and excitement. He adored that about her: the sharpened edge of her netherling instincts, warning her not to trust him, softened by human emotions forged during their shared childhood.

Before her, he'd lived his life in solitude, never needing anyone. He had no idea what spell she'd cast over him. She was beyond frustrating, always pledging her devotion to the wrong side. But her charm was undeniable. Especially when she defied him or glared at him with righteous indignation. It brought the most delicious snarl to her lips.

Morpheus set aside the hookah, although the burning in his chest had nothing to do with smoke. Alyssa was the only one who could quench the fire there, for she was the one who had first stoked those flames.

They'd spent five years together—childhood playmates—until

her mum ripped her from him, bloody and wounded, and he had to stew in remorse and guilt from a distance because of a foolhardy vow he'd made to stay away.

Being deprived of his friend gave him his first taste of loneliness. Even all the years he'd spent in a cocoon prior to ever meeting her, trapped and claustrophobic . . . even they hadn't prepared him for the desolation of her absence.

Then at last she'd come back to him, reviving all the old feelings he thought he'd mastered. That time, too, was short-lived. She'd left again, by her own choice. The resulting pain and loneliness were excruciating. Debilitating.

She'd only been gone from Wonderland for six months, and he didn't understand this sick emptiness inside that could only be filled by her touch, her scent, her voice. Solitary fae had no use for such nonsense. They required no companionship, abhorred emotional baggage. Their affection and loyalty belonged to the wilds of Wonderland and to no one or nothing else.

So what had she done to him to change that?

Each time he saw his reflection of late, he no longer recognized the moth in the mirror. He was incomplete, broken; and he despised it.

Despised it even more because she made him work so bloody hard to woo her, while she gave her affections freely to a worthless mortal.

Morpheus suppressed a snarl. He couldn't make sense of Jebediah's luck, how a human could wield such power over a netherling queen. How a mere boy could harness a royal half-blood heart so multifaceted, a spirit prone to pandemonium and madness. Jebediah was dragging Alyssa down, chaining her to the boredom and mundaneness of the human realm.

She must be set free.

Morpheus had considered killing his rival, but Alyssa would never forgive him. No. The time had come for creative measures.

If Morpheus knew what Jebediah had been thinking during his trek through Wonderland—all those times when the boy had been at his most terrified, his most discouraged—he would know the mortal's weaknesses and his strengths, *intimately*. He would see how to break Jebediah down, pit him against himself.

Those weaknesses would defeat him better than Morpheus could. Then, when he'd destroyed Alyssa's faith in her mortal knight, Morpheus would be there to comfort and win her.

He would once again hear her laugh the way she had when they were children, once again be the recipient of her dazzling smile.

Once again be complete.

"This way, please." The beetle motioned for Morpheus to follow.

Morpheus removed his hat and raked a hand through his hair. When the insect opened the door to a windowless memory compartment, the scent of almonds wafted from a plate of fresh-baked moonbeam cookies on an end table. A cream-colored chaise lounge was wedged against a wall, and an ornate brass floor lamp lit the space with a soft glow.

Morpheus's attention locked on the small stage across the compartment. His heartbeat thudded with anticipation, a deep and steady rhythm. Red velvet curtains waited to part at any moment, to play Jebediah's memories on a silver screen.

"Since you'll be riding in the boy's head to visit his lost memories," the beetle said, "I'm bound by policy to warn you . . . Human emotions can be a powerful thing. They can make you see things in an entirely different light."

"I'm counting on that." Morpheus smirked. "Ever hear the saying about friends and enemies?"

The beetle scratched his shaggy hide. "Um . . . keep your friends close and your enemies closer?"

Morpheus settled onto the cushioned lounge chair, smoothing his pin-striped pant legs as he crossed his ankles. "Even better to take a walk in your enemy's shoes. 'Tis the best way to control their footsteps. Or erase them altogether, should the opportunity arise."

The beetle, trembling again, punched a button on the wall with one spindly arm. The stage curtains opened, revealing a movie screen. "Picture the boy's face in your mind whilst staring at the empty screen, and you will experience his past as if it were today."

His spiel was rehearsed—mechanical, even—but Morpheus's pulse raced. He waited for the beetle to shut off the lamp. As soon as the insect had left the room and closed the door, Morpheus's body came apart at the seams—floating through the darkness as if he were made of dust motes. All the pieces reassembled themselves on the silver screen in vivid, cinematic colors, until he was inside Jebediah Holt's head, wearing his body, feeling his emotions.

In that moment, Morpheus gave himself over to the experience, seeing things as a human for the first time in his life.

MEMORY ONE: KRYPTONITE

Jeb woke up on a swinging bed.

He was naked. Why was he naked?

Before that fact could fully register, thirty or more moth-size sprites dropped out of the air, caressing and whispering over every part of him. He tried to move his arms and legs. The sprites' wings—purring at the speed of hummingbirds'—released particles like dandelion fuzz that somehow immobilized him. The seeds gave off the scent of cinnamon and vanilla and flooded his consciousness until the room blurred.

When the fog lifted, he was at home in bed. Night spilled through the window, and Taelor straddled him, half dressed. French-manicured fingers trailed down the hairs of his chest and abdomen toward the waist of his jeans.

This couldn't be right. He and Taelor had had a fight before prom, had broken up.

He gently flipped her beneath him and propped himself up on his elbows, dragging the hair from her face. But Taelor's eyes didn't meet his. Alyssa's icy blue ones did—staring in dreamy, innocent wonder. His fingers grew fat and clumsy at her temples.

Al was in his bed?

No. This couldn't happen. Alyssa hadn't even kissed a guy yet. And Jeb had never been any girl's first anything.

Al was untouchable to him. She'd experienced enough turbulence in her life. And he wasn't exactly the poster child for stability.

Jerking his hands free, he rose to his knees.

"Jeb, don't you want me?" Al asked, rubbing a palm over his chest.

He couldn't answer. His fingers itched and felt stretchy, as if they were growing. He held them up in the moonlight, watching in horror as they fell off one by one and morphed into caterpillars. The caterpillars then inched toward Alyssa, and he couldn't do a thing to stop them. He fell to the bed on his back, hands held above his face, staring in disbelief at the raw and bloody stumps where his fingers once were.

Screaming, Alyssa tried to scramble off the mattress, but the caterpillars caught her, creeping over her skin and spinning webs until only her wriggling form inside a cocoon remained.

"Let her go!" Jeb shouted. A light flashed across his eyes, and then he wasn't at home in his bed anymore. He was somewhere in Morpheus's mansion, and the sprites were rushing over his skin, hypnotizing him . . . using some kind of hallucinogenic pheromones.

They're holding me hostage so Morpheus can be alone with Al. The instant that reality came crashing in, the spell broke.

Jeb tumbled off the swinging mattress and out of his captors' seductive mist. Snagging a pillow, he covered himself. "Give me something to wear!"

The sprites floated in midair, their dragonfly eyes watching him.

Several golden baskets sat on the floor at his feet. Jeb kicked one over. His tiny captors swooped around the room in mass hysterics.

Gossamer, Morpheus's prized sprite, appointed five of them to pick up the spilled strawberries. They counted the fruits one by one and placed them back in the container.

Jeb knocked over another basket, this one filled with beads of scented oil. Five more sprites dropped to the floor for cleanup, stopping to count each bead before putting it away.

Soon he'd overturned every basket. Some were full of flower petals, some with lotion, others with grapes. By tumbling them over, he'd managed to preoccupy most of his captors. Only Gossamer and two others still fluttered around his head.

"Give me something to wear," he repeated, "or I'll start ripping the feathers from the pillows. There aren't enough of you in here to clean up *that* mess."

"He's not responding to our allure," one of the sprites muttered to Gossamer, her coppery bug-eyes turned in Jeb's direction.

"Or our magic," the other one added with a pout. "I conjured some girl from his memories, but his subconscious broke through."

"Yes, this one is indeed a challenge," Gossamer agreed in a voice that tinkled like chimes. After sending the other two sprites to pick up the contents of the latest basket, she offered Jeb a silk robe.

He turned his back and shrugged the covering on, taking in his surroundings.

Morpheus had put him in an opulent prison. The room was round with black marble floors that reflected orange candlelight. He was already intimately acquainted with the focal point: a swinging, circular mattress attached to the center of the domed ceiling with gold chains. Furs and pillows cushioned the bed, perfumed with rose petals.

For all its comforts, this room was missing one very important aspect. An exit. There was no door, window, or any other opening in sight.

Convex walls—painted dark lavender—had grapevines stretching around their circumference, winding in and out of the plaster and entwining lit candelabras. Fruit blossomed on the vines. At random intervals the grapes would spontaneously burst and drizzle their juice into stone basins set all along the walls to catch it. From there, rich purple liquid drained into fountains—a constant supply of sweet-smelling fairy wine.

He vaguely remembered tasting the wine when he'd first arrived. Suspicious of it, he'd tried to resist, but he had been so thirsty. No telling what kind of magic was inside the liquid.

He groaned and rubbed his face. How long had he been drunk and bewitched? He'd made himself useless to Alyssa, just like his old man would've done.

"Where is she?" he asked, ignoring the self-playing harp behind him, which picked up volume, trying to muffle his voice. "Tell me what Morpheus is doing to her."

Minuscule, glittering, and confident, Gossamer settled on a satin pillow. She patted the mattress next to her and crossed her green ankles. "Perhaps you don't realize what we sprites are capable of. We've had centuries of practice. We can show you rapture the likes of which you've only dreamed about."

Jeb regarded her, head to toe, then tightened the satin belt at his waist. "Sorry. I don't dream in green."

He found Alyssa's backpack under the bed and dragged it out. He'd noticed something in there earlier when he'd been digging through it: a wrought iron bangle bracelet she'd probably tucked inside at school and forgotten about. He'd done his share of research on fairies when he first started painting them, and he knew they didn't like iron—if the lore was true.

He slammed the backpack onto the mattress. The fur blankets billowed like a huge wave and knocked Gossamer from her pillow. Kick-starting her wings, she landed lightly on Jeb's shoulder.

"If it is Alyssa who inspires your passions, we can fulfill that fantasy." Gossamer clapped her hands. The others left their cleaning posts and hovered in a circle around Jeb. A sick spasm knotted his gut as every sprite took on the likeness of Alyssa—miniature replicas complete with platinum hair and sexy skate-glam outfits. They released their pheromone seeds again, blinding him with Alyssa's nectar-sweet scent.

Swinging a pillow, he shattered the illusion and scattered the seeds. The sprites screeched and hid in the vines on the walls, their glowing bodies like strands of white twinkle lights.

Gossamer fluttered overhead, scowling. "Enough! Report to our master that the mortal is loyal to the girl. We cannot seduce him to return to his world without her."

Jeb cursed as the sprites wriggled through pea-size holes in the wall where the grapevines wove in and out. If only he, too, could fit through those tiny exits. He gave a passing thought to using the shrinking drink in the backpack that he and Alyssa had found when they first arrived in Wonderland, but that would render him as small as his current captors, and he'd be powerless against Morpheus. Helplessness boiled in his gut, as deep as what he used to feel as a kid, hiding in a closet until his dad's rampages passed.

He clenched his teeth. There had to be a doorway hidden somewhere behind the vines. They'd brought him in here; there had to be a way out.

He took a running leap toward the closest wall and ripped some vines free, slinging them everywhere. Gossamer's tiny screech of surprise didn't faze him.

Grapes burst in his hands, releasing their sticky, potent scent. The ropy plants cut into his fingers like wires. He embraced the pain. This was something he could control—unlike the torment of his old man's glowing cigarettes boring into his skin, or the fists pounding his face and gut. The scent of nicotine, the taste of blood. Imagined or not, they fed the savage in his soul.

He plunged into a red tunnel of rage and trashed the room. When he at last came back to himself and leaned against the bed, he was shocked at the havoc he'd wrought.

Out of breath and sweating, he nursed the bleeding cuts at the bends of his fingers and searched the debris for Gossamer. Had he hurt her? If so, maybe he really was his father's son.

Jeb clenched his hands, disgusted with himself. "Gossamer?" He flinched at the sound of his voice, gruff and raw with emotion.

A flicker of wings stirred on one of the chains suspending the bed from the ceiling. He exhaled, relieved to see the sprite. Though it seemed stupid to care, since he was about to try using Alyssa's iron bracelet against her.

Gossamer settled on the floor next to the torn vines and the baskets he'd overturned yet again. Her shoulders were slumped in defeat. She probably didn't know where to start counting all the spilled contents.

Jeb began digging through the backpack. The harp had stopped playing, and the silence taunted him like a clock's ticking hands. Every second he spent away from Alyssa left her more vulnerable to Morpheus.

Cold metal finally met his fingers. He tossed the iron bracelet toward Gossamer but a few inches wide, hoping to weaken her without harming her.

She screamed and skittered into the air. "Please . . . put that away."

"Not until I get some answers." Jeb pinched one of her wings between his thumb and forefinger. He carried her to the bed and set her on a pillow, keeping the bracelet close enough to intimidate her. "Just cooperate, and I won't hurt you."

"It already hurts." She groaned, her greenish skin tinged turquoise. "Mustn't use my magic . . ." She slapped her palms to her face. "Will make me . . . hideous. *Abstain*." Her voice softened, as if she were speaking to herself. "Abstain until the threat of pain and contamination are gone." She gritted her teeth.

Jeb frowned. "So iron turns your power against you? The perfect weapon to use against your boss."

"A piece that size . . . will only work on the smallest of our kind."

Jeb bent over, holding the iron cuff closer to her. "Okay, then consider this a lie detector. Each time I sense you're holding out, the iron gets closer. Where is Al, and what's your creepy boss doing to her?"

The sprite's color changed to robin's egg blue. She rolled on the pillow, wings struggling to flutter. She pulled them over her shoulders and across her chest, as if to restrain her magic. "Your Alyssa is comfortable and cared for. Morpheus is watching over her as she sleeps . . ."

Jeb snarled. Last night, *he'd* been the one watching her sleep, in the rowboat. He'd rolled her to face him so he could make her a promise, even if she was too drowsy to hear it. He'd promised to watch over her, to get her home safely. He wasn't about to break his word now.

He had to fight the urge to trash the room again. "How do I get out of here?"

"Only Morpheus has the means to open the doorway."

Jeb leaned forward, his nose almost touching Gossamer's face as he held the iron bracelet over her head like corrosive mistletoe. "You're saying I'm stuck here until that winged cockroach decides to let me out? He's going to make Al face Wonderland alone?"

She whimpered, laying a palm on her brow. "No. Since you've proved yourself so loyal, he will allow you to accompany her on her journey. You will attend his feast and make plans."

"Feast?"

"Alyssa's introduction. Morpheus wishes to put her on display to the others."

"What others?"

Gossamer slumped in a purple heap and scooted off her perch. She dragged something from inside the pillowcase—a sketch of Al that Jeb didn't remember making. Slowly, Gossamer drew up her knees and studied the lines. "You did this while you were under our spell. You have power within your artist's heart—a light that can pierce any darkness. You've captured Alyssa's inner self perfectly."

"That sketch is pure fantasy," Jeb grumbled. He laid the iron cuff on the paper next to Gossamer.

She rolled to the middle of the drawing, trying to escape the metal. "There is more truth to this likeness of Alyssa than anything you can force me to say."

Jeb tugged at the picture, tumbling Gossamer and the iron bracelet onto the furs. He spread the sketch out on a pillow and traced the charcoal lines. This depiction was like all the other fairy drawings he'd made of Al over the years, but it couldn't be any more different from the girl he knew.

He'd drawn her with her hair pinned up. She never wore it that way. A black spaghetti-strapped gown flattered her curves. She wouldn't be caught dead in such a conventional dress. The only thing that looked like her were the lacy black fingerless gloves covering the scars on her palms.

Other than that, the drawing was a complete fabrication. Al was seated on a park bench. She held a rose. Mascara and tears streamed in graceful curls down her face. Come to think of it, it was similar to the way her makeup had looked the last time he saw her.

He still couldn't figure out why, after nearly drowning in an ocean of tears, her mascara hadn't washed away. Squinting, he studied the set of translucent wings spread behind her. The thin membranes shimmered in a single ray of sunlight slicing through the clouds. The wings made him uneasy, though he couldn't pinpoint why.

Maybe because they reminded him of Morpheus's wings, though a completely different color. Jeb's temples pounded. Nothing could be worse than her being alone with that bug man. The freak had some kind of hold on her, had gotten into her head when she was little. The subconscious could be very powerful, and if Morpheus still had access to Al's dreams . . .

"How do I beat him?" Jeb asked over the knot in his throat.

Gossamer's bulging eyes turned up to his. She was too weak to crawl away from the iron cuff, which now nudged her thigh. "He will not be defeated. He's waited years for this day."

Jeb grimaced. "Okay, so he's Superman. But everyone has their kryptonite. Something they fear."

"Confinement," Gossamer blurted, darkening to the color of a bruise at the confession.

"What do you mean?"

Gossamer pressed the back of her hand to her forehead. "Please . . . you're holding it too close . . . the iron . . . it's draining my energy."

Jeb fell back on the mattress and moved the cuff away from the sprite. Balancing it between his fingers, he studied the iron in the candlelight. It reminded him of his iron labret and the first time Al had seen it—her enthusiastic reaction. She'd begged to touch it, asking question after question about the process of getting a piercing. Her enthusiasm and naïveté. Her insecurities. Morpheus wouldn't hesitate to use any or all of them to manipulate her.

Jeb had to convince Al to leave Wonderland, to forget this quest to break the curse on her family, whatever it took. Something dark waited just around the corner for her, like in his dream. He could sense it looming.

"So, you want her to fix the original Alice's mistakes, right? What if *I* fix them instead?" Jeb tried reasoning. "You send Al home and let me take care of things."

"Impossible," Gossamer answered in a breathy whisper, her pale green color starting to return. Crawling toward the sketch, she ran a tiny palm along the rose. "She's already passed tests and proved she's the one."

"Tests? You mean like finding the rabbit hole to Wonderland and drying up the ocean of tears?"

She nodded.

"But I helped with those."

"She's the one he's waited for. Not you."

Jeb held the iron bracelet over her one last time. "What does he really want from her?"

Before Gossamer could answer, the domed ceiling started to shake. Pieces of plaster tumbled down in thick white chunks. Jeb held a pillow over his head and a palm over Gossamer to protect them from falling debris. The ceiling ripped at the seams, swinging the bed and pulling the chains in opposite directions so the mattress lifted several feet.

After the tremors stopped, Jeb glanced up. Morpheus's dark silhouette appeared in the jagged opening overhead.

Subtlety was low on this guy's priority list. "Anyone ever tell you you're a drama queen?" Jeb growled.

Morpheus leaned in low to glance at the messy room. "Anyone ever tell you you're a deplorable houseguest?"

His captor's grand entrance was partly responsible for the clutter, but Jeb bit his tongue, unwilling to risk his chance to see Al.

Morpheus eased back. "Alyssa awaits you in the mirrored hall.

And, by all means, wash up and shave. You are to be introduced to our dinner guests as an elfin knight, so you need to look the part. Gossamer shall give you tips on proper behavior." Morpheus dropped in some clothes and boots. They hit the floor with a clump. "Here is the uniform." He paused and gestured to the chains. "Too bad you haven't any wings or netherling magic. You will have to climb your way out. And I can assure you, it won't be an easy trek."

Jeb's muscles tensed as Morpheus vanished from view; he knew the warning referred to so much more than his exit from this room.

MEMORY TWO:
CARNAGE

Jeb wiped sweat from his brow. Morpheus had been right about the climb out of his gilded prison being difficult. But that was nothing to the trek through Wonderland he and Alyssa had taken since then. The entire day had been one crazy challenge after another, with danger and death around every turn. And now he'd lost Al. They'd become separated just before accomplishing the final test. She was facing the Twid sisters' cemetery alone, and he was stuck here in the bottom of a chasm.

Night had fallen the instant he'd hit the ground—such a fast transition, it was as if someone had flipped a light switch.

The kinks in his muscles tightened. He hated the thought of Al being alone in this wacked-out world after dark. Then again, she'd proved herself strong enough to face almost anything. It had been she who'd ended up saving *him*, in more ways than one . . .

He thought of how she'd looked—hovering overhead, glistening and wild, fluttering with the grace of a dragonfly. Seeing her sprout wings had been both terrifying and miraculous at once. He couldn't breathe while watching the transformation.

If he were honest, he still hadn't recovered his breath from when she had lowered him into the abyss and he'd shouted, *"You're my lifeline!"* before she shot up higher into the sky. He shouldn't have put so much pressure on her to save him. He had to do what he could to get out of here himself—meet her halfway. Otherwise, she'd never forgive herself if something went wrong.

A Jubjub bird's carcass had broken his fall. He wiped sticky goo from between his fingers onto his pants, turning up his nose at the rank remains of the army that had been chasing them and tumbled into the chasm. He pushed himself to stand in the pitch-dark gloom. His boots made sucking sounds as he walked. He'd never been squeamish; any aversion to blood and gore had been beaten out of him—a gradual desensitization reinforced each time he'd look in the mirror to find his cheeks and eyes swollen up, fat and bloody like raw steak.

But without a speck of light to go by, the carnage at his feet felt more alive than dead. His imagination pulled out files on everything from zombie movies to demons and hauntings. Nausea burned his stomach. He took solace that only the wind whistled through the chasm. He couldn't hear any ghostly chains or undead moans.

Besides, time was the actual foe here, more dangerous than anything he could imagine. Al still had to complete the final task in the cemetery. And then they had to find each other again.

He forced himself blindly forward until his palm skimmed the chasm's wall. Before he'd dropped all the way down, he'd caught a glimpse of Al's backpack snagged on a rock outcropping about a yard north. If he could find it, he'd have a flashlight. Hands scraping the crusty surface of the stone, he lifted his feet over obstacles, patting his toes across corpses to assess how wide each step should stretch.

Rubbing the scrapes on his elbows, he studied the sky. A shy smattering of stars wrestled the clouds and broke through to dimly light his surroundings, enabling him to wend his way around the queen's dead army. A damp breeze spun dust like tiny tornados. It was going to rain. And in this place, it was possible it would literally rain cats and dogs—the hissing and barking variety.

A chill that had nothing to do with the impending storm crept across his soul and shadowed any humor he might've found in the thought. What was with all of Morpheus's "tests"? Each time Al successfully completed one, her netherling form became more prominent. Was the goal to alter her completely, so she couldn't go back to the human realm?

Strands of hair blew into his face, and he shoved them aside.

Morpheus had said that all he ever wanted was to return Alyssa to her proper place. Her *home*. Jeb had hoped that meant back to their world, the human realm. But what if Al didn't have a curse on her at all?

He remembered from his fairy research that there were creatures called changelings—the offspring of fairies secretly left in the place of stolen human babies. Had Al's great-great-great-grandmother, Alice Liddell, been a changeling? Maybe that was how she'd found the rabbit hole as a child—by instinct. That would mean that this *was* Al's home, in some warped way.

Jeb shook off the speculations. They only dredged up more questions.

He'd reached the backpack. Opening it, he fished out the flashlight and flipped it on.

As he zipped up the bag, he brushed the landscape with swaths of light. The tattered guards looked like crumpled playing cards. Discarded playthings. Even the busted-up Jubjub birds could pass as children's toys with the stuffing pulled out.

Backpack in place, Jeb walked the circumference of the chasm without finding any openings. Displaced rocks filled any possible passages he might've tried. He might as well have fallen into a giant tube. There was no way out other than up.

He pointed his light at the grassy perch some twenty stories above—the clearing where Alyssa had landed. He was determined to find her before Morpheus did, even if he had to scale the jutting rocks in the dark without a safety rope.

He'd no sooner wedged the flashlight in his mouth and banked his foot on a crag to boost himself up than a familiar British voice rang out.

"Get to it, men. We need an accurate head count before the Twid sisters send their pixie brigade to gather up the dead."

Morpheus.

Jeb stepped down and almost collided with the winged nether-ling who had appeared from out of nowhere—as if he'd unzipped the air and slipped through. Twenty to thirty elfin knights filed in behind him, carrying lanterns and wearing the same uniform as Jeb, though much less frayed and dirty. They strode by without giving Jeb a second glance, too intent on the body count.

"Well, hello, pseudo knight." Morpheus smirked.

Every part of Jeb itched to rip off his cocky grin and pound his face. But he was outnumbered. If he wanted to get out of this pit and find Al, he would have to play nice.

"I hate to say it, but it's good to see you, Sir Morphs-a-lot." Jeb tucked his flashlight away. "You took the mirror route, I see."

"Glass is the only way to travel." Morpheus held up his lantern and examined Jeb's ruined clothes. "For one, it's a bit kinder on the wardrobe. And I'll let you in on another secret. By keeping my wings on that side of the plane"—he pointed a thumb at his back, where half of his appendages weren't visible—"the opening stays accessible for our return trip."

Jeb forced a smile. "Good to know." *Perfect, in fact.* He could go back with this fairy troupe, then take the mirrored-hall express to find Al. He would have to distract Morpheus first, though—get his guard down. "So, is that a new hat?"

Morpheus practically beamed. "How kind of you to notice. It's my Insurrection Hat. I've ne'er had occasion to wear it until today." He flicked several of the scarlet moths that made up the garland on the hat's brim, then leaned forward and cupped Jeb's ear to muffle a secret. "Their red wings represent bloodshed," he whispered.

"Uh-huh." Jeb clenched his jaw at the unwelcome rush of warm breath along his earlobe. He glared at the knights, discernible only by their lanterns floating in the blackness behind him. "So you're planning a revolt with the Ivory Queen's army."

Morpheus squeezed Jeb's shoulder. "Always knew you were smarter than the average mortal."

Jeb's muscles twitched at the contact. "Which means you were just sending Al on a wild goose chase for your own entertainment." *Careful*. He couldn't let his distrust show. Not yet. Instead, he bent down to adjust his boot laces and took a deep breath before straightening.

Morpheus tightened his crimson necktie. "Every task I've asked of Alyssa has had a purpose." He stepped to one side as someone new slipped through the mirror portal—a dwarfish skeleton with antlers and glowing pink eyes, trussed up in a red waistcoat.

"Rabid White?" Jeb whispered in disbelief. None of this made sense. Rabid was from the Red Court. Why was he here?

"What's the report, then?" Morpheus crouched down close to Rabid's height, still keeping his wing tips tucked inside the invisible mirror portal.

The little netherling kneaded his gloved hands and glared up at Jeb, his bald head reflecting the soft shimmer of Morpheus's lantern. "One of us, are you?"

Morpheus smiled and answered for Jeb. "Of course he is. He helped our Alyssa conquer the big bad Red army, did he not?"

Scratching his left antler, Rabid nodded. "King Grenadine, neutralized be. At both the front and back gates, the castle guarded by regiments three and seven. Flanking the queen, a circle of five. And not to dismiss, the crown and its keeper."

"Ah, yes. The bandersnatch. Well, once Alyssa brings me her prize from the Twid sisters' cemetery, I'll have nothing more to fear from that wretched beast. You've done well, Sir White." Morpheus tipped his hat.

Rabid clicked his cadaverous ankles together and bowed, then gave Jeb a final piercing pink glare before he hopped back through the portal.

"He's your spy," Jeb mumbled, feeling like an idiot for not guessing that sooner.

"Yes."

"So all those times the little bonehead threatened Al, scared her lifeless, that was to uphold the appearance of loyalty to Queen Grenadine?"

"The best spies are the ones that play both sides with equal vigor."

Jeb studied the swinging lanterns in the distance. The squeaking of metal handles and the shuffling of boots eclipsed the wind's soft whine. "Okay. Since we're laying out all our cards—"

Morpheus's snort interrupted him. "What a delightfully fitting pun, considering where we stand." His lantern motioned to all the card-guard corpses.

Jeb ignored the morbid joke. "I was going to ask why Rabid turned against the Red Court."

"He was Queen Red's royal advisor during Alice's visit. He wants to see the true heir upon the throne almost as much as I do."

"True heir." Jeb kicked up a puff of dirt with one boot, his chest tight. "So all of this has been to dethrone Grenadine and make room for a new queen."

"Yes." The lantern glazed Morpheus's face in an expression of dreamy indulgence. "And we're so close. Soon she'll be on her throne, where she's always belonged. In her proper place."

Her proper place. A hypothesis formed in Jeb's mind, outrageous and incomprehensible yet somehow the obvious answer to all the questions earlier churning in his mind. Every question except one . . .

"But first," Morpheus said with a dismissive sweep of his hand, "we have to be sure what we're up against when we raid the castle. You and Alyssa managed to take out quite a chunk of the opposition with your fancy footwork. We're here to assess if the numbers match up with the ones Rabid reported. We must ensure that Grenadine doesn't have any cards hidden up her sleeve." He slapped Jeb on the back. "See what I did there? 'Cards up her sleeve'?" He chuckled.

Jeb didn't crack a smile.

"Oh, come now. She has cards for guards. 'Tis a pun, like the one you made earlier, but much more clever."

"Yeah, yeah, I get it." Jeb scowled.

Morpheus's smile faded. "You're not a very fun date."

"Don't you ever take anything seriously?" Jeb gritted out. "Al's in danger out there."

"Nonsense. She's gloriously capable! Did you not see her fly earlier? Of course you did! You were dangling at the end of her chain." Morpheus swung his lantern over his head in celebratory sweeps. "Wasn't she a vision, coming into her own? Just like a fairy princess." He gave Jeb a sly glance. "Don't you agree?"

Fairy princess. There it was, out of Morpheus's own mouth, mocking Jeb for not realizing it from the very beginning. Jeb clenched his hands on the backpack straps to keep from jamming a fist into Morpheus's larynx.

Morpheus set his lantern down, then fished silver gloves out of his lapel. "Don't feel slighted, mortal knight. Your contribution did not go unnoticed. And I always repay my debts. So I'll be taking you out of this gully of death in demonstration of my gratitude."

"You can thank me by letting me help Al," Jeb managed, vocal cords tight. "She'll finish her assignment a lot faster with me at her side." If he could get to her, maybe they could hide from Morpheus in the Twid sisters' cemetery together until they figured a way out of this.

"Sorry," Morpheus said, pulling on the gloves as he motioned the elfin knights back over. "She needs to do this on her own. You shall see her soon enough; we'll all be reunited. One big happy family."

"No!" Jeb's control ripped loose. He lunged, but the elves were too fast and restrained him, fingers biting into his wounded elbows. "Just let her leave Wonderland, you son of a bug—"

Morpheus pressed a finger to Jeb's mouth. "Ah, ah, ah. Already used that one."

Jeb jerked his head back, leaving the netherling's finger hanging in midair.

The jewels at the edges of Morpheus's tattoos darkened to the color of dried blood in the lantern light. "Now, now. Is that any way to treat your rescuer?" He pouted. "Besides, how can I let Alyssa go if I don't *have* her? She was entering the garden of souls, last I heard. But once she's finished there, she'll find me. She has a very important role yet to play."

"Right. Because *she's* the heir to the throne." Jeb listened, incredulous, to his own words echo as if they'd slipped from someone else's mouth. "I don't know how, but it's her."

"Oh, ho!" Morpheus applauded. "Do you see what I told you, brethren knights?" Glancing over Jeb's shoulder at the elves, Morpheus patted his chest atop his red necktie, as if overwhelmed with emotion. "Smarter than the average mortal. Too bad he still has all the physical limitations of one."

"Doesn't matter," Jeb snarled. "She's out of your reach." He tugged against the elves, but there were too many holding him. "She must be inside the cemetery by now, and you can't force her to do anything. You said it yourself—the Twids won't let you in."

"True enough. But she'll find her way to the castle on her own.

The moment she realizes I hold captive the one thing she treasures above all else in the world, she'll come crawling to me, wings in tow." Morpheus raised a hand in some sort of signal.

The elfin knights released Jeb. He spun on his heel and flung his backpack at them, scattering the group like bowling pins. Throwing out a fist, he cuffed Morpheus's forehead and unbalanced him. One of the knights scrambled into place to maintain the mirror's opening. Before Jeb could catapult after him and leap through, blue crackles of lightning snagged his skin and clothes like static electricity. They dragged him around, controlling him like a marionette until he faced Morpheus once more. The lightning was coming from the netherling's fingertips.

Morpheus moved closer.

Jeb tried to step back, but his muscles shut down—paralyzed.

"Sleep," Morpheus said simply, and he laid a blue-glowing palm on Jeb's head. A pulse of light swept through Jeb. He tasted something sweet, like honey and milk, then smelled the scent of lavender. Fingers cinched in the silky weave of Morpheus's shirt, Jeb struggled to stay awake. But the light was too comforting . . . too soft . . . too warm. Against his will, his eyelids grew heavy, and he fell to the ground, sound asleep.

MEMORY THREE: CAGED

Jeb's skull throbbed, and blood drizzled from his hairline into his eyes.

He swiped away the stickiness to focus on his surroundings. Morpheus had brought him to the Red castle after putting the sleeping spell on him. Dumped him inside a birdcage in the dungeon. Jeb wished he hadn't drunk the shrinking liquid when he woke up, but the bug man had given him an ultimatum.

At first, he'd threatened to kill Al. But Jeb had called that bluff, knowing she was indispensable. Then Morpheus had pulled out another big gun, threatening to send Al's fragile mom completely over the edge of sanity. That he *would* do.

Al had fought so hard to save her mother. It would kill her to lose her to madness. So Jeb didn't hesitate putting the bottle to his lips.

His body swayed, but it wasn't from the woozy aftereffects of the potion. The platform beneath him was swinging from his attempts to head-butt his way through his prison's bars—a desperate move that had resulted in nothing more than the gash at his hairline. A piece of Morpheus's magic—a blue electrical thread—held the wire door of the birdcage immovably shut.

"Well, plenty of good that did, yes?" a nagging female voice intoned. "Morpheus chooses who has the power to coax his magic loose. Obviously, you're not a chosen one."

Jeb grimaced at his fellow captive. She was a lory—a parakeetlike netherling normally the size of a human. Since they'd both been shrunk, the only thing that set her apart from the birds in his world were the robes of creamy satin and red jacquard fitted over her wings, body, and bird legs, and her humanoid face slapped onto crimson feathers as if it were a mask. A beak that was more like a rhinoceros's horn jabbed at him from where a nose should have been, and her lips flapped furiously.

Worst of all, her voice could topple the Tower of Pisa with one syllable. Whenever she spoke, it was as if someone had surgically implanted speakers in Jeb's ears and locked the volume dials on "deafer than a stone statue." She was one of the many reasons he'd been trying so hard to get out of this bird prison.

Flickering light from the candles on the wall outside the cage illuminated her scowl and cast the rest of the dungeon into shadow.

"Listen, *Lorina*," Jeb said after her voice stopped echoing. "We wouldn't be in here if it weren't for your husband." He pointed to the creature snoring below the cage, who was just as strange-looking as his wife, with the body of a dodo, the head of a man, and hands protruding from the tips of his stubby wings. "*He* kept Alice Liddell in a cage just like this one all those years ago. It's his fault my girlfriend has what it takes to dethrone your queen. Did it ever occur to you that this is what you both had coming?"

"Charlie did no such thing!" shrieked the lory, fluttering in midair in the cage. "Did it ever occur to *you* that Morpheus is a brass-faced liar?"

Only every minute of every hour. Jeb leaned against the bars. His knees gave out, weakened by his efforts to strong-arm the wire bars with every available muscle. He clunked to the metallic floor, nudging a browning pear slice sitting on its side like a small couch. The cage was an impregnable fort in his miniature state. But it didn't matter. The bars could've been made of uncooked spaghetti, and he still wouldn't be able to help Al. Even if he escaped, at this size he couldn't take on anyone.

Charlie, Lorina's dodo husband, wasn't much help. He was bound in iron cuffs and manacles, napping against a wall. Though the birdcage hung on a peg just inches above the dodo's head, there was nothing Charlie could do about it.

Morpheus must've treated the giant birdman to the same sleeping spell he'd cast on Jeb earlier, though Charlie was starting to come out of it.

Lorina settled on the perch in the center of the cage, swinging over Jeb's head like an acrobat on a trapeze. Her face flamed as fiery as her feathers, which caused the red spade and heart stenciled on her cheeks to fade in comparison. "Since we're to be exiled in this urine-stenched facility," she bellowed, "you shall have plenty of time to hear the truth."

Jeb rubbed his head to ease the splitting ache. "If you could take your voice down about two decibels, I'd appreciate it."

"Take my voice *down?*"

"Augh." Jeb cradled his face in his hands.

The miniature trapeze squeaked with each swing, adding to the noise pollution. "For your information, my queen adores the sound of my voice. Praises it, in fact."

The dodo's snoring paused, and he smacked his lips. "That would be because she stops her ears with beeswax, O Loveliest of Lunatics."

"Fat liar," Lorina snapped, rocking her swing so fast, Jeb thought he might get seasick.

"I'm wearing iron chains," Charlie said on the tail end of a yawn. "I haven't the strength to lie." Then he dropped back off to sleep.

That seemed to shut Lorina up, at least temporarily.

Jeb took advantage of the silence to think. Morpheus must have told Al about her true lineage by now, about what was expected of her. She must be so shocked . . . so terrified. Jeb ached to hold her, to the point that his chest felt like an anvil sat on it.

That moth freak should've told her the truth from the beginning. She would never have chosen to stay. But Morpheus had known that, so he'd tricked her under the pretense that she could cure a curse on her bloodline. Jeb wanted to pluck off Morpheus's black wings and stuff them down his throat for misleading her, because there was no cure for family, as he knew only too well.

"It was Red who put Alice in a cage." The lory was off and running again. "Not Charlie."

"But your husband chose to keep her caged," Jeb inserted against his better judgment. He plugged his ears for the booming rebuttal, but Lorina only sighed.

"No. Charlie tried to do the right thing by the girl," she said, considerably softer now. "He planned to send Alice back to the human realm behind Red's back, but the queen found out and dragged them to a cave in the highest cliffs of Wonderland's wilds, without any of us knowing. She left Charlie with her victim, so she could enact her master plan, knowing Alice would be tended by a captive who could never escape. Because, of course, dodos can't fly. She stole my husband from me for years. He was a prisoner, just like the mortal was."

"Whatever helps you sleep at night, Birdie."

A flurry of dust-scented wings, jacquard, and satin dropped down and attacked him. "You will show respect and listen!"

Jeb held up his hands in self-defense. "All right. Sheesh. I'll listen." It wasn't like there was anything else he could do. Morpheus had told him that as soon as Alyssa was crowned queen, she could open the portal to the human realm. Whether Jeb believed that or not, he couldn't do anything other than hope. He had no power here. That knowledge gnawed at his insides with each passing minute.

Settled in front of Jeb atop a mountain of lush fabric, the lory looked through the bars and grumbled to her sleeping husband, "Worthless old fezzerjub. Leave me to do all your defending. Don't know why I ever married you."

The dodo snorted and murmured sleepily, "Because marrying the court jester was the only way you could have a spot in the Red Court, O Darling of Dirges." The snoring resumed.

"See how well that turned out," she grumped, her rouged, heart-shaped lips pouting beneath the curl of her beak. "Bony little Rabid and his black heart of stone." She preened the feathers on the back of her neck and tucked a sequined net around them.

Jeb reached over to retrieve the thimbleful of water their captor had left next to the pear slice. It was the size of a large coffee mug in his hands. He handed it off to his cellmate, who took it with her wings and gulped some down.

"Tell me something, Lori. If what you say is true . . ." Reading the defensiveness on her beaked face, he rephrased his question to save his ears. "Since you've chosen to share your side of the story, maybe you could tell me what role *Morpheus* played in Alice's captivity."

She patted water droplets from her lips. "He played no role at all. He was very fond of Alice and would've done anything to see her safely home. But the same hour he offered her advice as a caterpillar—warning her to avoid Queen Red's castle at all costs—his metamorphosis came over him. When he emerged, fully transformed, and learned what had become of Alice, he was furious."

"You're trying to tell me he actually has a conscience?"

"He did where Alice was concerned." The lory adjusted the regal robe that kept slipping from her lack of shoulders. "Morpheus used all his resources as a solitary fae and finally found her and my husband hidden away in the caves of the highest cliffs of Wonderland. Alas, it was too late for Alice by that time." Lorina returned the thimble to Jeb, half full now.

Jeb sat up straighter, causing the cage to rock. "So why does he want to help Queen Red get another queen on the throne, when he should hate her for putting Alice in a cage for all those years?"

"Mayhap he's angry that Grenadine didn't try to find Alice herself once the child was captured. But Grenadine lost her memory ribbon and forgot about the child."

"A good ruler would've had more than one ribbon to remind her, would've made sure everyone and everything was in its place."

"My queen *is* a good ruler!"

Jeb winced at the ear-splitting roar.

The dodo's snores stopped. "My vociferous wife speaks the truth, lad. Morpheus appears to be holding a grudge for what he perceives as neglect, even if it was simply an oversight."

Jeb shook his head at all the holes in everyone's reasoning. "No. There's more to this than that."

"You have good instincts, mortal knight."

Jeb perked up at the tinkling voice. A glowing light floated through the small window in the dungeon's heavy wooden door. Jeb stood and gripped the birdcage bars, angling his head to get a better look.

Gossamer.

The little sprite fluttered over and whispered something to the magical blue thread fixed around the wire door, letting herself inside the cage. The thread tied itself into a knot again after she'd reattached the latch behind her.

She sparkled like the lit fuse on a Roman candle as she hovered in place, studying Jeb with a sympathetic expression.

Since they were now the same size, she brought to mind a painting Jeb once saw by a Czech artist, Viktor Olivia. He was most famous for his depiction of a fairy who seduced men into getting drunk on absinthe. Gossamer embodied that creature: a woman's perfect form, dusted green and naked with glistening scales covering her like a string bikini.

He had sensed when he left the mirrored hall that she was on his and Alyssa's side.

"You came to help," he said, hopeful.

A copper key, the same color as her eyes and almost the full length of her torso, swung from her neck. Her gaze dropped to her dainty feet, as if she were battling herself. "I would've been here sooner, but Morpheus is always watching in the looking glass. Now that he's with Alyssa, preparing her for her coronation, he will be too busy to keep an eye on the rest of us . . . until the end."

"The end?" Jeb gripped the bar next to her, intent on her dragonfly gaze. "You have to tell me—everything."

The sprite glared at Lorina, who'd been inching toward the wire door. "You well know you haven't the power to leave this cage unless I open it for you."

Huffing, the lory fluttered up to the trapeze again.

Gossamer led Jeb to the pear slice, and they both sat down. The fruity scent overpowered the stench of the dungeon and calmed him enough to hear her out.

Gossamer curled her hands over Jeb's where they rested on his clamped knees. "I've already betrayed my master enough by being here, and his wrath will be great. All I can say is that, within the hour, Alyssa will be forever indentured—tethered to Wonderland for all eternity. Morpheus has planned all along to send you back, mortal knight . . . but without her."

A vein in Jeb's temple began to writhe like a snake on a hot plate. He leapt up and banged his head on the bars again, trying to shake loose the taunting blue thread, unable to control the helpless fury boiling through him. More blood dripped along his temple. "You have to get me out! I've got to stop this!"

"Yes, yes! Us, too!" the dodo and his wife piped up. "We must help Queen Grenadine keep her crown!"

"Of course," Gossamer said, grasping Jeb's hand to drag him back next to her. "You will all be given the chance to fight for your loyalties."

"But I can't fight like this." Jeb kicked a pear seed the size of his foot. "Did you bring an amplifying pastry?"

"No. It is not the strength of your body that will save Alyssa, but the strength of your artist's heart. Though I can assure you, you won't be leaving this place in your present form."

The lory dropped down from her perch and scowled at the sprite. "Now, you listen here, little mimsy silverfish. This boy has no part to play. He's secondary at best. I am the queen's handmaid, and Charlie is the court jester. *We* should be your priority. We're honored members of the royal court, the only ones who can put a stop to this travesty!"

Accelerating her wings to a misty blur, Gossamer floated and placed her hands on her hips. "For *your* part, Lorina, you can unlock your husband's chains, as I need to speak to the mortal alone and have little tolerance for iron." She opened the cage's door and handed off the key.

The lory went fluttering out in a flurry of flamboyance and ill temperament.

"Come, come, Sweetness of Savagery," Charlie encouraged his wife as she fluttered all around him, bouncing up and down, unable to maintain altitude. "Hurry, would you? The iron is stinging. Oh, really! It's not so very hard . . . do try again!"

Lorina's face fired even redder. "You try using a key the same size as your head with a wing tip, flufflesnot! Some of us weren't blessed with fingers, you know."

While the couple was preoccupied, Gossamer sat next to Jeb again.

"You said my artist's heart can save Alyssa," he whispered. "In the room at Morpheus's mansion, too . . . you said I have power within my artist's heart—a light that can pierce any darkness. My girlfriend is about to be dead to me and her family. It doesn't get any darker than that." Frustrated tears singed the corners of his eyes.

"Would you die for her, mortal knight?"

Jeb's spine stiffened. In the past, each time he'd protected Alyssa, he'd just jumped in without a thought. *Would he die for her?*

When his dad was killed in an accident, it was Alyssa who saved him. He couldn't believe he'd ever considered living in London without her. He needed her, every day. Her understanding smile, the way she made his scars feel like medals of valor under her touch, and her incredible eyes. Even though she'd seen just as much disappointment in her life as he had, there was a light inside her that never dimmed. And not only did it make her beautiful on the outside, but that same light allowed her to bring life to the incredible mosaics she made.

It was that light—both inner and outer—that had driven him to sketch and paint her over and over again.

He looked at Gossamer, hardly able to contain his emotions now that they'd been given an outlet. "She's my best friend." *My muse, my brush, my artistry, my heart. All of it's dead without her.* "I love her." Scrubbing his face, he smeared the moisture that had crept from his eyes along his cheeks. "Yes, I would die for her. Is that what I have to do?"

The sprite stared back, unblinking. "Are you willing to go

beyond death? To be lost to everyone, even yourself, in a place where memories wash away on a tide as dark as ink? For in order to free Alyssa, you will have to take the Ivory Queen's place in the jabberlock box where she's trapped."

Jeb pictured the dark water in the box he'd seen in the mirrored hall at Morpheus's mansion—the ghostly head inside—and his heartbeat stumbled. Self-preservation kicked in, his mind racing to find another way. But in the deepest part of him, he knew there was no alternative, and time was running out for Al. His only regret was that he wouldn't get to tell her how he felt just once with his own voice before it was locked away forever. "I'll do it."

"And so you shall." Gossamer stood and held out her arms. Weak and numb, Jeb stepped into her embrace. She clung tightly and flew him out of the cage, landing them on the floor. "The mortal has agreed to be your kingdom's hero." She fired the words at Lorina. "See that you honor his bravery."

Lorina had managed to unlock her husband. She sat upon his shoulder, fanning herself with a wing. Wide-eyed, she nodded in silence—the most heartfelt accolade she could've offered. The dodo knelt beside Jeb, a huge feathery presence. "We are forever in your debt, lad. What can we do to help?"

Gossamer pointed to a far corner of the dungeon, where a burlap blanket covered a cot, draping down to the floor. "Bring me what's beneath that bed."

Jeb watched, numbed by a mixture of disbelief and dread as the dodo carried over the jabberlock box.

Lorina gaped. "Morpheus had Ivory hidden down here?"

Gossamer nodded. "Upon Rabid's suggestion. He said this was the one place in the castle that no one would search for her."

After asking Charlie to open the lid and arrange a stone for them to stand on so they could see within, Gossamer dismissed the strange couple to a far corner of the dungeon for privacy.

Jeb stroked the white velvet roses flocked along the outside of the box, mesmerized by Ivory's beautiful face as it bobbed to the surface. Her haunted, crystallized gaze slid from him to the sprite and back again—cautiously curious. He shuddered at the thought of taking her place.

Did he really have to do this?

He felt Gossamer watching his profile. "I must ask one last time if you're sure," she said. "For, you see, since you are *choosing* to be locked within and sealing the choice with your blood, the box will never let you out. No one can save you. You're signing away your eternity for Ivory, a queen you don't even know."

Jeb gulped a knot from his throat. "No. I'm *trading* my eternity for *Al's*."

Gossamer smiled tenderly. "I once saw in your dreams your fear of not being good enough for the girl. After such a sacrifice, no one could ever question your worth as a man, or your love for her." She kissed his cheek, leaving warmth that trickled into his heart and managed to melt a small portion of the icy terror there.

Gossamer handed him a paintbrush and drew back. "Now, use the power only you can wield. Paint the roses with your blood."

Dizziness rushed over him. He mumbled . . . senseless, fearful things . . . agonized words that he knew would be his last.

Then he channeled all the anger, terror, and longing for a future he would never have into the sweep and sway of the brush. He stained each snow-white blossom red until he lost himself within the shadows of his work, and became one with his masterpiece.

THE MOTH'S
RESOLUTION

The scene stretched and blurred as Morpheus was dragged out of Jebediah's memories and deposited back into the chaise lounge. Darkness weighed heavily upon the room, yet he didn't budge to turn on the lamp. The pitch-black surroundings seemed to suit the murky thoughts in his head.

He ran a thumb along his thigh, tracing the ridges of the pin-striped fabric and smoothing the wrinkles.

Why was he feeling so out of sorts? He'd found exactly what he'd hoped to find. Jebediah's weaknesses had been there for the taking: a rage that could easily be coaxed out and manipulated, a sense of worthlessness fed by a violent and critical father, a jealousy that evoked a reckless protectiveness—even at the expense of his own life.

What Morpheus hadn't expected to find, however, was how similar he and the boy were. The demons from Jebediah's tormented past were not unlike his own. He'd often found himself jealous of humans . . . having never had a father or mother's tenderness. He also empathized with the fear that he might never know completely another's trust and affection, based solely on his place in the world.

Although, in the past, Morpheus had never considered that a bad thing. He'd enjoyed being a reclusive and self-reliant soul. At times he was vainglorious, of course, when it suited him to be the center of attention. But attention, affection, or trust weren't things he *needed*. Not until Alyssa came along. When she chose to ignore him, he couldn't function . . . felt bumbling and incompetent.

And now, after standing in Jebediah's shoes, Morpheus understood more than he wanted to about how the human side of Alyssa worked. Although one half of her had wings and could float past trivial, mortal insecurities, the other half of her was grounded and craved what any human would crave: reassurance and reliability.

Having seen Jebediah's courage, ingenuity, and loyalty to Alyssa firsthand, Morpheus knew without a doubt that that was exactly what the boy was offering her: a safety net of emotion that would keep her from ever falling too hard.

No wonder she was so captivated by him. No wonder he held her in his thrall. Hell, Morpheus himself was morbidly fascinated by the boy's honorable traits, unusual in a human so damaged. Morpheus was tempted to step back and let Jebediah have his moment of happiness. Some might even say he'd earned it by being willing to give up his future, his memories, his life for Alyssa.

Morpheus growled and slumped forward, hands clenched, trying to lighten the unfamiliar weight upon his chest. It wasn't as if the boy would be around forever. He was mortal. Someday he would die of old age, at the very least, and Alyssa would be fair game once more.

Fair game.

Morpheus's jaw twitched. Romance wasn't fair. Nor was it a game. It was war. And, as on any other battlefield, compassion and mercy had no place there.

The carpet beetle had been right. Human emotions were unpredictable and powerful things. They'd gotten into Morpheus's head, weakened his resolve.

Elbows on his knees, he held his palms up, unable to see even their silhouette in the darkness. He conjured a small strain of magic to gather at his fingertips in plasma electric balls the size of peas, then coaxed the orbs through every corner of the room, trailing blue lightning like static electricity. They climbed the walls before gathering together in the form of a woman. The light pulsed hypnotically.

Imagining Jebediah with Alyssa, showing her the ways of love, taming her savage spirit with his common human conventions, scalded Morpheus's throat with a bitter tang of envy.

He didn't want her wildness to be subdued by any other man, didn't wish to share any part of her. He wanted both sides: her innocence and her defiant spirit.

Where was the excitement in dependability? Where was the spontaneity in a predictable world? He could offer her an eternity of challenges and passion, of quiet, tender moments stolen in the depths of riotous flames and ravaging storms—tranquility amidst the chaos.

She belonged with *him*, wearing regal robes. He had so much to teach her about the nether-realm, about the glories of manipulation and madness. If he fed her gluttonous netherling side, her human insecurities and inhibitions would fade and, in time, vanish altogether. She would no longer crave Jebediah's safe love.

Morpheus called his magic back, reeling in the coils of blue light until he was surrounded by darkness once more. His wings swept the floor as he stood. He lifted them high in a determined arc that nearly touched the ceiling.

No more deliberating. He'd tried to do the *fair* thing in past instances, and, without fail, it always came back to haunt him. He could suppress the twinge of guilt stirring in his chest, but he could not give up his needs for Jebediah's. He would never be himself again without Alyssa by his side—the flame to his moth. He wouldn't stop until she was back where she belonged, in Wonderland.

To win, he would fight dirty, reap the spoils of her heart by any means necessary, no matter what it cost the mortal boy. It was the netherling way, after all. To do any less would make Morpheus human. And he knew, now more than ever, that that was the last thing he ever wanted to be.

SIX IMPOSSIBLE THINGS

SOMETIMES I'VE BELIEVED AS MANY AS SIX
IMPOSSIBLE THINGS BEFORE BREAKFAST.

—Lewis Carroll

✳ ONE ✳
MORTALITY

1

DEPORTATION

Some people might say it's impossible to die and then live to tell about it. They're the ones who've never experienced magic. As for me, I'm the great-great-great-granddaughter of Lewis Carroll's Alice inspiration. I've believed in the unbelievable for over sixty-four years, ever since I was sixteen, and learned Wonderland was real and populated with a whimsical, eerie, mad sect of beings governed by bargains and riddles. Yet sometimes, no matter how much you believe in the impossible, things don't quite work out the way you planned. Even magic can hit a snag now and then.

For example, I never expected my corpse to end up in a shoebox. That's what the cremation casket reminds me of . . . a human-size, corrugated cardboard box. The casket offers little comfort. There's no velvet lining to soften the plywood base. No cushion to cradle my curved spine. And no clothes, other than a crinkly paper gown, to cover my wrinkled and aged skin.

The scent of cardboard settles in my nose and the gurney's steel wheels roll along the tile hallway, squeaking somewhere beneath me alongside unfamiliar footsteps. I sense the transition from the cool, temperature-controlled room where the coroner signed off on my "deadness" (as the pixies in Wonderland would say). He then laid a stainless steel identification tag atop my chest and placed a lid over me, cloaking me in darkness.

There's a sharp jolt when the gurney takes a turn into a much warmer place. The rotten-egg stench of propane gas confirms our whereabouts. I've visited this room. I toured several local crematoriums late at night over the last few months, when no one else was around. So I'd be familiar with the giant brick-lined furnace that would be waiting to sizzle away my flesh. So I'd find the perfect layout, with a bathroom and a full-size mirror across the hall.

Once I decided on the crematorium at Pleasance Rest Cemetery, I prepared to die.

My original plan was to use Tetrodotoxin. In small, sublethal doses it leaves the victim in a near-death state for days, while allowing her mind to retain consciousness. But Morpheus didn't agree. He pointed out that the margin of error between a nearly dead state and a truly dead state is slim in the mortal world, and not something to be trifled with. He didn't want me to risk it. So he offered a Wonderland substitute: an enchanted cessation potion that works much the same way, but has a counter-inception potion with a one hundred percent success rate.

I drank down the cessation dose this morning, and ten hours later I can still taste the bitter and numbing flavor, like cloves swirling at the bottom of vinegary cider. I can't smack my tongue to relieve the potency. The magic has rendered me catatonic—my eyes closed and unblinking, my heartbeat and breath muted to a silent purr undetectable by any human means.

My netherling side flutters inside my skull, assuring me this is going to work, but my human side instinctively recoils as fear tightens my throat. I can't cry out to tell anyone I'm still alive. My vocal cords won't work. Claustrophobia, my old enemy, forms itchy tangles beneath my skin. I know what's going on around me, although my eyelids can't open and my limbs can't twitch. Every smell, sound, and tactile sensation is magnified by my inability to react to it.

The paramedic who answered my twenty-seven-year-old granddaughter's 911 call this morning pronounced me dead on the scene—struck down by a heart attack. It was unbearable, hearing her cry and wail. It triggered memories of my own greatest loss—of Jeb's death three years earlier. A knife still gores through my chest each time I remember our final good-bye.

But Jeb told me to be strong. And I taught my grandchildren the same—to always face things head-on. She'll be all right. I know it without a doubt because she's like me in so many ways, even beyond her blond hair, blue eyes, and inquisitive nature. She's stubborn, loyal, and a survivor.

Once the paramedic delivered my body to the morgue, everything went like clockwork.

My family was aware of the cemetery I'd chosen and the four requirements in my will: no public viewing of my body, no chapel service, cremation within twelve hours of my passing, and the sprinkling of my ashes where Jeb's were, beneath the weeping willow at our country cottage. That tree held special meaning, grown from a clipping taken off the willow that used to share our backyards as we were growing up.

Such unconventional requests didn't even faze my family, considering the eccentric old woman I'd become.

After Jeb's death, they watched me putter about my cottage, gathering up the mosaics I'd made throughout my life, filled with bizarre and mystical landscapes—with titles like *Winter's Heartbeat*, *Checkerboard Dunes*, and *Belly of the Beast*—and pack them away in the attic along with other heirlooms, including a tourism brochure for the Thames sundial trail in London. The last things I added were two keys: One had belonged to my mom and could make a mirror into a portal, and the other could open the gate to Wonderland's garden of souls. The latter was a gift granted to Jeb after he gave up his muse so he could fulfill the nether-realm's need for vivid, imaginative dreams, and bridge our worlds with peace in the process. He gave up what had once made him unique, to keep human children safe. A courageous act his own children and grandchildren never had the privilege to know. That memento was the hardest for me to let go of, for it was a tribute to Jeb's courageous heart and noble nature—the two things I loved most about him. But as Wonderland's Red Queen, I had no business keeping such a hallowed key.

I hid everything in a trunk in the attic and locked it. Then I stashed the trunk's key inside the pages of my well-worn Lewis Carroll collection. Jeb and I owned the cottage, and all the land around it, and insisted in our wills that it forever stay in our family's name. That way, if any of our descendants should ever need to find me, they can. All they'll have to do is look for clues like I once did. Follow the steps I've laid out, and believe in the impossible—in fairy tales and wishes and magic.

I've always kept them in the dark about our legacy, to give them a chance at a normal life. I even commanded the bugs and flowers to silence. I'm the only one who can hear those lines to the nether-realm now, and it will be that way as long as I'm the reigning Red Queen. But should any of my family members search diligently enough, they'll find the truth I've hidden for them.

All these years, they accepted my quirks because I've always respected and loved them, unconditionally. And now I'm counting on their loyalty. My entire plan to die hinges on the timeliness of the execution of my will.

Cremation was the only way to avoid draining my blood and pumping my veins with formaldehyde, sewing my eyelids shut—all the morbid and intrusive steps taken to embalm and preserve a mortal's body. I was blessed throughout my eighty years of human life with health and a sharp mind. I never needed a pacemaker and I have no prostheses, implants, or dentures, so there was nothing that might explode in high heat. That meant no incisions, no extractions. It was important that I remain intact—inside and out.

But if Rabid White doesn't hurry and get here with the inception potion to rouse me out of my stasis, it won't matter. I'll be a pile of glowing embers. And Morpheus will have to find a new home for my eternal spirit . . . a new body for me to inhabit.

He'll be livid if that happens, and he'll never let me forget it. An eternity is a long, long time to listen to *I told you so* pitched continuously in a deep, cockney accent.

"I don't care for it one bit," he had said two weeks ago, while we discussed my exodus from the human realm over tea during one of my Wonderland dream visits. He lifted a cup to his lips, his studious face as perfect and ageless as always. He took a sip, and then set it down once more. "Too many things can go wrong. I should be there to execute my plan."

"I'm doing it myself," I'd countered. I studied the canopied bed and fireplace, located diagonally from the tall Victorian parlor chairs where we sat beside a small oval table, seeking comfort in the familiar surroundings. "And we're going with *my plan*." Those would be my last moments in the human realm. It had to be on my terms. I suppressed a tug of sadness and attempted the same graceful control Morpheus had displayed with his cup of tea, but hot liquid splashed down my age-worn hand as a tremor shook through my wrist. I yelped.

"Alyssa, please. Allow me." He gently gripped my gnarled fingers in his elegant, smooth ones, wiping away the tea and soothing my scalded and scarred flesh with a cloth napkin.

Allow me. We both knew he referred to so much more than cleaning my spilled drink.

So many years we had spent together in my dreams—just as it was during our childhoods—with Morpheus training and teaching me about my kingdom and world. There weren't opportunities for us to be alone, since he kept the veil of sleep pulled away so I could interact with Rabid, Chessie, Ivory, the creatures, and my subjects.

That had changed once I'd become a widow. I would uphold my royal duties each night and fight to be strong until my grief for Jeb became so intense, tears built up on my lashes and blinded me.

Morpheus—sensing my shame, because queens don't cry—would insist it was time for tea, which we'd take alone in the royal bedroom that would one day belong to us as king and queen.

There in our solitude, hidden from prying eyes and surrounded by lush red carpets and curtains of gold, I would lose myself to my grief. *Allow me*, he would say. Holding out his arms, he'd hold me as I wept. Night after night for a year, until at last I was cried out.

Shortly thereafter, Morpheus's attentiveness changed. His touches became less comforting and more intimate. I was too embarrassed to respond, too self-conscious in my aging shell.

An eternally young fae romancing an elderly woman—I would've laughed at the absurdity, had I not been so deeply affected by his blind devotion and the depth of his love.

"Even *if* we go with your plan"—Morpheus's voice was low and cross as he dabbed the napkin between my fingers, sopping up remnants of tea—"I should still be there in the wings, to supervise how it plays out."

I frowned at him. His stubbornness, along with the firelight dancing across his wild hair and bizarrely beautiful features, reminded me of another night we sat in this room together—decades ago— when he first tried to convince me to wear the ruby crown. When I attempted to seduce him into giving me my wish back so I could escape Wonderland, cure my family curse, and keep Jeb safe. I was a different person then, brimming with youth, human aspirations, and innocence.

Our royal bedroom had become a painful reminder of just how creaky and decrepit I'd grown. I looked forward to making new memories here, when I was no longer trying to outrun Wonderland's chaotic brand of beauty, when I was crowned again and would remain sixteen forever—as eternally youthful, energetic, and alluring as the winged man who would rule by my side.

Until then, I didn't fit. I was a picture left out in the sun and rain, my vibrant colors fading to a melancholy yellow drab. My netherling powers were still strong, but trapped inside a timeworn vessel. My shoulders felt so hunched and heavy, I rarely let my wings free. I missed flying most of all.

I wondered if this was how Red felt in the end, and why she allowed Morpheus to talk her into going back to Wonderland and abandoning her half-human descendants. Ultimately, it was her plan to return anyway, although she had no desire to make that journey alone. She fought with Morpheus, unleashing a series of events and manipulations that ultimately led me to gain the crown and become queen. Something I learned to be grateful for, although back then I'd begrudged the gift. It took a lifetime for me to fully appreciate how precious immortality could be, and I would never take it for granted again.

After Morpheus finished cleaning the spilled tea, I dragged my hand free from his and self-consciously clasped the ruffled silken scarf at my neck, attempting to hide my droopy skin. People said I looked wonderful for my age. At least twenty years younger. But compared to Morpheus's unfading, otherworldly appeal, I felt ancient.

"I don't want you there," I pressed, determined to keep him away from the funeral home. "It's enough that you've seen me wither away to a prune all these years." Even my voice sounded rusty, as if the words were flaking off my throat and tongue in caustic, brown chips.

Morpheus leaned his elbows on the tablecloth, getting as close as he could with the tea set between us. His blue hair brushed his shoulders, animated and enchanted—a stark contrast to the white, dull waves confined in a bun at my nape.

"You are at the end of your chrysalis, luv. This step is the most difficult, take my word. 'Tis a harrowing and unsettling battle of identity, just before you break free and transform to the creature of flight and artistry you were always destined to become. I can keep you on task. Prevent any . . . distractions."

He looked down at my wedding ring, which I had yet to remove. It had become more than a symbol of my and Jeb's devotion. It had become a symbol of my human life, and I intended to wear it until the moment I left it all behind.

Morpheus's pinky outlined the ring, careful not to touch the diamonds or the silver band holding them in place. "It is important that you not allow anything to impede you from taking that final leap. You've mourned those you've lost long enough. They are at peace. Let their peace give you yours. Elsewise, you'll be crippled . . . unable to act with a sharp mind. Focus is key for any plan to work."

"I already know that," I answered, my chest pinched and tight. "You're worried I've become senile. That I can't handle this."

He sighed, stroking my thumb with his. "Not senile. Reminiscent. It happens to humans. You've told me so yourself, as I've watched you grow to refinement and wisdom."

"*Refinement.*" I ventured a tentative smile at his attempt to charm me. "Is that what we're calling it today?"

He held my gaze, unfaltering. "Your eyes have not lost their incandescence, nor your mind its wit. You are no prune. You're every bit my tart little plum, as you've always been. I've told you this repeatedly, have I not?"

At least once each night in my dreams, Beloved Moth.

I didn't answer aloud, just as I didn't reveal my deepest insecurities: I was ashamed for him to see me at my lowest point . . . I couldn't bear for him to have any memory of seeing me as a feeble corpse lying in a cardboard coffin—the way I'd had to see Jeb after his death, just before he was cremated.

"A queen should not require rescue," I said simply. I kept my eyes on his, mesmerized by those inky irises that looked back at me as they always had since our childhood, filled with awe and affection. Somehow, he saw past my aging shell to the girl I once was, and I craved to see myself as he did. "A queen must merit the respect of her kingdom and subjects. And the admiration of her king."

"Oh, I assure you." He captured my hand again and kissed each knuckle where they bulged with arthritis. "You've already merited that. In fact, I plan to show you just how *deep* my admiration runs"— the word *deep* grated in his throat like a growl—"however many times it takes for you to be convinced, the moment you're mine at last."

My cheeks flared hot. In spite of all the years he'd flattered and beguiled me with teasing innuendos, in spite of everything I'd experienced as a mortal wife, mother, and grandmother, he still had the ability to make me blush.

"Ah, there it is." He skimmed a finger across my crinkled cheek and smirked, far too satisfied with himself. "I haven't lost my touch."

"As if that could ever be possible, for the master of verbal seduction," I teased.

His mood shifted to potent defiance in one blink. "You'll soon see it's more than all talk, blossom."

I blushed hotter, feeling younger than I had in weeks. He always had that effect on me. Always made me feel desirable and alive. Aside from the times when he was challenging me or making me furious.

He leaned back in his seat, wings lifted. "Your body is bone-tired. Let me do this for you, so you can rest," he tried one last time.

"You've taught me to be strong and resourceful. I should make that final leap into the rabbit hole on my own." An unexpected surge of vulnerability made me shiver. I gripped my teacup to absorb its warmth. "But you'll be there, to catch me?"

"I shall be there expecting a mind-numbing kiss for all my troubles," he answered without pause.

Smiling, I took out the chess box. Morpheus watched intently while I animated the pieces to enact my grand design to leave the human realm and cover my tracks with the aid of my royal advisor, bits of bone provided by the pixies, a bag of ash, two simulacrum suits, a common housefly, and a handful of sprites. As I spoke, his jeweled eye markings glittered a lime green—uneasy, but hopeful. The anticipation emanating off of him was visceral.

It was inconceivable, that we'd shared a sixty-three-year courtship—platonic, though not without its share of tension. Although he took great pleasure watching me walk on my tiptoes across the tightwire of suppressed attraction, he kept his vow and respected my stand to be faithful to Jeb. He even waited for three years as I grieved my mortal husband's death and prepared my family for my inevitable parting. That was the depth of his respect for me. He'd earned the same respect in turn. And so much more . . .

Now the day and hour has come to reward him for his patience, and I'm starting to regret that I didn't let him plan my death . . . let him run the show. It probably would have gone smoother. I'd already be in his arms and in his bed—a young butterfly queen, ruling over my kingdom, drunk on power, madness, and passion.

No. I can do this. I can prove that I'm capable, calculating, and strong, *as all good queens should be.*

Morpheus's only role in my plan was to send the counter potion with Rabid. The moment my skeletal accomplice arrives, everything will fall into place and I'll make my escape into Wonderland. Since a body can't be exhumed once it's been reduced to ash and bone, no one will ever know that I'm still alive, only gone from this world forever.

A pang of sadness chases that thought as finality hits. It's over. I'm ready to end it . . . to start my immortal future. I've lived a full life here. My family is healthy and happy. We're on the best of terms. Every human dream has been fulfilled and my heart is strong and whole once more.

Yet *because* of that, there's so much to leave behind. There's no unfinished business, but it's still hard to say good-bye forever. Once the crown is placed on my head to jump-start my immortality, I don't have to wear it constantly to retain my youth, but I do have to stay in Wonderland. Just as Ivory once told me, time is tricky stepping back through the portal into the human world . . . one has to envision a specific hour, or the clock goes in reverse and will drop you into the exact same moment you stepped through.

If I try to cross the borders into the human realm after I leave, I'll either return perpetually to this moment and be eighty again over and over, or I'll automatically be aged however long I've been gone and turn to dust on the spot. Add to that the fact that I'll be dead in everyone's eyes—I could never explain my reappearance without causing undue terror or confusion—and going back and forth is no longer a feasible option.

An impenetrable wall is about to rise between my family and me, leaving us with nothing but memories.

Jeb's face resurfaces in my mind before I can stop it . . . the way his glistening green eyes held my gaze that last moment before he closed them in death. How they were so full of love and gratitude for all the dreams we'd shared.

My throat swells and there's a tug behind my lashes. The small metal identity tag at my chest feels like a pile of bricks.

Stop. I can't do this now. I have to concentrate on escape. Morpheus was right. Thinking of those I've loved and lost will only hinder me. I'll keep the memories at bay . . . suppress how I faced Mom and Dad's death, how I thought I'd never survive the grief. How Jeb was my rock, like always. Just like I was for him, when his mom passed.

It's futile to think of any of that now, because the moment Jeb died, the whole world distorted—took on a new form that I didn't recognize. Everyday things became foreign and unwelcoming. With him gone, I no longer belonged.

My metamorphosis was complete the moment my mortal husband stopped breathing. All that's left now is breaking out of my weather-beaten cocoon.

A new scent sifts through my cardboard surroundings—aftershave or deodorant—forcing me back to the present as two men converse on the other side of the lid.

"Last one tonight, Frank?"

"That it is, Brian. Just came in a few hours ago. Delivery only. And there's a rush on her. You want me to stay and help?"

I struggle to breathe. My plan doesn't allow for two witnesses. Only one. As I await the crematory operator's answer, my heart hunkers inside me, filling with dread. The organ seems to quiver, though there's no pulse along my wrists or in my ears. Just a cold, indiscernible quaking behind my sternum, like chilled gelatin sloughed quietly from its mold.

"Nah," Brian finally says as he rattles some papers. "I could do this with my eyes closed."

The irony is laughable. If all goes as planned, he'll not only have his eyes closed . . . he'll be asleep and dreaming.

"Go home to your family," Brian finishes. "Tell Melanie and the kids hi for me."

"You got it. See you tomorrow."

Hinges creak as the door shuts, and relief rushes through me, however short-lived. The click and clank of a mechanized hatchway shakes the cardboard walls of my coffin and rattles my stiff bones. A rocking motion tugs beneath my spine as my casket slips onto a rack of metal rollers. Flames crackle louder, warming my feet and toes where the panels under my soles come dangerously close to the incinerator's entrance as the rollers begin to move.

Rabid was supposed to be here before the temperature-controlled furnace was hot enough to trigger the opening mechanism. Things are happening out of sequence, too quickly. My muscles ache to shudder and come alive, but they're as rigid as steel. Immovable. A flash of another memory shivers through me: when Queen Red controlled my body that final day in AnyElsewhere. When I was her puppet. I feel as powerless now as I did then.

I'm about to be enveloped in flames. My body won't survive. Yet I have to somehow. I made a promise to return as myself. Whole and in one piece. It's a promise I can't break. Morpheus has waited too long for my return. I can't let him down.

Self-doubt raises its ugly head: What will I do? If I can't move, I can't get free . . . not without the counter potion. A hollowness stings behind my tear ducts as I wish for a flood to burst free and fill my box with an ocean of tears to save me from the fire. But my eyes might as well be filled with sand.

Enough with the dramatics, luv. Use your magic. Improvise and find a means of escape.

I'm not sure if it's Morpheus's voice in my head, or if it's mine. I've heard his accent and goading insistence so many times throughout my life, they're ingrained in me as if they're my own.

Whatever the case, it sparks my determination. There's a reason I came to this room last night when all was dark and quiet: So I could make a mental note of things I might animate if I needed them. So I could understand the logistics of the furnace. So I could use my magic *blind*.

I concentrate on the hatch's inner workings. I learned a thing or two being a mechanic's wife. The springs in the mechanism coil tightly as I envision them retracting. The movement triggers the hinges and the metal door snaps shut with a clang. My box jerks to a halt as it hits the obstacle.

"You gotta be kidding me," Brian grumbles. He jiggles the door handle and hammers at the hinges. "There. That'll do it."

He shoves my box to the back of the metal rollers once more, allowing room for the hatch to open. My mind scrambles for another way to stall him until I hear him shout: "What the . . . ?" and then the sound of his body slumping to the floor. The casket hits the closed hatch once more.

"Queen Alyssa," a tinkling voice drifts from the other side of the cardboard.

Nikki, you wonderful little spriteling. A tingle radiates through my lips, the ghost of a smile wanting to spring loose. My toes would twitch from excitement if not for my paralysis.

The casket's lid scrapes open and the wings of twenty sprites whisk around my face—little tufts of air scented with cinnamon and vanilla.

Teensy hands the size of ladybugs tug at my eyelids, opening them to a glow of amber light. I still can't turn my head, but in my peripheral vision, Rabid's antlers appear over the box's edge, then two glimmering pink eyes follow suit.

"Late, I be," he croaks an apology.

I try to nod in reassurance, but fail.

His entire face comes into view over me. "Fix you, Highness. Take you home, at long last."

Home. The word waltzes through my mind, filled with promise and hope. I imagine myself flying with Morpheus over Wonderland's bizarre, winding terrains. How lovely it will be to belong once more. To belong, and never have to leave anyone again.

Rabid's bony arm reaches inside and pours something from a bright red bottle down my throat. The faintest hint of berries mixed with menthol tickles my tongue. My heart jumps to life, pounding so hard against my sternum, I gasp. In moments, I'm able to squint without any help from the sprites. They disperse with jingly giggles and hover around the sleeping crematory operator where he's slumped on the gray cement floor.

I blink—hard and fast. My tear ducts reactivate and my eyes water. The saltiness stings and itches.

Next, my toes and fingers wiggle, then my muscles reawaken,

sluggish and resistant, like overextended rubber bands. As I pull myself to a sitting position, my old ligaments pop and snap.

Rabid perches on the edge of the incline and grips the casket, keeping him eye level with me. "Forgive Rabid of White. Forever-evermore, be at your side."

I pat his soft head. "No forgiveness necessary. What matters is you're here now. Did anyone see you coming out of the bathroom?"

Rabid shakes his head. "The fly on the wall kept an eye on the hall." He snickers at his rhyme and points to the top quarter of the door, which harbors the only window in the room. The housefly skitters across the glass on the other side in demonstration of its steadfast devotion.

Rabid offers the sly, frothy grin I've come to adore as his skeletal hand gives me a small backpack. I look inside and everything's there: my ruby-tipped key necklace, my wedding ring, the simulacrum suits, a bag of ash and splintered bits of bone, a change of clothes, a box knife, and three keepsakes from my human life that are the only things I'm taking with me across the border of Wonderland.

First, I pull on my necklace and press the key to my chest, savoring the power it holds.

The crematory operator snores from the floor. He looks cold and uncomfortable, but I know better. His dreams are warm and sensuous. The sprites flutter around him, tufted wings swishing at the speed of hummingbirds as they release particles like dandelion fuzz filled with pheromones. The seeds snow across the man's smiling face, coaxing his subconscious to envision his most carnal fantasies. I crinkle my nose, embarrassed even to conjecture what they might be. He's probably going to have a dream hangover for a week.

Although he won't suffer any lasting physical effects, the sprites are exploiting his private thoughts. When I was younger, I might've regretted using him as a pawn. Not anymore. When he wakes up in an hour or so, his splitting headache will prevent him from questioning how he managed to cremate me in his sleep. All he'll want is an aspirin and his nice soft bed at home.

The end justifies the means.

I use the box knife to cut a flap in the casket's side and swing my legs out, slow and careful. I can't move as fast as I once did. My bare feet meet the cold floor, paper gown swishing around me. Rabid turns his back as I peel off the gown and toss it into the box, then pull on a gray sweat suit and boots—the most comfortable and inconspicuous clothes from my closet. I kick myself for forgetting underclothes, but it doesn't matter what I wear now because in Wonderland, Morpheus has filled all the castle's armoires with lace-trimmed, satin and velvet gowns and lingerie—a wardrobe worthy of a queen.

Today, the simulacrum suit will hide my pedestrian outfit. I step into the enchanted fabric. All I have to do is pull on the hood, then concentrate on the surroundings, and I'll become like a chameleon, my body reflecting the background.

But first . . .

Rabid hands off the bag of ash and bone and my wedding ring without my even asking. I study the ring. Jeb made it for me when he had the magical ability to paint things and bring them to life. When his muse had become a living entity. It had served as both my engagement and wedding ring, and was indestructible. Or so we had thought. The only time it lost one of its twelve tiny diamonds was due to backlash from my own magic when I was practicing.

I had been standing outside our country cottage, coaxing the weeping willow to dance, when the diamond fell into the grass. We searched and searched, but never found it. Within a week, it showed up again, sprouting from the ground in the form of a glistening, glass-like flower. It was as if the diamond was a seed, holding within it a burst of Jeb's creation magic.

The scent of soil from the memory fades to the scent of the furnace's propane. I open the bag's drawstring and dump the ash and bones into the casket, keeping my movements methodical and precise so nostalgia won't overtake me again.

Upon emptying the bag, I kiss my ring and lay it atop the dusty pile. "Rabid, melt it with your magic."

My royal advisor hops over, peers through the opened flap, and sharpens his glowing irises until they radiate red heat. As he concentrates, the silver band melts, releasing the eleven diamonds into the ashes.

I place the identification tag within the casket and read what's etched into the steel: *Alyssa Victoria Gardner Holt.* A lump rises in my throat. It's the last time my human name will define me.

Repositioning the lid, I command the door's springs to retract and release. I squint against heat and flaring flames as the hatch swings up long enough for me to shove the casket down the incline, then slams shut. It seals so tightly, not even an orange glow can be seen from within.

Only a few seconds more and I would've been locked inside. Now, after the cardboard burns away, it will look as if I was. The shiny metal shelves along the wall house a multitude of small cardboard cubes. Inside are the remains of the bodies that came before me and are now waiting to be transferred to their urns.

But my "remains" are unique. Jeb's diamonds wait inside—little magical seeds. When these ashes are sprinkled where his have been absorbed into the earth beneath our willow tree, flowers will sprout there, a part of him and me. Uniting what's left of our shared humanness, in one final tribute to all the beauty he created throughout his life.

I grit my teeth against crying, and gather up my backpack as Rabid puts on the other simulacrum suit. It shrinks to fit his bunny-size form, and I send the housefly a mental query to see if the hall is clear.

It whispers back:

All is well, Queen Alyssa . . .
The other humans have gone. Nothing but a few lowly silverfish skittering about.

No need to be invisible quite yet, then.

"Nikki," I whisper, and the little sprite shakes her wings for good measure, releasing a final dose of fairy dust across the sleeping man. Then she gathers her spriteling companions and follows us out the door. The bathroom is only a few steps across the dim, long hallway. I hobble along, careful not to crush the silverfish skimming around my and Rabid's feet. I smile as the insects are joined by a long line of roaches, beetles, and spiders.

Queen Alyssa! Queen Alyssa! So sad to see you go . . .

The fly buzzes around my head, adding his good-byes to the mix.

"I'll miss you all, too," I say, fighting a swell of wistfulness. It's the last conversation I'll have with earthly bugs. The last time I'll hear their fuzzy, buzzy greetings. In Wonderland, the insects are . . . very different. Less innocuous and kind. Some are vicious and deadly, and far from small. But I know all their secrets, and all their weaknesses—thanks to Wonderland's wisdom keeper.

Our parade slips into the bathroom and stops before the mirror. Instead of dwelling on my wrinkled and frumpy appearance, I envision the little-boy sundial that covers the rabbit hole in a garden in London. The glass crackles like ice on a lake, and in the jagged reflection, the sundial appears, touched by a hazy pink sunrise. It's early enough that no one occupies the trail yet. As a precaution, I pull on my hood and Rabid does the same.

All we'll need is a thought or two about our surroundings, and we'll be invisible.

Using my key, I aim for a crack shaped like a keyhole, tiny and intricate.

The portal opens. Rabid nudges me with his bony knuckles, and I clasp my fingers in his. Together, with the sprites and our insect escorts, we step through the liquidized opening. A cool breeze flows through me, along with the scent of grass and roses tipped with sparkling dew.

The blossoms call out:

Fair faryn, Majesty. The years are behind you. You'll soon be in full bloom like us once more.

I grin. Rabid tugs me toward the sundial that's already been pushed off the rabbit hole. He's anxious to leave. More insects have joined our company, some along the ground: beetles, centipedes, and scorpions. Others ride the breeze: butterflies, moths, bumblebees . . .

They swarm out of the glistening foliage and spin around me and my royal advisor—an enchanted rainbow fog, thick and bright in the pinkish-tinged lighting.

The butterflies sing:

Long live Queen Alyssa. May you forever be young, mad, and free.

Several land on me, their wings caressing my cheeks and neck through the simulacrum, and I realize I won't have to make myself invisible after all. My insect friends are here to provide protection, like they've always been.

Rabid releases me, his cadaverous fingers scraping against mine as he follows the sprites and dives into the rabbit hole without looking back.

"Be not late, Majesty-y-y," Rabid's call echoes up to me, growing farther and farther away as he descends—weightless and lackadaisical as a feather on the wind.

Unlike my netherling entourage, I can't leave without one glance back.

I pause, peering through the cloud of a thousand beating wings at the shimmering landscape on the horizon. My chest cinches tight.

I take the keepsakes from my backpack. Three ornate glass bottles: the first filled with tiny stones, the second with seashells, and the last with silvery stardust. One look at the trio, and the memories I've been fighting illuminate my mind, graceful and slow, like sunlight creeping over a still and slumbering world.

CULMINATION

MEMORY ONE: STONES

Sixty-three years earlier . . .

It's morning in Wonderland, and Morpheus is whisking me back to the Ivory castle, where my family and Jeb wait to step with me through the portal, so I can live out the remainder of my human life.

My escort is pensive and quiet, his features hard as stone. Not one word passes between us during the enchanted carriage ride. The sound of the moths' wings beating a trail through the sky only intensifies the awkward silence.

My heart presses against my sternum, as if reaching for him where he sits across from me. I know if I looked beneath the silky fabric of my simple black dress and the jacket from his wardrobe he insisted I wear for warmth, the organ would be aglow with a violet hue. Just yesterday, my heart was ripping in half—the human and netherling sides killing one another—due to the curse Queen Red put upon me. Jeb and Morpheus intervened, combined their magic, and bound me together with enchanted sutures. They saved my life with their love. My body understands on some primitive level, and will never forget. It's drawn to both of them now, forming a bond beyond any human explanation.

But even without that bond, I could decipher the jewels on Morpheus's face and know what he's thinking. I woke earlier in his bed to find him seated on the mattress edge, stroking frizzed hair from my temples. Before I could even say good morning, he kissed my forehead and slipped away, stating that breakfast was in order.

We spent the night together, but nothing physical happened between us. Nothing will, for many years. Not until I've lived out my human life with Jeb.

I've made my stand on fidelity very clear; although Morpheus has made it clear he won't make it easy. Yet even with his ever-looming challenges dangling like loose threads, the newfound respect we've forged is wrapped securely around me. I know he'd never ask me to betray the humans I love—because that's part of who I am—as much as it pains him to step back and let me go.

After visiting Wonderland's landscapes together last night, I understand him on a level I never have before. And it's the same for him, because once we arrive and he takes my hand to help me out of the carriage, he doesn't hesitate to walk me toward the icy entrance where Jeb is waiting at the top of the snow-covered crystal stairs.

I catch a surprised breath upon seeing him. He's wearing his navy blue prom tuxedo, complete with the periwinkle dress shirt that complements his dark, wavy hair and the olive tone of his skin. The very shirt that had been fashioned into a pair of boxers in AnyElsewhere.

The tux is just the way it looked on prom night: fake webs, dusty streaks, and strategic rips along the velvet-flocked jacket and pants. For a moment, I'm taken back to Underland, when I first saw him waiting for us on prom night at the employee's entrance, and his wounded expression at my betrayal. I will never cause that look in his eyes again.

Strange. The last I saw of the tuxedo, it was on Jeb's doppelganger in AnyElsewhere. When CC fell into the pool of fears, the clothes disintegrated into puddles. Jeb must've painted them anew before he gave up his talent forever.

Maybe it was out of sentimentality, because his sister made the tux for him, or more likely because he wants to be wearing something familiar when we walk through the portal and back into his family's life.

Still, even in clothes from the human realm, he looks miserable and out of his element as he waits for me to take the stairs. Standing there in the daylight, seeing the beautiful landscapes he created for this world, must be killing him. Giving up his muse has to be the most excruciating thing he's ever done. He did it without hesitation, to help bring balance to Wonderland . . . to feed Sister Two's restless souls with his artistic dreams.

I'm still not sure if he's faced the full repercussions of that sacrifice yet. But I will be there to help him through it when he does.

As Morpheus and I ascend the lower quarter on our way to Jeb, we pass the netherlings who have come to see me off. A few of them are unexpected.

Hubert, beaded and polished like a Fabergé egg in an Easter

display, reaches out a praying-mantis claw to shake Morpheus's hand. "Couldn't just make it easy for me to hate her," the egg-man says to Morpheus as if I'm not standing there. "Little know-it-all queen. Not an ounce of manners or culture in that melon of hers. Yet she still managed to prove me wrong. Was so sure she'd end up in a casket. What a disappointment." In spite of the vitriol at the tip of his tongue, his yolk-yellow eyes reflect a begrudging admiration. To my surprise, he offers me a lifetime supply of eggs Benedict at his illustrious magi-kind inn should I ever choose to visit.

Next, we greet the odd assortment of netherling stowaways who'd been trapped in the memory train three days earlier. They all bow and thank me for opening the rabbit hole so they could return home. My nose tickles on the verge of a sneeze as we pass the dust bunnies.

Bill the Lizard stops us at the midway point. He holds out the two simulacrum suits I'd asked Grenadine to return to him.

"I'm sorry I lost one . . . that I stole them to begin with," I whisper, ashamed.

He shakes his reptilian head and his long tongue flickers out. "I am a subject of the Red Court. Ergo, they belong to *you*, Majesty. Your thieving craftiness pales only to your application of their magic. You will make better use of them than I ever would."

Stunned, I place my hand atop my chest. Underneath my dress, the ruby key necklace that opens my kingdom presses back. "Really?"

Bill holds out the suits.

I look to Morpheus.

He smiles and nods, encouraging me to take the translucent fabric. I tuck it beneath my arm and thank the lizard, who bows low to let us by. Rabid is waiting for us on the next step—dressed in a red vest and matching trousers. He opens his arms to carry the suits for me. My perfect little gentleman advisor. I pat the soft skin between his antlers as we climb.

Elfin guards line the upper half of the steps on either side. They draw their swords and touch the tips overhead, forming a glistening silver archway.

Jeb waits at the end, jaw clenched as if it's killing him not to run to me.

While Morpheus and I ascend the stairs beneath the swords' shadows, I nod at Jeb in assurance. His whole body relaxes. The circles under his expressive green eyes attest to a lack of sleep. The twelve hours we've been apart had to be torture. As strong as he was when we said our good nights, it's obvious he feared they might actually be good-byes. That I would decide to spend my future in the human realm alone without him.

I can't be in the same world as him day after day and not have him in my life. We love each other. We both want the same things. We will share those dreams and grow old together. A mortal life is precious and short in comparison to forever. It should be lived, and never wasted. Something that Morpheus understands now in a way he never did; otherwise, he wouldn't be letting me go without a fight.

My face feels numb, less from the cold than the agonizing, uncomfortable situation I've placed them both in. I remind myself that this is the worst part . . . that once I step through the portal into the human realm, my two lives will mesh, yet at the same time never cross wires, unless it's necessary for someone's safety or well-being. That's what we all agreed on.

A crust of frost grinds beneath my boots as I take the final step. The elfin knights salute us and return their swords to leather holsters. The jeweled blood beaded along their cheeks and temples shines like berries against the wintery background surrounding them. Clicking their heels, they descend the stairs to surround the castle at their posts.

Frowning, Morpheus offers my hand to Jeb. It's the strangest gesture, grand and dignified, as if he's walked me down the aisle and is giving me away. In a way, he is. For one human lifetime.

His wings rustle when Jeb takes my palm, an involuntary spasm. He's straining not to take my hand back. "You know the protocol . . . should something happen to her body in your world, you or Alison must contact me immediately. Alyssa's spirit must be housed for it to survive."

Jeb nods. "I got it." His answer is succinct and his tone even, but the worry in his expression gives him away. It's something none of us like to think about, something we all hope will never have to be addressed.

Rabid's pink gaze turns up to me, his pale face bewildered. I send him toward the door to rescue him from the morbid subject matter.

Morpheus waits for the skeletal clacking of bones to vanish within the castle, then drags a pair of gloves out of his pocket, proceeding to work them into place. "And I suppose it is unnecessary to tell you to treat her like a queen," he grumbles to Jeb.

Jeb weaves our fingers together. "Just like it's a waste of breath to ask you to lay off the seduction tactics in her dreams."

"Is that jealousy I hear in your voice, pretty pseudo elf? Never fear. I'll still think of you every day, whilst she's with you."

"I prefer you think of me every night, when she's with *you*." Jeb helps me peel Morpheus's jacket from my shoulders, replacing it with his tuxedo coat—still warm from his body heat. "I'll send an owl, as a reminder." He hands Morpheus his clothing back.

Morpheus takes the jacket and folds it over his arm, patting the wrinkles out of it. He chuckles, though it's mirthless and hollow. "I'm going to miss your bumbling attempts at wordplay."

Jeb forces a smile. "Not as much as I'll miss your pompous-ass condescension."

They stare at each other, a mixture of amusement and restraint in their expressions. Begrudging respect bridges the underlying tension—a link that grew, without their even realizing or encouraging it, during the month they spent together in AnyElsewhere.

"You two want to be alone?" I ask, desperate to end the weird exchange.

Morpheus narrows his eyes. "I will see you tonight, Alyssa. And from this moment on, when you're with me, I expect your mind to be as it was in our childhood. Fixed on Wonderland matters, and not the humdrum mundane of the mortal realm. Mend things there, so they won't be a distraction while you're fulfilling your royal obligations. Are you sure you don't need my help to clean up all the messes? I've had some practice *handling* humans." The smug grin he offers Jeb is filled with innuendo.

"We got it, Mothra," Jeb says. "I can relate to their innocent sensitivities better than you ever could." He raises an eyebrow, delivering his own underlying message.

There's a muffled thud at the giant, crystallized door. Jeb and I glance over our shoulders where my parents are peering out. They both look beautiful and rested, but also anxious.

I tip my head in greeting and they wave, then withdraw deeper into the hall, to give the three of us privacy.

Jeb turns back around, his arm snug at my waist. "Are you coming in to see us off, Mort?"

Morpheus glares at Jeb pointedly. His bejeweled markings flash through a pastel palette, like a glittery sunset. Resolution flickers inside his inky gaze. "I want nowhere near the portal. I've had enough of your stagnant realm to last me a lifetime and then some."

"I hope you mean it," Jeb says. The statement isn't barbed, just sincere.

"Oh, I most assuredly do. With the exception of that precious part of your world which will one day belong solely to mine." Morpheus tips his hat my way and the bluish gray moths at the rim quiver, as if bowing. As he turns his back and takes the stairs, wings dragging through the snow behind him like a cape, a part of me aches with a deep sadness.

A gust stirs in his wake, kicking up a whirlwind of snow.

It's better that we're leaving through the Ivory portal. This painful parting would have been compounded by all my subjects' faces looking back at me. I chose not to say good-bye to any of them last night when I visited the Red castle. It would've felt too final and strange, somehow. I take comfort knowing I'll see them and Morpheus in my dreams.

After the moth-driven carriage lifts to the sky, Jeb turns me to face him. He brings my hand to his mouth and nuzzles my knuckles. His intense gaze roams every feature, from my eyes to my nose to my lips, as if he's studying a painting again.

The silence twists my stomach into knots. "Are you going to ask?"

"Ask what?" he says against my hand.

"If anything happened." My and Morpheus's time together feels private and sacred, but if Jeb needs to hear what we talked about and the places we visited to ease his mind, I'll be open and honest.

Jeb links our fingers again. "You took *my* hand today, and you're standing here beside *me*. That tells me all I need to know. You're a queen, and you have responsibilities." The admiration behind his words surprises me, although it shouldn't. Not considering his emotional ties to my world. "I don't have to have an update each time you return. You would tell me anything that might affect us and our life."

I smile, awed by his faith. "I would. I *will*. And thank you."

He gently grasps the hair braided at the nape of my neck and presses our foreheads together. "Thank *you*." His voice—deep and husky with emotion—forms a haze of condensation between us. "Thank you for coming back to me."

I caress his face and the hint of whiskers along his chin. "Okay, I won't feel like you need an update each time. But please, don't think you have to say 'thank you' every morning when I wake up beside you, either. I want us to be normal."

"Normal." He draws back and grins, his dimples finally making an appearance. "This from the girl who sprouted wings and gave me my first colossal wedgie while we sand-surfed over Wonderland. When was the last time we were normal, huh?"

I snort, remembering how I couldn't carry him across the chasm and had to leave him behind, that even when he was every bit as scared as me, he made me laugh and gave me the strength to do what I thought would be impossible. Just like now.

His grin softens, causing his labret to glisten in the light. I touch it, circling the warm metal so his whiskers tickle my fingertip.

The action, intimate and sensual, hits me with an almost inconceivable truth: There's nothing standing between us now. Our lives together will begin today, the minute we cross the border. I'm both happy and overwhelmed.

"I'm ready for my ring," I manage over the tightness in my throat.

His expression sobers. Dragging the chain from under his shirt, he pulls it over his head and slides the ring off. Eyes locked to mine, he slips the silver band into place onto my right hand, where it will remain until he places it on my left once we've said our wedding vows. The diamonds glisten—a heart with wings—and my own heart flutters as if it could fly.

The band fits my finger perfectly and feels like coming home.

"You'll always be my lifeline," Jeb whispers, then presses his thumb to the dimple in my chin and pulls me in for a sweet, gentle kiss. I wind my fingers through his hair and taste him—free of cologne or paint or turpentine. Just him. Human, masculine. *Jebediah Holt.*

I could drown in the sweetness of the simplicity.

With our chests pressed together, my sutured heart glows and hums, trying to close the space between us. His body tenses, as if he senses the pull.

He breaks the kiss and tucks my head against him, his stubbled jaw scraping my temple. "I have something to show you." His lips caress the top of my ear and warm me to my toes. "I wanted to wait until we were back. Until we were alone. But I think you need to see it now." He withdraws something from his pocket and reveals what resembles a clear glass marble—though it's soft like a bath oil bead.

"A wish?" I swipe tears from my face with the back of my hand, shocked. "How? When?"

"Last night at Ivory's party, after our slow dance. A Mustela fae pulled me aside . . . licked my face to thank me for all I'd done for Wonderland."

"*Oh my gosh.* So, that's why you left early?"

He rolls the little ball around his palm. "I was about to cry my eyes out." He holds up the sparkling tear to the light. "Couldn't have the Red Queen see me bawl like a sissy pants."

I let out an impromptu giggle, adrift in an unexpected swirl of emotions.

Jeb's brow furrows in thought. "We could use it to help us fix things, in the human realm."

My happy smile fades. "No. This wish can only be used for you."

"I was holed up with Morpheus for a month. The one thing I learned is that magic is flexible. It's all about the wording."

I shake my head and cover his hand, hiding his tear. "Magic is *precious*. You have to save it, Jeb. You could wish for so many things!" I pause, because we both know there are two monumental things he can't wish for. He can't get his muse back without unbalancing Wonderland again. And he can't ask to live forever. Magic won't change who you are inside. He chose to forfeit his immortality by giving away Red's powers. He's mortal and there's no altering that now. "Jeb, don't waste the power. Save it for something of consequence."

He grows somber, and I know he's already been struggling with the same thoughts. He puts the wish into his pocket and his jaw ticks.

Before either of us can say another word, the castle door opens and Dad and Mom step out. I'm shocked to see her wearing the same backless cocktail dress she wore at prom. Although the layers of blushed chiffon on the skirt and wispy cap sleeves are frayed from her fight with Wonderland's eight-legged cemetery keeper, the dress is still intact.

I frown, piecing things together. "Wait." I point from her to Jeb. "So . . . you're both wearing the same clothes you disappeared in. Is this part of a master plan?"

"Yes. Jeb came up with it," Mom answers. "We still need to sort out the details. But first . . ." She and Dad draw me into their arms.

After a long hug, they celebrate our news. Dad teases Jeb that he almost had to sell a kidney to buy Mom's engagement ring. Mom tweaks Dad's ribs so he yelps, and then she gently catches my right hand to admire my ring finger.

She looks at my face. I know what she sees there: the same anticipation for a human life that she wanted with Dad after saving him from Sister Two's lair. Her smile is so bright with hope, I could be looking directly into the sun.

As she turns to give Jeb an impromptu hug, Dad pulls me aside.

"Butterfly," he says, tucking a stray strand of hair behind my ear.

"Dad," I answer, catching his hand and holding it at my temple.

He shakes his head. "Throughout all the craziness . . . I didn't get the chance to say how proud I am of you, Alyssa Victoria Gardner." The tenderness in his brown eyes reminds me how the two of us faced the world alone together as I grew up, and how I always felt safe. If only I had known then that my life was being guarded by a genuine knight. "My little girl is a queen. A *queen of Wonderland*."

I smile. "Slightly different from my wimpy dress-up versions, right?"

Dad laughs and kisses my head. "You can say that again. More like a ninja."

I laugh and hug him, blissfully surrounded by his warmth and strength.

"You ready to go home?" he asks, rubbing my back.

"Well, not exactly *home*," Mom says in response, returning to my side. "We have a detour to make."

"Detour?" I ask as she and I step into the castle, arm in arm, with the guys behind us. Our shoes clatter along the glassy floor. Ivory stands at the top of a winding crystal staircase, where the portal waits at the end of a long corridor. Rabid is next to her with Finley at her other side, hand secure on her lower back beneath her wings.

"Jeb's house will be the first stop," Mom answers as we ascend a few steps.

I'm puzzled for an instant, until the maneuver makes perfect sense. "So we can scope out any police activities going on at our place. Very smart."

"More than that," Dad corrects me from behind. "We're going to need some outside help to set the stage for Mom and Jeb's absence for a month, and your escape from the asylum. If we don't handle this right, I could get arrested for breaking you out while you were a suspect in their disappearances."

"Help from whom?" I ask, gripping the cool, glassy rail. This is starting to sound more complicated and dangerous than I imagined I never considered Dad going to jail. Maybe we should've taken Morpheus up on his offer after all.

"Help from someone who's been working with the police on the investigation," Mom answers. "Someone who's not a suspect and who everyone trusts because she's been grieving her brother and best friend ever since they've gone missing."

My pulse hammers in my wrists as I look over my shoulder to where Jeb's coming up the stairs behind Dad. "You can't mean . . ."

Sunlight streams through the crystallized walls and emblazons Jeb's features, magnifying the cautious resolve there. "Unless you can think of another way, Al"—he says, an obvious reference to the wish waiting in his pocket—"we're going to have to tell Jen the truth. All of it."

Though I won't say it aloud, I'm not willing to let Jeb give up his wish for anyone or anything. After the violence she's faced in her life, Jenara is tough. She also believes in the power of crystals, voodoo, Ouija boards, and tarot cards. She's only one quirk away from tipping the mad scale already. Making her an honorary netherling is the most logical step in this illogical situation. And, honestly, it will feel good to stop hiding my Wonderland side from my best friend. She's going to be my sister-in-law. Our family life will be less complicated if we can talk openly about everything.

Before we step through the portal into the human realm, Mom, Dad, Jeb, and I discuss the plan, since we have different places to go during the setup.

Last night, after I'd reopened the portals during my tour with Morpheus, and while Jeb was weeping a wish, Mom and Dad went into the human realm and did recon. From the safety of our attic, they waited to be sure the house was empty, then went online and gathered up all the news reports they could find about the Underland tragedy on prom night, Mom and Jeb's disappearance that seemed in some way to be tied to it, and my escape from the asylum a month later.

APBs had been issued for me and my dad within twenty-four hours after we left. We'd been officially missing for three days.

The most helpful piece of information was Mr. Traemont's recent interview with the local paper about his ruined activity center. The devastation had been so severe—busted concrete walls, collapsed floors, and water leaks—it took two weeks to clear away enough to fully assess the damage. He brought in the construction team who'd originally converted the old, abandoned salt dome into Underland, so they could offer insights as to what had triggered the accident. After they reviewed the layout and blueprints, they determined there must've been a weak point in the foundation caused by workers mining for salt decades earlier. This sinkhole effect sucked everything into one of the mining tunnels deep beneath the underground cave.

Their reasoning made more sense than the truth no one could see: that a Wonderland queen had unleashed a cloud of powerful nightmare wraiths that dragged the contents of the activity center into the rabbit hole with such force, half of the cave folded in on itself.

Like I once told Morpheus, most humans would rather believe they're alone in the universe than ever admit they might have an otherworldly audience. And like he said in response: Their ego is their weakness.

Since the accident, Underland had been abandoned—all the entrances to the giant cave condemned and cordoned off with police tape for public safety. That's where Jeb's idea fell into place. He pointed out that a few months before the construction on the activity center began, the mining tunnels had been used for storing bulk goods for a military base close by: wet wipes, first aid kits, combs, dry shampoo, powdered deodorant, toothpaste packets, crates of dehydrated meals, bags of dried soup, and bottled water. He saw inside one once after he started working there, and the supplies had yet to be cleared out.

Thank you, procrastination. Human nature had given us our perfect alibi.

All we had to do was magically maneuver enough stones and

debris aside to get into one of the caved-in tunnels. Once there, we could set the scene of Mom and Jeb being trapped for a month and living off the military supplies. It was so simple, which is what made it perfect. The fact that no one had even considered that possibility was mind-boggling. They'd been so busy pursuing the crazy girl's alleged involvement, no other venue had been explored.

As for me and Dad, our story would be equally simple: I had managed to get his keys and escape the asylum using the gardener's entrance that day while we were unsupervised in the courtyard. He didn't have time to run for help, so he chased me and jumped into the truck bed as I was driving away. I took him to Underland . . . and while there, retraced my steps on prom night. Upon seeing the wreckage, a terrifying memory came back to me—of seeing Jeb and Mom get eaten by an avalanche of stones and rippling cement.

I had suppressed it . . . was too traumatized to face their deaths.

Only they weren't dead. Because while Dad and I wept for them in the darkness amid the debris, we heard a clacking sound and followed it down to a pile of stones covering an opening. We managed to dig our way in and were reunited with Jeb and Mom—but the gap was unstable, and more rocks and pebbles closed us in again: the four of us trapped together.

That's where Dad and I had been for the past three days.

Jeb's idea was brilliant. Even Morpheus would've been impressed.

So, we had a plan of action, which only required my and Mom's magic and the two simulacrum suits. Other than that, all we needed was a catalyst: someone to tip off the police as to our possible whereabouts.

That was where Jenara and her Ouija board would come in.

Although it's morning in Wonderland, it's nighttime in the

human realm. Wrapped in simulacrum suits, my parents enter the portal first, stopping by our house so they can pick up one of Dad's uniforms and an asylum gown Mom had tucked away. The gown will be for me. We all have to be wearing what we were last seen in, to make the plan work. After Mom and Dad hit the house, their next stop will be Underland, to lay the groundwork for our grand unveiling.

Jeb takes my hand and steadies me as Rabid and I step with him through the long mirror on the back of Jenara's door into her bedroom. It closes up to a reflective pane of glass, taking with it our view of Ivory and Finley waving good-bye.

We made sure Jenara wasn't in the room before stepping through. We're going to have to break this to her in increments. It'll be enough of a shock at first just to see us alive and safe.

When she's ready, I'll show her my netherling traits and powers. Rabid's here as backup, in case she needs more proof than my wings to convince her that Wonderland is real.

I tuck away my key necklace. The pink and white vertical stripes on Jenara's wall glow a silvery hue, gilded by the moonlight streaming through translucent curtains draped across the arched window. Vines of black flower silhouettes stretch across her ceiling—immaculate shadows painted by Jeb's masterful hand a few years ago. A mural worthy of an art museum.

I catch him staring at it before he tightens his jaw and looks away. The sadness in the action knots me up inside.

"Jeb." I stall behind him and wrap him in my arms, my mouth pressed to the clothes hugging his broad shoulder. "You'll find your way. I promise . . . there's so much you have to offer this world still."

He tenses, but crosses his arms so he's clutching my elbows in place. "I'm not sure how to let go of something that once held me together."

"You don't have to let go. That part of you is still intact. In frames, painted on walls, sketched on squares of paper. Your muse lives on here, through the people who are getting joy from your artwork every day. That's more magical than anything. Let that hold you together until you find a new path."

He brings me around so we're facing each other, then kisses me. "You're pretty smart, for a netherling."

I laugh. "And you're pretty tough, for a human." I drag his head down for another kiss.

Rabid coos and stares up at us, wide-eyed and fascinated.

Embarrassed, I pull back. The momentary reprieve was nice, but I know it won't be so easy to brush aside everything Jeb's lost. It's something we'll deal with together, day by day, until he finds his way again.

For now, we have this situation with Jenara to tend to.

Jeb clears his throat, obviously thinking the same thing. "So, I guess I should check the house."

"Do you think she's at work?" I peel off my boots to let the plush shag of the pink area rug cushion my toes.

He cracks Jenara's door and peers into the hall. "I know Mom has to be. She always takes the evening shift. You two wait here."

Once he steps out, leaving the door ajar behind him, Rabid clambers onto Jenara's bed. His spindly fingers and toes wrinkle the black-and-white damask comforter. The pink dust ruffle and shams remind me of how Jen and I used to play dress-up in this room. How we fashioned wedding gowns out of sheets and pillowcases, told secrets, ate junk food, and stayed up till all hours of the night.

It seems so long ago.

Two white, faceless mannequins stand in front of her window with luminary shades tilted on their heads like hats. Jeb wired their hollow insides and threaded lightbulbs through their craniums to make lamps for her fifteenth birthday.

I turn one on, casting a white, starry pattern across the wooden floor and Jenara's bedspread.

"Ooooh." Rabid stands on the mattress and dances through the glowing shapes created by the luminary. I face the mirror, watching his reflection in the glass. He's like a macabre ballerina in a busted snow globe. So out of place in this room filled with normal, human things.

Then I see my own reflection. My netherling eye markings haven't fully faded yet. My skin is glistening, and if my hair weren't caught up in a braid, it would be rustling—alive and enchanted.

I'm an alien.

Come to think of it, we're all aliens now. Even Jeb. After what we've been through and seen, this tranquility seems more dangerous than the chaos we faced. I wonder if this is how soldiers feel after returning home from a war. How do they get past it? How do they learn to belong again? To feel safe once more?

The fuzzy buzzing whispers of a few bugs break through my thoughts, a welcome comfort. I close my eyes for an instant, but snap them open as a high-pitched squeal from the other end of the hallway makes me jump.

I shoo Rabid off the bed and into the closet. "Don't come out unless we call your name, okay?"

He nods, burrowing into a pile of sewing accessories—scarves, belts, and swatches of fabric—on the floor.

I stand in place, arms at my sides . . . trapped.

Jenara's hysterical sobs grow closer as Jeb leads her toward the cracked door. He talks in gentle tones, so quiet beneath her crying I can't make out what he says. My heart hammers in time with the hinges squeaking open.

When they step in, she's wrapped up in his arms, gripping the lapels of his shirt, head tucked against him and face hidden behind a curtain of wet pink hair—fresh from the shower. Jeb must've caught her just as she came out of the bathroon. Her green satin pajamas remind me of past slumber parties and giggling games.

I've missed her so much.

"Jen?" I murmur tentatively, without even knowing what to say next.

At the sound of my voice, she turns her head in my direction.

"A-Al?" Her freshly scrubbed pink cheeks bulge as she tries to suppress her sobs. She loses the battle and cries out, running to me.

I hold up my arms to hug her and we crash onto the mattress together, the springs bouncing beneath us. Catching my breath, I bury myself in the citrusy, bubblegum scent of her shampoo. A smile radiates from my heart to my lips and I hold her tighter against me, tears dribbling down my temples. Hers or mine . . . it doesn't matter. The sensation is wonderful.

Jeb rubs her back. "J."

"No, no, no, no." She sobs into my neck. "Don't wake me up. I'm dreaming, I'm dreaming."

He puts one knee on the bed next to our embracing bodies, and the concern in his eyes for his little sister is enough to make me forget we ever left.

"It's okay, Jen. It's not a dream," I reassure her. "We're here."

Jeb strokes her head, purposely skimming my cheek with a fingertip in the process. He doesn't want to hurt his sister—he's spent so many years protecting her. But he knows this is best for all of us, in the long run.

Still, it's obvious he's struggling and lost, like that little boy he once was.

I clasp his hand and drag him down so his body falls against me on my right side. He snuggles close enough that his soft breaths graze my ear, putting his arm across me and Jen so I'm sandwiched between my two favorite people. Together, the three of us cry and then laugh until we're hiccuping.

For the first time in weeks, we're together again. A family.

This feeling. Maybe this is how we find our way back to normalcy.

Once Jenara calms enough, she sits up, trying to slow her ragged breath. "Where have you *been*? We looked everywhere for you!" The accusation is directed at Jeb. "We thought you were—"

"I'm sorry," Jeb rises to his knees, interrupting her before she can admit that they were thinking the worst.

I stay put, spine anchored to the mattress. Afraid to move.

"Al, maybe we should just tell her everything all at once," Jeb says, his voice wavering.

"Including how I sent you there?" I grasp for the right words and fumble terribly.

Jenara's watery green gaze falls on me. "Huh?" Understanding crosses her face. "Wait." She scoots off the bed and stands, wobbly but determined. "The police were right? You knew where he was all along? But why would you . . . ?" She sobs again. "What about your mom? Where is she? And your dad? What's going on?"

I study her tear-streaked face, her pink hair dripping onto her ruffled pajama top, the three tiny freckles on the bridge of her nose. She looks so vulnerable. Do we *really* want to bring her into this? There's no turning back once we do.

Jeb forces me to sit up. "You're the only one who can show her. Make her understand."

I gulp. "I don't even know where to start."

"Somewhere right around here." He trails a finger down the slits in my dress that reveal my bare shoulder blades. My wing buds tingle at his touch.

Heat scorches my face. "But, I can't just . . . we need to prepare her."

Jenara inches backward toward the door. "Prepare me? You guys are freaking me out. I'm calling Mom." The doorbell rings and she stalls, her face brightening. "Corbin," she mumbles, and turns toward the hall to let him in.

"No, J." Jeb tries to stop her but she shrugs him off.

"Wait, Jen!" I jump off the bed. "Corb can't be here for this."

"Why not?" She spins, hands on her hips. "He's been here while Jeb's been missing. And while you were committed. He loves me, Al. *He's* been taking care of me and Mom. Anything you can tell me, you can tell him." She turns and marches through the bedroom door.

"We-we've been to Wonderland!" I blurt, stopping her in her tracks. She does an about-face midway into the hall, her mouth agape.

"Show her your wings," Jeb adds, narrowing his eyes. His long lashes cast shadows across his cheeks and the luminary lights sparkle across his skin, making him look as much like a netherling as me.

"*Wings?*" Jenara snaps, stomping back into the room. "Seriously, bro? You *want* her locked in the asylum again? You have no idea what she went through while they were trying to knock the Wonderland out of her. Don't enable her delirium!"

"Al . . ." Jeb guides me toward her. "You're gonna have to own it. There's no gentle way to make someone believe. It took me a crash course via the rabbit hole."

Upon hearing the word *rabbit*, Rabid bursts from the closet, his skeletal form tangled in scarves and belts. He stumbles into Jeb and knocks them both to the floor. Rabid inches along toward me on his belly, looking like a demented caterpillar with only his antlers and pink eyes showing.

"Rabid of White, I be!" He announces in his hissing voice as he rolls around, trying to get liberated.

Jeb curses and Jenara screams so loud all sound deafens to a dull roar, as if my eardrums are stuffed inside a seashell.

The front door slams open and footsteps pound down the hall. Jeb scrambles up to shut Jen's bedroom, but too late. Corbin arrives at the threshold, panting, reddish-blond hair shimmering in the soft light. He clenches a house key in his hand. His eyes fall on Rabid, who's managed to peel off the accessories from Jenara's closet and is standing there, baring all his netherling creeptitude.

The little creature opens his arms in a grand flourish. "Ta-da!" he shouts, froth spritzing from his mouth. I scowl at his showmanship. Morpheus must've taught him that move.

"What the hell?" Corbin drawls in his deep Southern accent, grasping Jenara's elbow and backing her trembling body toward the hall with him.

Jeb frowns, intent on the key chain in Corbin's hand. "I was about to ask the same thing. Why do you have a key to our house, Corb? Since when are you living with my sister?"

I stare at Jeb. The netherling side of me laughs out loud before I can stop it, reveling in the ridiculousness of the entire situation. It seems we're all driven by instincts. For Jeb, giving his sister and best pal the shock of their lives takes a backseat to protective-big-brother mode.

Hearing Jenara's sobs reins my wicked side back in. I grab her robe from the chair by the nightstand and toss it over Rabid. He growls and the smell of singed fabric sharpens the air as his eyes become two glowing red orbs underneath, making smoky holes in the terrycloth.

"No fires, Rabid!" I scold.

He turns off his eyes and hunches lower to the floor.

"*Jeb? Al?*" Corbin mumbles, as if he's just now noticing us. He looks dangerously close to passing out. The freckles around his nose appear dark against his pale face. His intense blue gaze stays nailed to Rabid's hunched and wriggling form beneath the terrycloth robe. "Where've you . . . how did you . . . ? That thing. It's gotta be a robot . . . right?"

"Rabid no robot be!" My royal advisor screeches from under his covering, offended.

"Into the closet," I command. Rabid mumbles something indecipherable and hops out of sight, dragging the burned robe behind him like a wedding train.

Jeb and I exchange glances. "There's always forgetting potions," I offer.

He huffs, studying Corbin and Jenara where they're propped against the wall outside the room, confused and shaken beyond words. "Losing your memories isn't all it's cut out to be. Trust me."

"So we tell him, too," I offer. "It's that, or he forgets and we send him home."

"I'm not going anywhere without Jen," Corbin grates out, the color returning to his face. He holds Jenara against him as she buries her nose into his button-up shirt, struggling to breathe normally.

Jeb's lips turn on a slow, daring smile. "Not going anywhere *tonight*? So, you plan on being devoted to her for another day or two?"

Corbin's jaw clenches. "Try forever." His embrace tightens, drawing Jenara so close her pajama pants cling to his jeans, popping with static.

"Forever's a long time," Jeb says, and the twinge of sadness in the statement tugs my insides, as if they were a harp strummed by his fingertips. Sniffling, Jenara turns to look at her brother, her expression bewildered. Jeb's mood shifts again as he shakes his head—an affectionate gesture. "Looks like you have yourself a regular white knight, sis."

I catch Jeb's wrist where a raised scar has replaced his tattoo. "You would know a little about how stubborn those can be. Yeah?"

He chuckles softly and winds our fingers together. "So, Corb. You want to be a part of our family? What say we make it official?"

Corbin and Jenara both squint at us, holding their breath. The house falls deathly quiet. Nothing can be heard but a few whispering insects—on a frequency only I'm attuned to—and Rabid's grumbles from the closet.

Jeb lifts my hand and kisses my engagement ring. "The thing you both need to know about Al?" he says to our audience. "That asylum never had a chance at curing her. See, you can take the girl out of

Wonderland, but you can't take Wonderland out of the girl." My hand slips from his as he steps back to give me room. "Show them what you got, fairy queen."

I put on my most regal smile. And there, in the middle of the pink-striped bedroom, with my best friend and the love of her life staring wide-eyed, I free my netherling wings, and confess all my lies.

⊰·I·⊱

MEMORY TWO: SEASHELLS
Four years later . . .

PLEASANCE, TX., JUN 29 — Two Pleasance locals who were reported missing four weeks ago, along with two others who vanished last Wednesday, were discovered alive early Saturday morning, with only a few scrapes and bruises, trapped within a collapsed mining tunnel beneath a condemned activity park.

Another local, a sibling and close friend of the missing persons, had reported suspecting their whereabouts after receiving a tip via her Ouija board, according to Officer Riley Hughes.

"Normally, I don't put much stock in spiritual hokum," Hughes said. "But the girl had been fully cooperative with police during our monthlong investigation for her missing brother and next-door neighbors. She was insistent we at least look. Since several cave-ins took place at the park on the eve of the Pleasance High prom weeks earlier, and considering it was the missing

persons' last reported whereabouts, we thought it was worth a
follow-up. We went there expecting to find nothing. Score one
for hokum."

"Al, are you *kidding* me?" Jenara's piqued voice pulls my attention from the four-year-old newspaper article. An ornate glass bottle filled with the stones I collected during our "rescue" from Underland sits next to me on the wicker couch. I rub my temples, fuzzy from my trip down memory lane.

Jen rushes across the threshold and shuts the door behind her. "I can't believe you haven't even put on your underskirt yet! What's with you? Twenty-one years old today and already showing signs of senility. Maybe you need some fresh air."

She cracks the window behind me. A salty breeze drifts in, stirring the turquoise starfish-patterned curtains above my head. My hair flutters, the platinum waves skimming across my bared shoulders and lacy white corset.

I trace the hem of my matching lacy boy shorts, surprised to be sitting in nothing but my underthings. What was I doing before I sat down? First, I ate the birthday cupcake Mom left next to her card on the bedside table.

As if triggered by my thoughts, the paper cupcake liner flutters to the floor on a gust of wind and blows over to Jen's bare feet. She picks it up and frowns at me. "Ummm?"

"Cupcake from my mom." I smack my lips, still tasting the bright blue, cloyingly sweet, honey-anise icing.

Jenara crumples the paper and tosses it into the trash. "So, this is you coming down from a sugar high?"

"Maybe?" I attempt to recall the rest of the afternoon's events. After my snack, I took off my robe to get dressed. While digging through my suitcase for the brand-new choker necklace I had borrowed from Jenara for today, I was sidetracked by the keepsakes I'd packed. Somehow, I ended up on the couch under the window with scrapbook and bottle in hand.

I study the newspaper clipping again. *Is* this me crashing from a sugar rush, or is it something else?

I feel so strange. My body and mind are relaxed, but my blood is the opposite. It races through the veins under my skin—white-water rapids branching off into a thousand tributaries.

"Come on, zombie girl, let me see *some* sign of life," Jen says, only half-teasing. "It's one hour to sunset, and we still have to fix your hair and makeup. And FYI, that icing stain around your lips does *not* count as your 'something blue.' That's what the garter is for. How are we supposed to get that off?" Her gaze falls to the bottle of stones beside my thigh. She picks it up and rattles it in front of me. "Unbelievable. Jeb's out there with Corbin getting sand between his toes, pacing the shore to check every little detail. And here you are, reminiscing."

Jenara's wound up about more than just the wedding details. She had to leave a fashion show in New York two days early to get here for this. She's been in constant contact with her design partner, and their line is stirring up quite a buzz. I have a feeling her career is about to take off big-time. We tried to plan the wedding around her schedule, but this was the only week the beach house was available. So we compromised and made it for the tail end of the fashion show. I told her she didn't have to come, but she said she'd die before missing it.

Even now, when she's hitting me with her harshest green-eyed glare, I can tell there's no place she'd rather be. She's a vision of softness in her shin-length, flowing periwinkle sundress. Her pink hair sits atop her head in a chic chignon. Dark blue pygmy roses are tucked in at strategic intervals, forming a halo. A few stray pink tendrils coil at her neck.

"You look perfect," I tell her, dreamily.

She fights a grin and rolls her eyes. "Wish I could say the same for you."

"Has Corb seen you yet?" My question is rhetorical. The two have been joined at the hip for years, and now that Corbin has almost completed his bachelor's degree in advertising, he's planning to move with her to New York by the end of the summer.

Just last month, he asked for "her hand in marriage." Dressed in medieval chain mail, he rode up to our duplex in a horse-drawn carriage. Jeb had helped him refinish an old Chevy they found in a junkyard. Jeb took the body and scrapped all the clunky, unnecessary parts, making it a shell lightweight enough to be pulled by the two white horses Corbin borrowed from a friend. After adding a sturdy harness, replacing the tires with buggy wheels, and painting the body a glossy white with red trim, they had the perfect Texan knight's carriage. When Corbin pulled up in Jen's driveway with three dozen roses in hand and asked her to ride off with him into the sunset, she nearly fainted.

It was old-fashioned—yet modern—and oh so sweet.

Lost in her own nostalgic haze, Jenara admires the sparkly engagement ring on her finger. Her grin breaks loose, along with an attractive blush to her cheeks. "Well, yah. My betrothed approves of my latest creation. But you're the one who's about to be in the spotlight." She tosses the bottle of stones into my opened suitcase and then reaches into the closet for my dress. Jeb and I had decided Jenara's beautiful creations got a bad rap at prom, and deserved the spotlight in a good memory.

Over the past few weeks, Jenara did a masterful job stitching rips and patching holes with sequined appliqués—one of which she'd found in an antique store, so it was also my "something old." Any stains were masked with airbrushed periwinkle dye followed by a sweep of glitter. Now the strapless white dress looks brand-new. Or as new as a vintage wedding gown can look when it's been modified to resemble shadowy, moldering fabric fresh from the grave.

"Come on, Al, get the lead out," Jenara scolds, losing patience.

I grunt in response.

She tosses the sheer purple-gray underskirt my way and it drifts over my head, surrounding me like a perfume-scented cloud.

"I'll prep the makeup," she says. A loud clatter follows as she dumps her cosmetic bag onto the table next to Mom's birthday card. "Maybe nail polish remover will work on your lips."

I crinkle my nose. "Yuck . . . really?"

She shrugs. "Desperate times call for disgusting measures." On the other side of the iridescent netting covering my face, she sorts out eye shadows, liners, brushes, and blush.

My body feels light, like I could float away. It's partly elation . . . partly nerves . . . and something more. Something I've never felt before.

Or have I?

The skin around my eyes tingles, as does the skin at my shoulder blades.

Muffled laughter and footsteps drift through the living room's paper-thin wall. It sounds like part of the crowd is headed out for a while. The beach house my dad rented has seven bedrooms, a loft, and four and a half bathrooms, but is still barely big enough for my and Jeb's combined guests. I can't imagine how packed it will be once the rest arrive.

Gathering my energy, I drag off the netting and slide the newspaper clipping back into its spot in my scrapbook. I'm tempted to flip through the other pages. To glance over pictures of our art sales—limited edition paintings that Jeb will never be able to replicate, and my glass gem mosaics—along with goofy snapshots of the past four Halloweens, Christmases, summer picnics, snowball fights, and college pranks. Just one last glimpse of our time together as an engaged couple, captured between sleeves of polypropylene film, before we start this next chapter in a new scrapbook, embellished with white satin and tiny strings of pearls.

Every inch of my skin flushes, thinking of what comes after the ceremony. It hadn't been easy to wait the past few years, but life was complicated enough, working through Jeb's grief over his lost artistic abilities, going to college, and balancing my royal duties in Wonderland with our human life. It never seemed to be the right time, until now. We've adjusted to our new roles, learned to make compromises while being honest, and have always been there for each other emotionally. And after tonight's physical commitment, our bond will be unbreakable.

There's no more perfect start to our new life together than this: his strong arms holding my bared body as I trace each of the scars along his chest with a fingertip, healing his wounds with just a touch.

"What's with the goofy smile, Al?"

I glance up, grinning despite myself.

Jenara snorts. "You're worthless today, you know that? Give it over." She pries the scrapbook from my hand. "Most maids of honor don't have to call on necromancy skills to get the bride ready. You're paying me extra for this, right?"

I lift my legs off the floor so she can help me with my underskirt. "Sure. Ten thousand times more than the wages we agreed on."

"Hmm, ten thousand times zero . . . I knew I should've had a lawyer look over those terms." She holds the netting open as I plunge my feet inside, then grasps my hands to lever me off the couch.

As I settle the elastic under the corset's hem at my waist—so the slip puffs out to just below my knees—that tingling behind my shoulders escalates to a burning sensation. Before I even realize it's my wing buds, they burst free: opaque white and glimmering with rainbow-colored jewels, splayed around me like a butterfly's wings fresh from the cocoon.

I screech.

Jenara gasps, her eyes as big as quarters. "Al, what the heck? You can't do that now!"

"I—I didn't mean to!" My shout reverberates around us.

"Shh." She smacks a hand over my lips and looks at the paper-thin wall. When we hear nothing but the steady hum of oblivious chatter from the guests in the other room, she lets her hand drop. "Okay . . . but you'll have an audience within the hour. Put them back."

I try to absorb them, but my wings won't budge. "It's not working." I try again. "I *can't*." My pulse spikes.

Jen's expression grows wilder. "Oh, huh-uh. You're sparkling. And your eyes . . . you're seriously not doing this on purpose?"

I shake my head. A thousand glimmers of light reflect off

Jenara's face and the sunny yellow walls surrounding us. I tap my fingers along my cheeks, envisioning what I know must be there: black markings like curvy tiger stripes beneath my lower lashes that resemble Morpheus's without the jewels. "My patches . . . how prominent are they?"

Jenara's gaze is nailed to my eyes. "It's not just the markings, Al. It's your irises. They're . . . purple."

"*Purple?*"

Jen nods. "And it's not a subtle shade . . . it's otherworldly weird."

My stomach drops. "This can't be happening." My hair begins to sway around me—a taunting dance of magic unleashed.

"Holy crap," Jenara blurts as a few of the strands reach out to her. "Is this like a netherling flu or something?"

"I—I don't know." Fingers trembling, I capture my unruly waves and knot them at the nape of my neck. "What are we going to do?" Panic coats my vocal cords, making me hoarse—as if I swallowed liquid sandpaper.

Jenara kneads her hands. "Well, you can wear your hair up, and we can say we got creative with your makeup. The wedding veil will hide your eyes during the ceremony. Afterward, you can tell people you're experimenting with special-effects contacts. But the wings . . . I—I don't think we can possibly disguise those."

There's no looking glass for me to check the full extent of my netherling display, for obvious reasons. I didn't want any mischief weaseling its way into today's festivities, so I chose the smallest room because it had no mirror, trusting Jen to do my makeup and make me presentable for the wedding. The drawback to choosing this room is there's no lock on the door, which now makes me even more vulnerable and accessible.

Blasted hindsight.

The flush in my maid of honor's cheeks fires to an anxious red. "I'm getting your mom." She starts to leave but pauses. "Just . . . stay here and watch the door. Try to keep calm until I get back. We'll fix it, okay? Nothing's going to ruin this for you and Jeb."

I nod, but it's only for her peace of mind. How can this *not* ruin things? I can't face our unwitting human guests with all of my dirty Wonderland laundry hanging out! This isn't prom night at Underland. Having wings on a beach can't be explained as easily as wearing them to a masquerade under black lights.

Once Jenara is gone, I wedge the chair beneath the doorknob and tug a wing over my shoulder. The gems blink through a rhapsody of colors, just like Morpheus's eye markings when he's anxious or perplexed. A while back, I discovered that my moods show through my jewels like his. It's something Morpheus kept to himself, and one of the reasons he likes to have my wings on display . . . so he can read me.

But *I'm* the one who gets to decide when to let them out. I've been managing my netherling aspects effortlessly since I've been back in the human realm. Never once have I lost control. There's trickery afoot here. And it started with that little blue cupcake that tasted of anise and honey.

Anise . . . a flavor startlingly close to licorice. *Licorice tobacco.*

I grit my teeth. "*Morpheus.*"

Last night, before I returned from my dreams, I hugged him, something we don't often do. We've laid out strict boundaries for physical contact, to honor my human life. But he'd been grumpy and ill-tempered with my subjects, which he rarely is, and I knew he was suppressing his feelings about my pending marriage. So I wanted to comfort him, to assure him his patience had not gone unnoticed or unappreciated.

He hugged me back for all of five seconds, then pushed me to arm's length. When he looked down at me, his expression was the furthest thing from sad or troubled. It was utterly composed, which is never a good sign.

"*I've decided to give you and your groom a wedding gift tomorrow, plum,*" he said, opening his hand. An electric blue orb ignited in his palm, then took flight, hovering between us. "*Since Jebediah gave up his ability to dream for Wonderland, you may share your dreams privately on your honeymoon. You will not come to Wonderland for that one night. Instead, Jebediah can step inside with you and your dreamscapes will belong solely to him. But only if he can prove himself worthy of marrying a fairy queen.*"

Before I could capture the floating blue light, Morpheus shoved me out of my dreamscape.

My hands fist in the netting covering my thighs. When I woke in this room this morning, I considered telling Jeb about Morpheus's cryptic words, but didn't have my cell phone because Jenara's been doing her bridesmaid's best to keep her brother and me from seeing or contacting each other until the ceremony.

There's no more time to waste. He needs to be warned that Morpheus has arranged another test for me to pass. Or, rather, one for him.

I stumble over to the table for a second look at Mom's birthday card, maneuvering my wings around the furniture arranged at odd angles in the too-small room. I lift the card, studying it carefully. Beyond the cute owl's face on the front—*subtle*—and the "Whoooo's birthday is today?" sentiment inside, Mom's signature is in print.

She always signs cards in cursive. Why didn't I catch that? Or the fact that Dad hadn't signed it, too? Come to think of it, I should've caught it all because I should've had my guard up. Morpheus has trained me better than this.

But he *knew* I would be distracted with my brain in wedding mode. He was counting on it. And to make matters worse, there were no bugs to warn me. The beach house was fumigated a week ago due to an ant infestation, and the silence has been deafening since we got here. I suspect he had a hand in that, too. Yet he's still keeping his vow not to come between me and Jeb, because he's managed to make it my netherling traits that are causing all the issues.

I'm on the verge of impressed, but it pales to the anxiety tying me in knots. How could I have been so careless?

"*Bloody mastermind moth*," I seethe, expecting to hear an echo of smug laughter stirring in my mind. When there's no response, I clench my teeth and rip the card in half, angry there are no answers to be found there.

"Okay, you got me. But you have to know you're underestimating *him*," I say aloud, in the hope Morpheus is at least listening. I sound strong and confident, even though nervous tears sting my eyes. "Jeb will find a way to make this work . . ."

"You're right, Al." Jeb's deep, determined voice pulses through me from behind—an electric current, setting all my nerve endings alight.

I turn to see a single white rose wiggling through the cracked door.

"Let me in."

Almost tripping over my wings, I rush over and scoot the chair away so it's in the middle of the floor, then I back up to give him room.

He steps inside—dripping wet in the remains of his prom tux—and shuts the door. He leans against it and stares at me. Sand and droplets of water sparkle on his forearms where he's rolled the periwinkle dress shirt to his elbows. The placket, half-unbuttoned, bares his glistening chest. His navy pants are rolled up, too, stopping at midcalf. He must have left the blue velvet-flocked jacket outside, hanging somewhere to dry.

"Jen tried to tell me about your eyes," he murmurs before I can ask what happened to his clothes. "But there's no artist's palate, no comparison in this world for that color. Al, you're so *beautiful*."

I was just thinking the same about him.

"And you're so wet," I say stupidly. It's hard to think past the way the soft light reflects off the sheen of his olive complexion, sparkling silver labret, and dark, unruly waves dripping water across his forehead and along the bridge of his nose.

He doesn't respond, too busy taking me in with his deep, mossy gaze. If Jenara were here, she'd insist I cover my corset and underskirt. No, she'd insist I kick him out. But being away from him since the reception dinner last night has been long enough. Even the chair standing between us feels like a mountain. I should move it, but he has me entranced. His gaze traces every turn of my body—a mental touch as intimate and thorough as a real caress would be.

"Maybe we shouldn't have chosen a beach wedding," I tease, trying to suppress my overactive imagination.

Jeb's resulting sexy smile reveals that crooked incisor that I hope our future sons or daughters will inherit. "You mean, given our past experiences with large bodies of water?"

I laugh.

He laughs, too, but then his mood turns serious. "We found our way back to each other on a beach in AnyElsewhere. You made a vow to me there. It's only fitting I make my vows to you on one. No matter what happens before or during our wedding. No matter what kinds of hoops Morpheus makes us jump through today, it's worth it. *We're* worth it. And we're going to prove it to him."

I've never seen him look more confident or . . . energized. "Wait, are you . . . ? You're enjoying this." I grin tentatively.

He shrugs and smells the white rose in his hand. "I like a challenge."

"Morpheus is going to hate that he can't push your buttons."

"Psssh. We both know he's thrilled I'm up for the game."

I shake my head, smiling. It's strangely comforting, how well they know and understand each other now. "So, he's the one who made you fall into the water?"

Jeb forces his eyes from my half-dressed body to my face. "Well, technically, it wasn't him. He's keeping his word about staying away from our world. Corb was getting the ring bearer's pillow ready when something pinched his big toe and made him drop the rings. A rock lobster plunged out of the sand, scooped them up, and scuttled into the waves."

"An actual rock lobster? Like the ones in AnyElsewhere?"

Jeb tucks the rose's stem into his pocket, then plucks his shirttail from the waist and starts unclasping the remaining buttons. "Yeah. I painted some for Wonderland before we left, when I reinvented the landscapes. Morpheus had requested them specifically. Proof without a doubt he sent that one here."

It's a struggle to follow the conversation because all I can do is watch how the wet clothes cling to Jeb's toned form with every movement. "So . . . you dove into the ocean to get the rings back?"

"I tried, but couldn't outswim our thief." He peels the soggy fabric from his shoulders and arms, revealing water-slicked abs and droplets beaded along the dark hair dusting his pecs. "I asked your mom to contact Ivory through the mirror in her room. She had a magical flute at her castle. I saw it while we were there. Come to find out, the instrument works on the clams in our world, too. They flushed the lobster to the shore. The rings are now tied safely in place. Corb's keeping the pillow with him until the ceremony."

I think back on the clams we met in Wonderland on our first visit there . . . how I played a flute that called and commanded them. How in a sweep of dingy gray, they came rushing to our rescue when we were being chased by an army, and carried our pursuers away on a surge of rattling shells. I'm even more grateful now than I was then. I just hope no one saw anything.

"Don't worry about the guests," Jeb says as if reading my thoughts. "Your dad kept everyone preoccupied. He took them on a tour to the other side of the beach where the sailboats dock."

Relief washes over me. But it's only temporary, considering everyone is going to see *me* soon.

"Shouldn't we address the flying elephant in the room?" I ask, flapping my wings.

Jeb lays his dripping shirt over the chair's wooden arm. His Adam's apple moves on a slow swallow. "You mean the fact that you're the most radiant and magical woman I've ever seen?"

Woman . . . I don't think he's ever called me that. His gaze is so intense, my legs wobble. I inch toward the bed, needing its support against the back of my calves and thighs.

His gaze stalls on my blue lips.

I rub them. "It was dumb. I ate a cupcake that came out of nowhere . . . I know better than to eat anything strange."

"No. Mort would've found some way to make this happen, with or without you eating anything. He's making a point. I've proven my worth to be a husband to your human side by almost dying for you more than once. But he wants me to be worthy of your netherling side, too."

My mouth gapes. "That's what he said in my dream!"

Jeb frees the rose from his pocket and strokes one of the petals. "I shared his magic once. I know how he thinks. He's proven his love for your human side when he wouldn't let Ivory crown you and destroy it. So, he wants me to prove myself like he did. I've got no problem with that. It will be my honor to marry you today, in front of God and everyone, with your wings and netherling attributes in full view."

As lovely and sincere as the sentiment is, I can't get past the logic of it all. "But this"—I spread my wings out behind me and they cast shadows over both of us—"I don't know how to face an audience of humans without giving myself away. This is impossible."

"Nothing's impossible. You taught me that a long time ago. On the bright side, we know the effects of the cupcake are temporary. Morpheus cares too much about your mending heart to endanger it by ruining your ability to live a fulfilling life here."

I nibble the end of my thumb, careful not to mess up Jenara's meticulous French manicure. "Temporary can be anything from hours to a whole day."

"True. It's going to last through the ceremony at least. But we can handle it. Just let me worry about what everyone thinks or sees. I'm going to fix this with human ingenuity and a touch of magic."

A touch of magic. "Wait . . . you're not going to use your wish, are you?"

"No. I promised you I'd find the right time to use it. It's safe still. Your mom and Corb are taking the mirror portals to a few costume shops."

"For what?"

"It's a surprise." He glances over his shoulder at the door, then again at me. "I should leave before Jen gets back. I was supposed to just hang my shirt outside on the doorknob so she could fix the stains and iron it. She's going to flip if she knows I looked in on you before the wedding . . . but I wanted to tell you happy birthday." He holds out the rose, a bit too far away for me to reach.

"Come closer," I plead.

His clean-shaven jaw ticks. "Bad enough I saw you. Who knows what havoc would be unleashed if I touched you."

"Let's find out."

His expression grows fierce and hungry. He shoves the chair aside and starts toward me.

The gusts from the window pick up the scent of his cologne mixed with the rose he carries. He stops just a few inches away, free hand fidgeting at his side, as if considering his options. A sweet, torturous tension stretches between us—like the charged lull before a lightning strike. Three strands of my hair break free from the knot at my nape and twine around him and the rose. One brings the flower to me and I capture it in my right hand.

Jeb watches, captivated.

I try to contain my other strands of hair where they lock around him, but he grasps both my wrists and brings my left palm to his lips.

"Let it be," he murmurs against my scars, and reaches behind my neck to loosen the rest of my waves. "You know I love you like this." His voice grinds, rough and raw.

My hair whips around us both, rapturous to be liberated. It encircles his biceps, shoulders, and waist. With gentle force, it brings our half-clothed bodies together and his lips find mine. He tastes of the ocean, sparkling cider, and chocolates. He's been sampling the reception food.

I drop the rose and run my hands across his chest. His skin is wet and warm and his muscles twitch with restraint.

"This is worth any amount of bad luck," I whisper against his full, soft mouth, returning his feverish kisses.

"We've never had good luck anyway," he whispers in return, dragging us down to the bed together while careful not to crush my wings. "But we're damn good at making our own."

He eases me onto my back, his weight ensnaring me in a most delicious trap. His knee wedges between my thighs, his damp pants snagging my underskirt. A breeze rushes over us, cool on my bared skin. So strange, to burn like a furnace, yet still get chill bumps.

Jeb's hands glide along my curves—an intimate expanse that he's familiar with, but has yet to fully explore. "You're cold," he says as his lips move across the chilled flesh at my neck.

My bones feel like they're turning to liquid, my blood to molten lava. "Furthest thing from it," I answer, breathy.

Eyes heavy with desire, he rolls away—freeing me. He reaches behind my back and drags a corner of the lavender and turquoise striped coverlet around to wrap my body and wings, separating my skin from his.

I groan. "Jeb. I don't want anything between us."

His fingertip traces the shape of my lips. "After the ceremony, there won't be. I'm going to make you mine tonight, and it will be all we ever dreamed of."

My body lights up, sparks of anticipation igniting in every part of me that he touched earlier. I'm about to tell him that it will be even more than we imagined—because he can literally share my dreams this one night if we can pull off our wedding—when the door crashes open.

"Oh, come on!" Jenara shouts.

Jeb boomerangs off the bed and gives me a sheepish grin as his sister herds him toward the door.

"Are they back? Did they find everything?" he asks her just before she pushes him out.

Jenara scowls. "Yeah yeah. Not that it matters, now that you've tempted fate by seeing her."

Jeb ducks in one last time and smirks at me. "As if fate has anything on a fairy queen."

I smirk back, still tasting his kisses.

"Meet me on the shore at sunset?" he asks.

"A stampede of wild Jubjub birds couldn't keep me away," I answer.

He laughs and then disappears around the corner, leaving me with a grumpy maid of honor, a thousand questions, and a glowing heart.

MEMORY THREE: STARDUST

Fifty-six years later . . .

Rain slaps the window in fat droplets curdled with ice. It's only six o'clock in the evening, but autumn dusks come early in Pleasance. I stare through the glass, rain filling my skull by osmosis, blurring my thoughts as I lean against the chilled pane. The soft blue walls behind me close in, reaching for the dark grounds outside and forming a tunnel. Claustrophobia, my old nemesis, lurks in the shadows.

My curved spine hunches lower. Ammonia singes my nose. I taste the bitter purity in the back of my throat, and it stings.

The movement around Jeb's hospital bed reflects back through the glass's reflection. He's surrounded by family: our two sons and our daughter, along with their spouses, children, and grandchildren. Jenara and Corbin are absent—she's in a nursing home, and he's in a cemetery. But our nieces and nephews have all sent flowers, plants, and well-meaning texts meant to comfort and give hope.

Hope is the last thing I feel.

Just two weeks ago, Jeb was perfectly healthy. Then, after a routine exam, our whole world turned upside down. Ugly words like malignant, aggressive, and inoperable ate away at our happy life, leaving it as crippled and depleted as Jeb's body would soon be. The doctor said only six weeks at most . . . that to offer a chance for any longer would be impossible.

But he's wrong, because he doesn't know that my husband has a wish yet to be spent.

Clothing rustles and shoes clomp on the tile floor as part of the crowd leaves the room, headed to the cafeteria for dinner. All that remains are our three children, who—like me—have no appetite, and our two great-grandchildren, who've already eaten.

Jeb is being strong, making up silly stories about the bruised purple pinpricks in his arms. He won't dare let the little ones know the truth: that they're from his first bout of subcutaneous chemo treatments, which have only served to make him achy, nauseated, and miserable.

Our great-grandchildren, ages three and five years, take turns perching on the edge of his mattress, trying to be closest to him.

"No. *Not* beetle footprints, Pop-pop," our blond and blue-eyed Alisia scolds as she pats the wrinkles on his face lovingly. The timeworn etches only serve to make him more distinguished and handsome—his almost eighty years in this world notwithstanding.

He smiles and kisses her plump fingertips. He loves both of our great-grandchildren, but Alisia holds a special place in his heart. She's the spitting image of me as a toddler, with the same cynical and serious nature, which presents him with an irresistible challenge to make her smile and laugh.

"They most surely are footprints," he teases. "They've been stepping in ink and trekking across me as I sleep. Drawing maps on my skin. They think there's buried treasure in my hair. That's because it's made of magical silver thread." Faint purple light streams through the window, dancing across his thick, silvery white waves. I dread to think of them falling out in clumps and leaving him bald.

Alisia giggles—a lovely, tinkling sound that echoes in the cold room and warms the ears—a wonderful reprieve from my morbid thoughts.

"Really, Pop-pop?" Scotty screeches, nudging his way into the conversation. The rough-and-tumble five-year-old tries to shove his younger sister aside to get a closer look at Jeb's hair, nearly toppling her.

I spin, panicked, but our elder son catches her and settles her back into place by the pillow. "Scotty, I told you, no roughhousing around the bed. There's too many wires and plugs. Be good, or you'll get down."

"Yes, Grandpa." Scotty bows his dark head, his brown eyes penitent.

"Ah, he's all boy, this one." Jeb rubs Scotty's head.

Lying beneath the blankets, pale and sallow, my husband seems so much smaller than I remember.

We both do.

I sigh and face the rain again.

The clock on the wall ticks out a dead man's march. I wring my wrinkled hands.

How many hours do we have left? How many minutes and seconds to say our good-byes? I adore our family, but while they're here, each private sentiment I want to share sits silent on my tongue—dormant thoughts, aborted whispers.

Lightning strikes and the walls blink with yellow illumination.

Our younger son—forty-four-year-old Jackson—sits in the corner chair not far from me, concentrating on the sketching tablet in his lap. He's always been the most like me. Quiet, introspective, serious. He has a tendency to escape into his designs when he's troubled or upset. He's probably perfecting his latest assignment from the architectural firm.

"Mom, you have to see this one," my daughter's voice reaches out. I know that tone. She's trying to pull us out of our emotional tailspins. She's always been the family cheerleader and mediator.

I turn to face her and press my shoulders against the window, the chill numbing my dormant wing buds. Victoriana lifts a photo from the shoebox on the nightstand and holds it up. Across the bottom is a white sticker with black marker script that reads: *David Nathanial Holt—fish out of water.*

"Do you remember when Uncle Corb took this?" she asks.

I nod. It's from forty-nine years ago. Jeb is thirty, and I'm twenty-eight. We're laughing and wading in the ocean with our first child. My belly bulges with our second, and we're totally unaware it's a girl. The beach was one of our favorite haunts for family vacations. Mom and Dad would come, along with Jeb's mom, Jenara and Corbin, and their two kids. I study the happy couple in the picture. It feels like a lifetime ago. Jeb and I hold two-year-old David's dimpled hands between us, lifting him so his bare feet can skim the waves. He's the only one of our three children who never liked to swim. He wasn't afraid of water . . . he took baths and showers happily. He just didn't like getting his swimsuit wet. It always "stuck to his skin" and made him grumpy.

Victoriana's tear-streaked face begs silently for help as she looks at David where he's still standing guard over his grandchildren. He scoops up Scotty and moves to the other side of the bed beside his sister, leaving Alisia to fuss over her pop-pop's enchanted hair.

David taps the dimple in Victoriana's chin reassuringly, then leans down to let Scotty dig through the pictures. David's head almost touches his sister's. They both inherited their father's dark hair and green eyes. In fact, had it not been for the two years' difference in their ages, and my daughter's delicate loveliness—so different from her brother's masculine, muscular features—people would've thought them twins.

Victoriana pokes his shoulder with the corner of the picture. "*Ick, don't get my clothes wet! It feels gwoss!* You were such a wimp, bro."

A bittersweet smile creeps over me. There are times she reminds me so much of her aunt Jenara, I ache from the nostalgia.

David snorts. "Well, at least there's such a thing as nude beaches for people with my . . . sensitivities. On the other hand, there's no escaping birds. They're *everywhere*." He finds a snapshot of his nine-year-old sister running from a chicken at a petting zoo and holds it up for everyone to see. *Victoriana Violet Holt: learning to fly* is written on the sticker. "Yeah, Vic." David grins. "*I* was the wimp."

"Hey," she elbows her brother. "I don't have ornithophobia, jerk. I like birds fine . . . just can't stand for things to flap their wings around me. Especially bugs." She shudders and turns to little Scotty where he's propped on his grandfather's waist. Joining her hands to form wings, she flutters them around the child's chubby cheeks. He snickers and snorts, then grabs her hands and wrestles them.

David laughs again. "Right. All because a moth got stuck in the kitchen once. Most kids who live in the country survive that kind of trauma without any long-lasting effects. It didn't affect Jack."

Jackson sweeps a curtain of blond bangs from his forehead and pushes his glasses up on the bridge of his nose, at last setting aside his sketch. Blue eyes like mine dance behind the round, brassy frames, and his mouth lifts to a wide smile with a crooked incisor that matches his dad's. "Uh, I wasn't born yet, Dave." He stands and walks over to me, putting an arm around my shoulders. I lean into him, breathing in his cologne—a mature version of the little-boy scent of sweat and outdoors that used to cling to him in his skateboarding days.

"Yeah, our handsome Jackson Thomas was still tucked safely

inside Mom's uterus back at the time of the great moth caper," Vic pleads her case, her dimples deepening as she casts a teasing smirk at me.

Jackson holds me closer, nose wrinkled. "Really, Vic? Do you have to paint such a vivid picture?"

I laugh halfheartedly.

"Oh, right," Victoriana says. "David's the famous artist. I should leave the painting to him."

David rolls his eyes. "Sculpting and painting are completely different animals. Just like chickens and *bugs*."

Everyone laughs—Jeb the loudest of all, which triggers another bout of giggles from Alisia.

"That moth was big enough to *eat* a chicken!" Of course, Vic isn't letting it go. Her tenacity is part of what makes her such a good mechanic, and part of why she's the official owner of her father's garage now. "Also, I was five. Hard to get past a memory like that."

"Tell me about it," I say, under my breath. Jeb, hanging on to Alisia's ruffled dress to keep her anchored on the mattress, catches my gaze. His green eyes are still as expressive and clear as they've always been, in spite of how pale his skin is and the weary bags under his lower lashes. He knows what's going through my head. After almost sixty years of marriage, he could write on the pages of my mind without ever needing an eraser.

We're both remembering secret things the children will never know. It was the only time Morpheus ever visited our family, and it was due to some emergency Red Court business I needed to attend. Had Jeb not been magic once, too, and come to love Wonderland as a part of himself, he might've helped our oldest son swat the giant moth with his plastic nunchuks, especially considering Morpheus had said he would steer clear of the human realm. Instead, Jeb captured the moth to rescue him from David's "sticks of wrath," then put Morpheus in our room until I returned from the grocery store and could fix things.

"Hey, here's a shot of Dad's marble run blueprints," David blurts, shaking me from the memory. He raises the picture toward me and his younger brother. "Jack, you gotta check this out. They're plastered like wallpaper all over the garage. So weird that I've never seen this . . ."

Jackson takes my hand and tries to pull me over with him, but I squeeze his fingers and start for Jeb's bedside instead. I don't need to see the picture. I lived it.

It was two years after we came back from our final Wonderland adventure, and Jeb had been cleaning out his mom's attic while she was at work and I was at college taking one of my finals. He stumbled upon a trunk, and inside were all the sketches he'd drawn as a kid when he and his dad used to make marble runs. There were even some he'd sketched that he had one day hoped to make with his dad, before he'd lost him in the accident. Jeb hadn't known his father kept them all those years. He figured he'd thrown them out. Each was so intricately designed and planned, Jeb didn't have to do anything but follow the blueprints—no artistic vision required.

Jeb had plastered my garage walls with the hundred or so papers before I got back from college that day. When I pulled Gizmo in, I was surrounded by our future. I'd never seen my fiancé look more fulfilled, because he'd found a way to continue to create, and his dad had helped him do it.

Arriving at Jeb's bedside, I touch his face and he holds my hand in place to kiss it.

"Nanna! Pop-pop talks to beetles!" Alisia sings.

I laugh—though it's bittersweet at best. She stands precariously on the mattress with Jeb guiding her, and bounces along until I capture her and nuzzle her sweetly scented hair.

"Oh," Victoriana gasps from beside the nightstand. "This one's always been my favorite." Her smile is both bright and trembling.

One glimpse of the picture she displays, and I'm at our wedding again with my groom, surrounded by white rose trellises. Every female in the wedding party—even the flower girl—wore wings that lit up thanks to fiber-optic threads and battery packs. Only mine and Mom's were real, with netting strategically wrapped around their bases to hide where they sprouted from our skin. I had a sparkling tiara, and all of the guys, including the ring bearer, wore chain mail tunics.

Jeb gave me a fairy-tale wedding on the beach, complete with knights and fairies, all of us glittering and gilded with the pinky-purple rays of sunset. The moment our vows were spoken and he kissed me, a small blue orb floated down from the sky and landed on Jeb's head before bursting like a bubble. Those who attended thought it was some sort of atmospheric anomaly precipitated by the humidity and dim lighting, but they all agreed it was the most magical wedding they'd ever seen.

Little did they know how right they were: that the man who'd given up his dreams would be dreaming that night with his new bride—an unexpected gift from a netherling who had once been his bitter rival.

Jeb's eyes trail over me like they did that evening, the first time we were together as man and wife, full of love, trust, hope, and desire.

Looking back and forth between us, David clears his throat and gathers up the photos that Scotty scattered across the nightstand. "You know, on second thought, I think I'm ready for some dinner. You guys want to come?"

Jackson skirts around the activity, clutching his sketchbook as he moves the chair behind me. "Sit down, Mom. Stay awhile."

I give him a sad smile and he helps me settle at Jeb's side.

Victoriana sniffles and drops the lid on the picture box. She leans over to kiss her father's forehead. "Be back soon, Dad."

He grasps her hand and presses his lips to it. "Okay, angel."

Jackson and David hug him and gather the little ones.

"Wait, kids." Jeb's plea catches them just before they step out. "You all know I'm proud of you, right? How happy you make me and your mom?" His eyes sparkle with unshed tears.

They nod.

"Good. I love you."

"Love you, too, Dad," they say simultaneously, their voices quavering. The door closes behind them, and the only sounds are the clock and the rain.

Jeb pulls me in for a long hug and we softly cry together.

It's difficult to regain composure, but once we do, he drags something from under his pillow and holds it out to me: a white rose . . . crushed and slightly withered, but the most beautiful flower I've ever seen.

Taking it with a shaky hand, I hold it to my nose. "Where . . . how?"

"I still have a few cards up my sleeve, skater girl."

I try to laugh, but it turns into a sob.

He strokes my cheek. "Shh. Did you bring my wish?"

I drag it out of my pocket, fighting back more tears.

He closes his hand over mine. "Come on, now. I've waited so long to use it. This is the *something of consequence*. No one needs to suffer through my illness."

"Least of all you," I whisper on the edge of tearing up again. "But you could use it to be cured and live a little longer. At least long enough to see Alisia start kindergarten. Magic can work miracles."

His finger traces invisible lines around my eyes where my netherling markings lie in wait. "You were the only miracle I ever needed. You've always blamed yourself on some level, for me losing my muse. But don't you see? I never lost anything. *You* are my muse. Even with my creativity gone, you stayed by my side and were always there, inspiring me to be the man I wanted to be. Because of you, I'm leaving behind a legacy. A well-adjusted and happy family who will carry on our memories and traditions. That's how I'll live forever, Al. No mortal man could ask for anything more."

Tears stream hot down my face. It hurts to breathe. If I didn't know it was impossible, I'd think my heart was breaking.

"As for Alisia and Scotty, we both know that the older they are when I go, the harder it will be for them. We also knew it would come to this one day. That one of us would end up going where the other couldn't follow—either way. There was no escaping that. Because we're from different worlds. Magic can't make me into someone I'm not. I'm human. Death is part of who I am. But it's not part of you. You have another life waiting. I've had all I ever dreamed of. Because *he* stood back. Now it's his time."

Deep inside, I know he's right. But to imagine never being able to see Jeb again . . . to never hold his hand . . . to never laugh with him—it cuts me to the core.

"I'm scared for you." It's a lie, because it's me I'm scared for.

Facing this much pain alone is paralyzing. "How can you be so sure ... so calm?"

He presses our foreheads together so all we can see is each other's eyes. "Because wherever I'm going on this new journey, I get to go peacefully. I have the easiest walk of all. You're the one who has to stay behind and comfort those who're still here."

The pressure builds in my throat. I want to be furious with him for leaving. But all I feel is love and admiration. I can't even imagine closing my eyes forever ... facing the unknown. He's so much braver than I could ever hope to be.

I bury my face in the blankets covering his chest, weeping. "Morpheus once told me it would be harder than I thought . . . I didn't want to believe him. I thought . . . I thought I was stronger than this."

Jeb tenderly wiggles the bun at the nape of my neck. "You are. You're Alyssa Victoria Gardner, the girl who broke through stone with a feather and crossed a forest in one step. You held an ocean in your palm, you changed the future with a fingertip. You—"

"*We* defeated an invisible enemy with Tumtum berries," I interrupt, looking up through my tears. "*We* trampled an army beneath our feet. It was us together meeting those tests head-on." My voice cracks.

"But it was you *alone* who woke the dead, and harnessed the power of a smile. You alone who defeated Red and all of AnyElsewhere. You who earned the crown." Jeb's voice is husky with emotion. "A magical kingdom is waiting for your reign. You've just suppressed that side of you for so many years to belong here, you've forgotten what you can be when it's fully unleashed. It's time to remember. To never forget again." He catches my face and presses my mouth to his in the gentlest kiss we've ever shared. "Now, we have a chance for one last perfect moment, fairy queen. Let's make it count." With his thumb, he blots the wetness that has gathered in my wrinkled cheeks.

I grit my teeth, and hand over the gelled tear.

Holding my gaze, Jeb squeezes the wish to release the scent of longing and brine, then speaks the words he's practiced over the past week: He asks that he relive the dream we shared on our honeymoon night, so we can be together one last time, young and free, and then that afterward, he never wakes again.

I've barely closed my eyes when I'm there, inside his room of dreams where we spent our honeymoon. Silver pillars wrapped in purple garland surround me. At my side, a wicker bench sits beneath an arch swathed in purple and white tulle; shiny Mardi Gras masks hang from rafters on varied lengths of string—purple, black, and silver.

I'm twenty-one again, wearing my wedding dress—white lace, pearls, and airbrushed shadows. I've just released a magical ribbon from the box in my hand, and a golden, glittering fall of letters dances around me:

Things I once hoped to give you:
1. A magical wedding . . .

All my earlier fear and sadness vanishes as Jeb appears beside me in his tux—twenty-three years old, smooth olive skin, muscled body, glistening labret. Full of health and vitality. Choking back happy tears, I hold out my left hand where his ring already sits.

He smiles that dimpled smile. We confess how much we'll always love each other until death do us part, and then he pulls me in for a kiss. A spark, hot and electric, jumps between us. Shock and sensation shimmer through me, aglow with his heat and flavor—just like the first time I tasted his lips. He eases us down onto the bench, and we indulge in passion until we're spent. In the aftermath, we touch one another's faces, sharing soft kisses and whispered sentiments. We treasure each moment, each glimpse, each smile and sigh, no longer two singular entities, but one united force.

We lay there in each other's arms as the scenery transforms around us. It's still his dream room—although the background changes to allow us to relive every dream he had that has now been fulfilled.

The picnic basket on the ground becomes weightless and hovers overhead. Jeb unties the ribbon on the handle, releasing a new glimmering parade of letters:

2. Picnics at the lake with your mom . . .

We walk through a green meadow, following the basket, then relive the moments laughing with Mom and Dad beside a lakeshore. We're famished, and feast on berries, chocolates, and wine.

After our appetites are sated, I tug a ribbon loose from a mosaic drifting along the water like a boat. Another glittering sentence is released:

3. A lifetime of shared successes and laughter . . .

I let my wings out. Jeb takes my hand, no longer needing any help to fly. Together, we rise up to the rafters and watch our surroundings flip through other scenes—all of our hopes becoming fulfilled, with each new accomplishment and birth of a child.

Catching me by the elbow, Jeb points to the other side of the room, where his motorcycle idles high up in the rafters, amid strands of white Christmas lights.

It's the one dream left incomplete, and it will be our final moment together.

We float across and release the bow tied on the bike's handlebar.

4. Midnight rides across the constellations in Wonderland . . .

Snowflakes and a soft breeze wind around us. The rafters open up to a fathomless night as I settle behind him in the seat. He revs the motor, and the Christmas lights transform into a spiral of white stars coiling and uncoiling in feathery sparks, like curls of lightning. We've entered the same Wonderland sky we slept beneath a lifetime ago while in a rowboat on the ocean of tears.

My arms wrap around his sturdy form and we sway back and forth, our movements synchronized as we climb higher and higher. Jeb gives the throttle some gas and we pick up speed, my wings spreading behind me and catching the wind. I whoop and holler and Jeb's laughter joins in.

I clutch his waist tighter, the wheels skimming through the moon and leaving streaks of phosphorescent light on our zigzag race through the constellations.

I reach out and capture one star. It fizzes in my hand before crumpling into glistening dust.

DESTINATION

I squint at the sunrise, then look again at the bottle of stardust in my hand, determined to be stronger than the agonized ache behind my sternum. When my family had returned to Jeb's hospital room that night three years ago, they found me asleep with my head on his chest. They thought he was sleeping, too, but he had quietly slipped away.

As they woke me, I felt something in my fist and opened it to reveal the last token of our time together. Everyone was so busy grieving, they didn't notice that I had captured a star, or that I slipped it into my pocket—another secret to keep, the final magical stitch to complete my heart.

Sniffling, I tuck the bottle into my backpack along with the other two, and zip it up. The flock of butterflies and moths that have been my veil grow impatient, and herd me toward my final destination.

I turn my back on the human realm, staring into the rabbit hole at my feet.

"Alyssa, luv. Take the leap."

This time, there's no question who's speaking in my mind. It's the voice of my Beloved Moth.

It hits me how tired and depleted I am. How ready I am to break the bonds of mortality—to step into my forever.

Without another moment's hesitation, I let my body crumple and fall. I drift, like a feather, and shut my eyes against what I know passes me on my descent: Open wardrobes filled with clothes, pieces of furniture, stacks of books on floating shelves, pantries, jelly jars, and empty picture frames pinned by thick ivy to the dirt walls.

I won't look because I want his face to be the first thing I see.

At last, I feel his strong arms catch me and set me on the ground. Morpheus—ever waiting—just like he promised.

My eyes open to his immaculate fairy features, untouched by time, flickering in the firelight from the upside-down candelabras. The scents of wax and dust fade to the familiar perfume of hookah smoke.

There's a grinding sound as the rabbit hole closes overhead, leaving only the candles to light up the windowless domed room.

"Welcome to your new reality, little plum." He takes my wrinkled and age-freckled hand, holds it to his warm, soft mouth, and drags me in for a kiss—right on the lips—despite that I'm old and frail. He sees beyond that, to what I am inside. To the ruler he's helped shape in my dreams since my childhood.

Just when I think I'll drift away on waves of madness and passion, he breaks the kiss. "Let's get you out of those hideous human clothes, aye?"

A knot of excitement and nervous anticipation scrambles through me as he peels off the simulacrum and removes my tennis shoes. But I stop his hands before he can touch my sweats.

After years of riddles and wordplay and manipulating my subjects in the Red Court, my mind is finally Morpheus's match. But my body is inferior now. I'm weak and ancient—a sluggish mass of gnarled skin, pitted bones, and atrophied muscles. He's always been elevated, either in thought or form. From this day forward, I want to be his equal in *every* aspect—body, spirit, and mind.

"First," I insist, with a voice more royal and commanding than I ever thought myself capable, "make me young again."

"As My Queen commands." Bowing, he reaches around me to the table in the middle of the room, lifts my crown off a pillow, and then places it upon my head.

There's an enchanted beat . . . not one that I can hear, but one I feel—a rhythm of life and magic that starts in my heart and throbs through every nucleus of every cell, waltzing across the expanse of my DNA. My hair thickens and warms with the pale blond of youth. A few wispy strands twirl around me, shimmering and alive with magic. I hold out my arms, and my skin, breasts, and muscles lift and smooth to suppleness. I release my wings, gasping in rapture as they rip through the back of my shirt and spread tall and proud behind me. Colors bounce off the walls, reflecting the jewels that span the length of my gossamer appendages . . . showcasing every mood for Morpheus to see.

His study of me intensifies, mesmerized and reverent. He's so quiet and somber, I'm afraid something went wrong.

I touch my face, tapping the soft, flawless skin. "Did it work?" My vocal cords quaver. "Am I normal? Am I me?"

"Not quite, Alyssa," he answers, his voice gruff. "You have ne'er been normal. You are exquisite. You are transcendent. And you are *mine*."

His stake of ownership coils through me—a dare. For one whisper of a moment, it's disarming, to feel my youth and vibrancy brimming at the surface, tempting me to turn on my charms and meet his challenge. To summon that power—after so many years of being trapped inside a withering mortal shell, of relying on my intellect and wit to nurture confidence and self-respect—is both frightening and exhilarating.

But my hesitation passes in a blink. I'm not intimidated by my sensuality like I would've been when I was a naive girl. Now I know to embrace it. When combined with my netherling fierceness and cunning, my feminine wiles will make me invincible *because* I am a woman . . . and a Red Queen.

I'll never take my status in either court for granted again.

Morpheus's admiring stare alerts my competitive side, awakening it. After such a long wait, he's earned the right to claim me . . . for now. But after we're married, I'll claim him right back.

On that thought, I remember I'm completely naked under the sweats hanging baggy on my youthful body. "Did you bring me some clothes?" I ask.

Morpheus clucks his tongue. "As if your footman would let you appear before your subjects in anything less than lace and softness." His blue hair lights up his smile as he drags some red satin lingerie from his jacket pocket.

I take the skimpy bra and panties, blushing. "Thank you. But . . . where's the rest of it?"

"Hmmm." He taps his lip with a fingertip. "What else could we need? You already have your crown. And I brought boots."

"Morpheus," I scold, half-mortified and half-giddy.

"Oh, of course. There's this." He holds out a freshly clipped red rose embellished with a lace bow. The flower wriggles in his hand as if alive.

I bite my lip, holding back a smirk. "Pretty. But corsages don't provide much coverage."

"You think this a corsage? How adorably human of you." He snorts. "Absolutely no chance of that. I've written off proms and everything associated with them for all eternity."

I'm the one who snorts this time. I trace a fingertip along the flower's stem. My finger skims his thumb. An electric spark races through my hand at the contact, a delicious sampling of the magic he possesses.

Stepping back, he folds one wing across the rose and blue lightning sparkles behind the satiny veil. When he withdraws his wing, the blossom has flourished into a crimson gown of living rosebuds, lace, and netting.

My heart pounds, because I recognize this dress, and how it matches the suit he's wearing.

He turns his back so I can slip into the lingerie. As I step into the gown and pull the stretchy lace into place, each rosebud I touch disappears into the fabric, only to bloom again once I've moved my hand. It fits perfectly.

"Did you peek?" I ask the moment I'm fully clothed and Morpheus is facing me. The question is rhetorical. I caught him looking at least three times.

He draws me close. "I'm wounded, luv. We both know I'm a perfect gentleman. Now, let's get you to the palace. You've had a long journey. Tonight, you will rest in solitude. I shall give you time to grieve." His voice is deceptively sincere as he coaxes the rest of my spirited hair free of its bun so it can wind around his arms and fingertips.

I tilt my head. "I won't be spending tonight alone. After all these years, you're still lying to me."

His dark gaze glimmers through thick lashes that only half hide the voracity lurking there. "What gave me away?"

I touch the bejeweled face I've come to love so dearly. Not in spite of his infuriating tactics, his word wizardry, his tender malice . . . but *because* of them. "Oh, I don't know. The desire blinking through your eye patches." For the first time, I notice he's not wearing a hat, and there's no question why: because by the end of the day, a crown will be sitting on his head. I trace the lapels of the crimson suit tailored perfectly to fit his lithe, graceful form—the very suit he wore in my vision of our fiery honeymoon so long ago. His body trembles in response to my touch. "Or maybe because we're both dressed for a royal wedding."

His black wings rise behind him, smoke and shadows. His slow-burning smile widens. "What? You expect me to marry you in these old rags?" He rolls his eyes. "Well, I suppose. If My Queen commands it."

I bark a laugh.

His white teeth shine, his jewels flashing between amusement and adoration, and I know he sees the same thing in the gems blinking along my wings.

"No more looking back," he says, his gaze settling on the backpack behind me, next to my old clothes.

The sad pang triggered by his statement softens as I concentrate solely on his face. "I have many treasured human memories. Even without keepsakes, they'll be with me for eternity."

Morpheus nods. "Your mortal knight was an honorable man . . . he wanted what is best for you. He would want you to be happy."

I suppress the burn behind my eyes. "Yes, he said I should move forward. You know as well as I, that memories are often the key to that."

Morpheus purses his lips, restraint and wildness battling for control of his features. "So, does that mean you're ready then? To move forward?"

"What do my wings say?" I ask, fluttering them softly so he can decipher the jewel tones.

He grins. "They say you want to race me across the clouded skies of Wonderland, and that you think I'll let you win."

A tingling thrill skitters from my feet to my wing tips. "On the contrary," I correct. "They say we're *both* going to win this time." Balanced on my tiptoes, I throw my arms around his neck and give him the mind-numbing kiss I promised, deepening it when he groans in pleasure. His tongue dances with mine, flavored with dense, sweet black licorice and storm-swept forests—all things exotic, lush, and untamed.

He lifts me into his arms, pressing our bodies together and spinning us around until my dress's long train trips us. We crash against the purple-striped wall, laughing like children.

My face pulses hot with vitality. "Morpheus."

"Yes, my blushing blossom," he whispers, breath ragged along my neck as he helps me untangle my right wing from a red velvet curtain and satiny gold cords of rope.

I'm the one trembling now, imagining being tangled up with him in satin sheets and velvety blankets. "Let's not put the wedding off for another second. The Red Court needs a king, and I want to sleep in his bed tonight. You've waited long enough for your queen, for your dream-child."

He makes a sound, somewhere between a relieved moan and a blissful sigh, then lowers himself to his knees, using his hands and mouth to appraise the way the dress clings to my curves on the way down. The rosebuds vanish and reappear with his touch.

"Something tells me"—his voice rumbles low against my abdomen as he clutches my hips—"you will both be so very, very worth the wait."

It's the first time he's ever been so intimate with his explorations. I weave my fingers through his silken hair and nuzzle his head, struggling to contain the emotions and sensations rocking through me. Somewhere, locked inside my young body, is an old woman's wisdom and worldliness. So why do I suddenly feel so inexperienced and exposed?

His hands find their way to the hem of my dress at my feet, and he raises the enchanted fabric just enough to expose my left ankle in the candlelight. He traces where my netherling birthmark is bared, no longer covered by a tattoo. "I must admit, I'm going to miss your tribute to me. But small price to pay, to have everything back as it was the moment I first confessed my love for you."

I frown, determined to tease him. "I told you, the tattoo wasn't a moth. It was wings."

Morpheus slants his head, smirking. "Look at my words from every angle, luv. Consider what they mean, beneath the surface."

It takes his prompting for me to stop and think . . . for things to fully register—the depth of the change in my body. *Everything back as it was when he first confessed his love. Beneath the surface.*

My tattoo is gone. Which means I'm sixteen through and through, *exactly* like the moment I was first crowned in the Red castle. Before I got wings inked across my ankle to hide my netherling birthmark . . . before I became a mother and grandmother. Before I even became a bride.

Against every impossibility, I'm innocent and untouched once more.

I inhale loudly, shocked by the revelation.

Morpheus looks up at me with smug satisfaction.

"You knew all along," I say, caressing his face. "You knew it would end like this."

"Of course I did. Isn't magic a splendid thing?"

I answer him with a shy smile, but there's something behind it that wasn't there sixty-four years ago—something coy and expectant.

"Mmmm," Morpheus murmurs. "Now there's a smile with scads of potential. Let's get this forever started, shall we?" He drops my hem back into place, guides me to my knees beside him, and from his pocket drags out a bottle labeled: *Drink Me.*

We toast to new beginnings and, between greedy kisses, take turns sipping until we've shrunk enough to step through the tiny door and into the outskirts of Wonderland.

❋ TWO ❋
ETERNITY

PREPARATION

"I'm not supposed to *feel* this much, Alyssa. 'Tis impossible for my kind." Wearing a tortured frown, Morpheus holds my hand to his smooth chest where his nightshirt hangs half-open, exposing the waist of his black satin sleeping pants. His heartbeat races and his voice grinds, no longer silken and sweet like the one he uses in my lullabies, but wretched and bewildered. It scrapes through my ears and plucks at my heart.

I want him to be happy, and I know he is, in the deepest part of himself. This anguished tone means something else entirely: surrender, and the easiest victory he's granted me in the nine months since we've been king and queen, not to mention all the years he occupied my dreams before that.

To think, this is all it took to win without a fight. I almost smile, but can't get my mouth or jaw to release their clenched muscles.

I squint through my lashes in the candlelight given off by floating, self-sustained wicks that never burn down, studying him where he sits on the edge of our bed—the bed that once belonged to him alone. He arranged to have it brought here from his manor, along with his moth and hat collection, the moment we were married and he moved into the Red castle.

I'm on my side, naked beneath the covers, knees pulled tight to my swollen abdomen in a futile attempt to ease the electric pulses radiating along the muscles there. The waterfall canopy holds its trickling stasis wide enough for me to see around the outline of my king's body and his blue hair, still messy from sleep. Other than when he moves to trigger them, the curtains refuse to open any farther than a few inches from him, as if allowing us this sanctuary out of respect for the monumental event that's under way.

On the other side of our canopy, the royal bedroom is a flurry of activity.

Morpheus's harem of sprites buzzes about: some coaxing pieces of blue, fluffy, cotton candy clouds through the door to line the cradle, and others herding wasp-size flying elephants with antennae on their heads and pollen sacs on their legs toward a cluster of luminescent flowers.

The flowers were sent by Grenadine. She's found she's happiest tending the gardens. Something about the scent of the plants helps her remember how to care for each one; they're the sensorial equivalent of the whispering bows she wears on her toes and fingers.

The blossoms she sent to our room are colored like rainbows and shaped like bells. They hang from vines secured upside down from the ceiling, just above the cradle. When the blooms are pollinated by the winged elephants, they jingle and release a honeyed fragrance while spinning, which paints the velvet-draped walls with prismatic light. An enchanted baby mobile, made especially for an enchanted prince.

Lorina, the dodo bird's wife, carries a bucket handle with her wing tips and leaves the sloshing, thick liquid a few feet from the bed. Her humanoid face shimmers with excitement. "I brought the treacle sap Gossamer requested!" She ruffles her red feathers as her booming words reverberate. "I also woke the royal advisor so he might boil it."

The jarring timbre of her voice shakes Morpheus's moth-filled terrariums on their shelves and rattles my spine. Morpheus winces and I grind my teeth impatiently, hoping the bird-woman doesn't stay. I can usually overlook her lack of manners for her kind heart, but I'm too high-strung tonight.

There's a clatter in the corridor, and two seconds later, Rabid White hops over the threshold wearing a nightgown of wrapped fabric that resembles toilet paper. His matching nightcap drags the floor behind him, hanging askew off one antler. He blinks his pink eyes sleepily and rubs them with skeletal knuckles. "Late be I?" He yawns. "The Red Prince, at last arrived did he?"

"Not yet, sleepy bones." Gossamer flitters in the door and pushes Rabid toward the bucket of treacle beside Morpheus's feet. "Now, remember what I told you. We need this heated."

My royal advisor brightens the light in his eyes and concentrates on the floor.

"What in bloody hell?" Morpheus bellows at Rabid as his bare soles turn bright red.

"Your feet cold, were not?" Rabid asks, frothy lips pouting. "Gossamer said . . ."

We all stare at Gossamer.

"I said his feet would do *well* to be cold," she scolds Rabid. "Master displays a startling lack of caution when it comes to certain aspects of his life." She smirks and flutters around us, trying to look busy and innocuous in spite of how her coppery eyes flash with mischief.

When I first left to live my human life in reality, the sprite and I had mended fences. But since my and Morpheus's wedding, she's become increasingly prickly and envious, as if living all those years as Morpheus's confidante in my stead rekindled her unrequited affections for him.

Rabid frowns remorsefully at Morpheus. "Rabid White gave you a hot foot . . . not necessary?"

"No, blast it!" Morpheus barks, lifting a sole to observe the flaming, tender skin. I grasp his hand, a reminder to be gentle. He squeezes my fingers in response and his furious expression softens to annoyance. "My feet were not cold." He casts a warning glare Gossamer's way. "Nor will they ever be where Alyssa's concerned."

The sprite looks down, green skin darkening with a flush.

"Sorry I am, Majesty." My apologetic advisor bows so low he nearly tumbles headfirst into the bed.

Morpheus catches him by his antlers then nudges him toward

the bucket of treacle. "There, Sir Bumble-noggin. That's what you're to be heating. Get to it."

Rabid nods and readjusts his visual aim until the metal bucket glows orange. The syrupy liquid bubbles and pops, filling the room with a cherry scent. Having done his job, the rabbit-size netherling gathers some fallen cloud residue to make a pallet on the floor, curls atop it, and starts to snore.

"I don't understand why you sent for treacle," Lorina caterwauls to Gossamer, so loud my eardrums clash inside my head like tambourines. "Humans always use boiled water. I've seen it in their box pictures."

"You mean their tellie-visors," Gossamer corrects, and as if to make up for her earlier wickedness, hustles Lorina out the door and offers a polite thank-you for her services, assuring the bird-woman she had brought the right bucket.

"Tele*visions*," Morpheus growls to everyone and no one at once while rubbing a still-red foot. "Also, what in the name of Fennine and all the fairy saints is the treacle for?"

"Perhaps we use it to christen the baby?" a chorus of sprites twinkles.

"Yes, yes. We christen it!" echoes another. "Wait . . . what does that mean?"

"Dunk it, headfirst," a lone sprite chimes.

I yelp, horrified.

"Everyone, shush!" Morpheus barks the order. He strokes my hair in a calming rhythm. "Do not worry, blossom. No one is dunking our prince in boiling syrup."

Gossamer returns, rounding up her sprites like a drill sergeant. "Treacle sap comes from the sassyfras tree, Master."

"I'm aware of its origins, pet."

Her bulbous, brass-colored eyes brighten, a sure sign she's pleased to have his full attention. "Being as it's the most flippantly happy of all the trees in the wilds," she says to him, intent on holding him captive for as long as possible, "I sent for undiluted syrup to sweeten and tame the beastly toys."

"Ah, well played."

Gossamer beams at his praise.

"To your posts then." Morpheus shoos everyone off the bed. "Our queen needs her rest."

Pouting, Gossamer leads the sprites away. They settle beside the boiling treacle as Chessie and Nikki drag over a box. Inside is an octopus-like creature the size of a half-dollar with rattlers similar to a rattlesnake's tail sprouting from each tentacle—venomous and creepy enough to entertain even the most cynical member of the Red Court; a self-playing xylophone made of living fish bones; and some teething rings formed of actual snapping teeth, among other oddities.

Using Chessie's tail as a rope, the sprites dip one of the snarling teething rings into the boiling syrup. It resurfaces—nothing but gums . . . soft and rubbery. They do the same with the octopus-creature, transforming it into an eight legged rattle—colorful, brittle, and harmless.

Upon seeing the fate that awaits them, the other toys hiss and clamber over each other in an effort to escape the box, desperate to retain their wild, dangerous forms. The sprites screech and give chase.

The scene is morbidly chaotic and funny enough that I giggle. It's a mistake, for the muscles in my abdomen respond with a set of contractions hitting me in a flourish of electric pain. I wail as it runs the length of my torso, then through my lower back and upper thighs. Fingers of blue light, so like Morpheus's magic—yet entirely unique to the one causing them—follow the path of the spasms beneath the sheets and inside my belly. I tuck my head under the edge of my pillow, whimpering.

Gossamer and the other sprites give up their chase to poke their heads through the space between Morpheus's body and the water canopy, curious and concerned.

Morpheus rubs my abdomen and glowers at them. "Why are you all flitter-flattering in midair like mindless twits? This isn't some pageant put on for your amusement! You've no business being in this room lessen you have a task, aye?"

Gasping at his ill-tempered outburst, they retreat to chase the toys once more.

"All this hovering is inane and senseless . . . and not in the good way," Morpheus grumps. "May as well have charged admission. We should keep that in mind for next time."

"Next time?" I sob, trying to breathe through a contraction. "No, no next time. I won't survive *this* time."

"Of course you will. Do you not remember? We both saw the vision in your blood mosaic a few weeks ago. We'll be welcoming a daughter after our son turns five." His is the voice of gentle and measured reason, a stark contrast to the teasing lunacy he usually emanates. "Now, stop worrying about what's happening out there. For you hold me captive *here*." He lifts his wings so I can no longer watch what's happening outside, so I'm grounded on our bed where it's just us and our own little island adrift on raw emotions and soft-spoken ploys. "This is the perfect opportunity to take advantage and regain your pride. Or perhaps you don't mind that I trampled you at chess yesterday morn."

The pain recedes and I unclench my jaw. "No, *I* won," I manage.

He narrows his eyes. "I had the checkmate, luv."

"But it was strip chess, remember?"

His gaze tours my body. "Oh, I remember that detail vividly."

"So, with each counterattack you executed . . . I dropped another piece of clothing. With each glimpse of skin . . . you found it harder to concentrate. In the end—chessmen and checkmates aside—all you could think of was how much you wanted *me*. Isn't it me then, who ultimately captured her opponent's king?"

An appreciative laugh rumbles in his chest. "Sneakie-deakie."

I laugh with him, and then stop myself. As unbelievable as it seems, tears glisten along his beautiful face in the candlelight. Not only the gems, clear and pristine, but rivulets of water that capture the glow like tiny currents of lightning along his luminous skin. He hasn't realized they're there yet.

"You've been crying," I accuse, gently.

"Have not," he retorts.

"Have, too."

"Well, I'm not the queen, so I can cry all I like."

He said those very words to me on our last night together before I left to live my human days in the mortal realm. It's the loveliest of rarities—to have his feelings exposed and him helpless to stop them. He's usually either in complete control or manipulative enough to force my hand before he shows his.

As moved as I am, I'm holding the ace this time, and I can't let human tenderness sway me. I'm one of the two most powerful netherlings in the Red Kingdom, and I won't miss this chance. Who knows when my rival will surrender again without making me work for it?

"Flatter me," I insist with a wicked, teasing smile. "As the official winner of the chess game, I get to choose your penalty. I demand words of persuasion and praise."

Morpheus glares at some sprites wriggling through the water curtain's spaces. They pause at my lips to offer sips of cooled cherry treacle to give me positive energy. Afterward, they fluff my pillow and move down to straighten the blankets.

He waits until they're pulling up the sheets at my feet before focusing all his attention on me. "Your beauty terrifies me," he says, swiping his tear-slicked cheeks with the back of his ruffled sleeve.

I smile wider, because it's exactly what I want to hear, and he knows it.

The sprites stall in midair and swoon at their master's unprecedented lovelorn display, their reflective dragonfly gazes moonstruck.

"Privacy, pets," Morpheus snarls, and they scramble out from the canopy. He folds his wings low around my head and arms, shutting out everything and offering solitude within the shadows. My sparkling skin reflects across his face. His elegant fingertips trace my neck and collarbones, warm and soft. He watches the trek, still fascinated by the same curves he's felt a thousand times by now. His hand stops atop my breast, thumb pressed to my sternum, seeking my heartbeat.

My breath catches.

"Your savagery dazzles me." His sweetly scented whisper warms my face. "I desire you endlessly. More than a precarious fall through the constellations, more than a game of malice upon the checkerboard sands, more than a treacherous traipse through the wilds."

"So you admit it," I gloat, clutching him by his shirt placket, our lips a hairsbreadth apart as I suppress my instinct to raise the stakes in our game with a flurry of pandemonium. "You expect me to hide such blatant disregard for the rules of your kind, solitary fae? A Red Queen never rations out favors . . . even to her Beloved Moth." I lose my hold on his shirt as another surge of contractions shudders through me. Gripping my abdomen, I groan. "Unless there's something in it" —I struggle to find my voice— "for her or her kingdom. Give me whatever I ask, or I will make a royal proclamation. *King Morpheus worships* his bride *more than Wonderland itself.*"

"You wouldn't dare," he croaks, playing along. He lowers his wings, exposing us to candlelight again.

"Everyone will know." I laugh the words through my own tears as the cramps relent for a moment—though it will be short-lived. They're getting closer now, only minutes apart. "All of our enemies, all of our allies, each and every denizen of this world will see that you are still my footman."

"Then you would give them the key to our defeat. You're speaking madness."

"Your native tongue," I quip without hesitation.

There's a potent glint of lust behind his gaze. Playfulness twitches at his lips, accentuated by the impish yellow flash of his jeweled markings. Even in a moment like this, he's relishing my provocation. It's in his nature and mine, too. On a typical night, such banter would lead to a scintillating duel of magic and word wizardry, and end in passionate ravishment.

But nothing is typical about tonight, and come to think of it, ravishment is how we got into this predicament in the first place.

"Ask what you will, My Queen," Morpheus offers in humble

submission, so unlike him. He cups my face in both hands and wipes the tears from my cheeks with his thumbs. "Toy with me, trap me, lock me in chains. I'll give you anything so long as you bide my secret."

A fluttering movement rolls within the cocoon of my flesh, just beneath my rib cage. At first it's tiny and knotted, but then it spreads as if opening. An elbow, a fist, a wing tip? No. He can't be trying to fly again; shouldn't he be rolled into a ball, preparing to arrive? As if in answer, the unmistakable sensation of flapping stirs inside me.

A highly charged contraction follows the movement—rips through my belly, hot and grinding—as if to force the release of my prisoner. I scream, stiffen my legs, and arch my back. "Get him *out!*"

Acute regret shimmers in Morpheus's inky eyes and his wings tug his shoulders to a slump. "Alas, you ask the one thing I cannot give."

Snarling, I dispense punishment in fits, my powers as unruly and unpredictable as they were before I learned to control them. I attempt to throw off the blankets; instead, they take flight and dive-bomb us like temperamental ghosts. Morpheus curses and struggles to keep my nakedness covered. I try to fling the water curtain away, but push too hard. It becomes a tidal wave and washes across my king and our attendants, soaking them and snuffing out the candles. The only lights left to go by are the glimmering bodies of the sprites and the luminous flowers.

The wave crosses the room and shakes the shelves along the walls. Moths and caterpillars scatter in their terrariums. The current comes to rest only after it has shuttled Morpheus's hats off their perches and scattered them across the floor where they float, adrift beside Rabid's snoring form and a bevy of swimming toys.

Morpheus howls and lifts a foot from the puddles, prying a teething ring's snapping jaws from his big toe. He drops the creature into the treacle that is somehow still boiling.

My king's wet hair hangs limp as he grimaces at me in the dimness. By some miracle, my covers are still dry. Only my face and hair got splattered.

"Any other time," he mutters darkly, concern overshadowing the madness and beauty that so often call to me from within his long-lashed gaze, "I would be tempted to ravenous by your challenge for dominance. But right now, you need to preserve your strength." Igniting his blue magic, he uses the strands like a fan's rotary blades to dry himself and me. "Someone capture the baby's playthings and salvage the cradle!" he grouses to our attendants.

The sprites shake themselves off and putter about the room, bumping into one another in a rush to straighten the mess my wayward monsoon left behind.

"Fetch more clouds!" Their combined shouts tingle like a clatter of coins.

Chessie and Nikki appear with a mop to clean up the puddles. A few sprites assist with sponges. Others use miniature nets to scoop up the toys and return them to their box. Our attendants' glimmering bodies reflect off the wet floor and form rivers of stars, small and distant. *Disorienting.*

I moan and close my eyes to fight a surge of nausea. My magical hair slaps my face, taunting me. Morpheus captures the long waves with his fingertips and wrestles them into a braid to contain them. It would be easier if he used his magic to do it. But he always insists on managing my hair with his hands. It's his "honor and distinct pleasure to tame my tresses with his touch."

A residual water droplet wriggles from my hairline, down my temple, and stops at my jaw—a benign itch that's oddly grating against the backdrop of the electric currents racing through my torso.

"Little plum." My king's knuckles sweep across my eye markings and swipe away the water—leaving a gossamer trail as delicate as a spider's web. "Let nature take its course. Stop fighting it."

My eyes open to narrow slits. The candles have spontaneously relit.

"*Nature?*" My voice is earsplitting and terrible, the one I reserve for disobedient subjects. "I'm ready . . . you're ready. Our entire kingdom is ready. But no. He's too busy flying around in there. He's the one fighting it. He doesn't want to leave! Nothing about that is *natural.*"

Hues of purple and gray glisten through Morpheus's jeweled eye markings. He drops to his knees on the damp floor and sculpts his hands around my swollen abdomen beneath the sheets. "All right, Trouble." His term of endearment for the baby incites an irascible arm or leg to jut from inside. "Stop playing games. Wrap up your wings. 'Tis time to meet your subjects. Your mum is tired."

Our son reacts to his father's voice in an excited tizzy. The flapping intensifies, stirring more contractions. I glare at Morpheus. "You just had to teach him to use his wings. You couldn't have waited a few more weeks until he'd actually *need* them!"

Morpheus's head bows, a blue curtain hiding his features. With a trembling hand, I push back the strands, regretting my harshness. He's on the opposite end of the same situation as me. He has no idea how to act, what to do.

"Forgive me," I whisper.

He clasps his fingers over mine and meets my gaze. "No need. I would've already taken off the heads of everyone in this room were I being tortured like you."

With all the magic my king and I have between us, neither of us can control what's happening to my body, or appease this lightning storm that brews within me, refusing to come out. But the pain doesn't quench my maternal desire. My longing to see our prince . . . to cradle his tiny, magical body to mine, nuzzle his downy blue hair, smell his scent. To love him eternally. Unconditionally.

It's overwhelming to consider how important he's going to be, to more than just me and Morpheus. He's going to improve our way of life here, by teaching the netherlings how to dream so they'll never again need to rely on humans for that rare resource crucial for peace among the restless spirits in the cemetery.

Innocence and imagination, the components of dreams, have been missing in the fae lineage for so long, no one can even remember when they possessed such traits. Ivory once told me that it's why Wonderland's occupants don't have childhoods. The nether-realm is founded on chaos, madness, and magic. Innocence and imagination fell by the wayside long ago, replaced by manipulation and murderous intent on their children's playgrounds.

But Morpheus experienced innocence through me, each time we played together in my dreams, and he learned to wield an imagination because of it. So our son will be the first child to be born to two netherlings who've shared a genuine child*hood*. He'll possess Morpheus's dream-magic, and my imagination. Somehow, he's going to pass on this unprecedented power, so the fae children will learn to dream again. They will experience childhood, in every sense of the word.

I don't know all the details, I only know the prophecy, and the fact that Morpheus and I are to guide our son so he can master his gifts and impart them to all of Wonderland. I'm both honored and nervous to have a role in such a prestigious commission. Our prince is arriving not a moment too soon. The dreams Jeb left behind will begin waning now that he's been gone for several years. That's why I joined Red's spirit to his muse, to buy us a little extra time. Sister One has assured me the substitute will last for a while longer. Still, I've no idea how old our prince will be before he comes into his full power.

Another contraction needles through me, and I bite back a howl.

Our kingdom has been on high alert over the last few months, preparing for their dream-child. But Morpheus and I have waited even longer to meet our son. Decades. So why is he determined to end me before I can even kiss his head?

I'm exhausted and scared like the human I once was. I've forgotten the process completely. When I experienced childbirth as a mortal, my mother was there to hold my hand, to guide me. I feel alone and fragile without her wisdom.

A sob clogs my throat as the thought of her provokes another: that she and Dad are gone forever, just like Jeb. That nothing is left of the human husband I loved except my memories and our children and grandchildren—a mortal family in a human realm I'll never see again.

A deep sadness flares inside my chest. When I came here to reign as the Red Queen permanently, I made the choice not to have contact of any kind—even to view them through the looking glasses— although I couldn't resist sending out scouts to watch over them. But aside from their reports of well-being, I ask for no other details out of respect for my king. As long as my earthly family doesn't need me for anything life-threatening caused by my Wonderland ties, I have to stay away. To step in and intervene with magic under any other circumstance would only cause problems for everyone.

Still, there are times I long to know their everyday lives, times I grieve for those who died before I left. I've become strong, the master of my sentimentality. But tonight, I'm vulnerable, and the bittersweet memories threaten to drag me into their undertow.

I can't reveal something so human to the Red King. He'd be disappointed by my weakness, maybe even wounded by my wistfulness. My mask is slipping, and I won't let him see.

"You should leave until it's over," I mutter and writhe as another wave of contractions contorts my body.

"Like hell." Morpheus scowls. "I made a vow never to leave you when you were hurt. Not that I would go otherwise. Your bandersnatch's serpentine tongues couldn't tear me away."

"Listen to your king." The Ivory Queen's wise and gentle voice breaks from the doorway.

Morpheus tenses, as if torn between greeting our dear friend and holding on to me so I won't drift away on crashing waves of pain. Although we sent a message via sprites, we haven't had a chance to personally offer our condolences since Ivory lost her love, Finley. Though she'd been able to extend his life expectancy by retaining his physical age with a youth potion, his mortality finally took him from her just a few weeks ago. No human can live forever, as I know only too well.

Instead of going to Ivory at the doorway, Morpheus stays by my bedside, and I love him even more for it.

"Neither of you can get through this alone," Ivory continues. "It will take both of you working together to bring this child into the world, just as it took both of you to create him."

"I am at a complete loss," Morpheus moans, and I know by the rasp in his voice that it's physically painful for him to admit he can't manipulate a way to fix this situation.

Ivory kneels beside him in a swish of skirts and wings that match her glistening skin—the lavender frost of snow beneath a winter moon. "This is the first birth between a full-blood and a half-blood in the history of Wonderland," she answers. "Of course you're befuddled. We all are. The best you can do is comfort her. *Strengthen* her. Show her your faith in her fortitude. But remember, the labor itself is upon you both."

Ivory strokes the bump on her own belly. This event holds personal interest to her, considering that she'll be following in my footsteps and giving birth to Finley's child in a few months. By some magical surprise, it's the last gift he gave her. I only wish he could've lived long enough to see their baby born. But Morpheus and I plan to be there to help every step of the way. Ivory won't be alone.

Gossamer ducks into view and perches atop Morpheus's shoulder possessively.

"I don't understand. What is my role in such a thing?" Morpheus murmurs to Ivory.

"Support her," Ivory answers. "Emotionally and mentally. Remind her she's not alone in this."

I cringe against another labor pain.

Morpheus frowns in sympathy. "But she is alone, in her suffering. I don't understand why it's taking so long. She's done this before as a mortal." His finger soothes circles across my scarred palm.

"Shouldn't she fall into old habits? Is it so different for our kind?"

Ivory blots my hairline with a soft, damp cloth. "Of course it is different. Wings are involved. But that's irrelevant. Don't forget, it's *all* new to her. Her mind remembers her human life, but she physically never experienced any of it. Being a lover and a mother became foreign terrain the moment she returned to her sixteen-year-old form."

Gossamer clucks her tongue. "Good thing for you, Master. Elsewise, why would anyone want to wait sixty-some years for such a *privilege*?" Her tinkling voice holds a jealous bite.

She's lucky the unrelenting contraction still holds me captive. If I wasn't concentrating so hard to keep from wailing like a banshee, I'd launch her across the floor using Chessie's wet mop as a hockey stick.

Morpheus flashes the saucy sprite a threatening grimace. "Never speak of our queen or her past life with such disrespect." His deep voice slices the silence, both royal and brutal, making even my hair prickle. "Know your place. *Or risk losing it.*"

The sprite averts her dragonfly gaze, blushing a darker green—more a splash of reverent fear than shame. She flaps her furred wings and lifts from his shoulder. Bowing to me, she flutters away.

Ivory stands and squeezes my and Morpheus's hands where they're joined. "You can help your queen by reaching out to your son together, as a united front. Your prince needs to realize what he's missing by hiding. Make him understand . . . help him see the magic and vicious beauty that awaits him. Once he does, he will want to be born. And then all of this will be behind you. Your new life as a royal family will begin." Smiling kindly, she glides toward the baby cradle to help some sprites arrange cotton candy clouds within.

Morpheus rises to sit on the mattress again. His jeweled markings shift from midnight blue to impassioned purple. He lifts my hand, kisses my wrist, and murmurs in my mind so only I can hear: "*You're giving me a gift tonight, luv. Worth more than a king's ransom and all the white gold in Wonderland. I am forever in your debt. But tell no one of my weakness.*"

His sweet concession shatters my barriers, exposing the unbreakable bond between us.

He leans in to kiss me. Lips, silky and flavored with a hookah smoke haze, press upon my chapped and strained mouth. My fingers weave through his hair, pulling him closer, begging him to deepen our connection. To take me away from here as only his kisses can.

His tongue teases mine to join his, and I'm lost in the salty-sweetness of our yesterdays, forgetting the agony and fear of the present. We're back again, after our eternal wedding vows and the resulting manic celebration with our subjects, when we escaped to be alone and waltzed on Wonderland's sun; when our clothes burned to ash and I went to him—naked and bared, body and soul, without reservation; when he put a stop to our lovemaking because I was innocent again, and cloaked us in clouds to fly me back to our room in the Red castle so he could romance me throughout the night with patience and gentleness. In spite of how long he'd waited for that moment. In spite of his feral nature.

Falling back to the present, I break his kiss and watch the gems around his eyes flash through calming hues. It's clear why he wanted me to remember that night. It was to remind me that he understands the human in me, that he adores her as much as my netherling side. I don't have to admit how scared I am, or that I sometimes miss the mortals I will always love. He already knows. Just as I know he will never be my footman again, because I respect, adore, and need him as much as he does me. He is my partner in every way.

"Your secret is eternally safe, *solitary fae*," I whisper and draw his face to mine, giving in at last.

His mouth curves to a smile and drags across my lower lip, then glides from my cheek to my temple. His fingertips trail my jawline and skim my neck, then lower.

So intent on his touch, I almost miss the flutter of wings at my cheeks and brow. My eyes pop open to find five sprites hovering around us, along with Chessie's decapitated head and grinning face—all of them mesmerized by our impassioned spectacle.

"Blast it!" Morpheus shouts upon looking up. "Do you not have better things to do?"

Chessie gestures his whiskered muzzle toward his body where it continues to mop the floor on the other side of the room with the help of Gossamer and Nikki—as if that excuses his nosiness.

"Step off, or you'll all lose your heads," Morpheus grinds out through clenched teeth. "*Permanently.*" It's a promise, not a threat.

Chessie's head and the naughty spritelings hustle to escape, crashing into one another in midair in a clumsy race off the mattress. The commotion causes the baby to flutter again, triggering another influx of high-voltage pulses through my abdomen. I double over, dragging Morpheus with me as I bite down a scream.

"He's going to stay in there forever," I cry between panting breaths.

My king caresses my back. Although he's trying to help, it only antagonizes me, too small a comfort for pain this intense.

"How are we supposed to convince him to join us"—I force the words through constricted vocal cords—"if he's intent on never leaving all he's known?"

Morpheus tips my chin so our eyes meet. "The same way I once convinced you. We entice him with a journey through the terrible and beautiful wilds, via our memories."

"But we have so many memories . . . I can't wait that long." I grit out the response, the relentless contractions intensifying my pessimism.

"Then choose three. Three of your most indelible memories. Let him see Wonderland through your eyes . . . the moments and places that hold the most meaning to you. All we need is a glimpse. We have my dream-magic and your imagination to set the scene."

I study my husband's face, thankful for his brilliant, maniacal mind, and grateful that a once self-serving fae can harbor such patience and compassion for a half-human girl. That he even rations out such qualities in smaller doses to our subjects . . . when he's feeling generous.

Touching his jeweled markings, I whisper, "I love you, Morpheus. Thank you for showing me all I could be."

His eyebrows lift in the most endearing expression—the same look he used to offer as a child when I caught him off guard. He pauses for a moment, as if struggling to regain his composure, then answers, "And I love you. But this is just the beginning. We've yet to see all you can be." He tweaks my nose. "Now, shall we meet our son?"

I nod.

My king takes my hands and presses them to my abdomen. He weaves his fingers through mine. Warmth radiates in the spaces between us as his blue dream-magic pulses through my body and distracts me from my pain.

His voice fills my mind:

"Little prince, so keen to hide, traverse your kingdom far and wide. Follow us through mental flights, and share the dangers and delights."

Though he sings for the baby, Morpheus's beautiful lullaby captures me in a dizzying whorl of music, so irresistible I become the notes themselves. He leans down and his lips meet mine with a spark of enchanted supplication. I surrender and fade from the present, reappearing in our convoluted and mad past . . .

MEDITATION

MEMORY ONE: IN WHICH
I FACED WONDERLAND

Mommy and Daddy think I'm sleeping, but they're wrong. I'm dreaming in Wonderland, brought here by my playmate, the blue-haired boy named Morpheus. Minutes ago, he lifted the veil so Wonderland's creatures could see me like I do them. In the five years I've visited, I've only watched them from behind the wall of sleep, like seeing fish inside a tank. This is the first time for me to meet them, and it makes my heart knock and my face hot.

But it's my own fault. I made it happen.

Earlier, we were at Wonderland's historical library. The Secret Keeper—as pink as a sunset, with the long neck of a flamingo—

helped Morpheus find some books filled with netherling lore. After she patted his eight-year-old head and left the room, Morpheus lifted the veil that kept me invisible to Wonderland, and called me over to a table. He opened a book's pages, exposing thousands of words written in red ink. I don't know how to read . . . but it didn't matter. The sentences and letters floated off the pages, dancing around my head, blending into a real voice—high and whiny like an out-of-tune violin. For an hour, the droning book lectured me about Wonderland's citizens: their habits, what food they like, their weaknesses and strengths.

"But where's the pictures?" I asked after the fifth lesson, yawning. "I want pictures . . . like the ones you draw in the Alice book. Talking is BORING."

Offended, the book slammed itself shut. A waxy red substance oozed from between the sheets of parchment, as if the ink melted. It coated the pages' edges, sealing them closed. The circle of wax then shaped itself into an angry face, hardened, and huffed.

It refused to peel off, no matter how much Morpheus sweet-talked it.

"Now see what you've done." Morpheus's young brow tightened to sternness. "There will be no opening it. The only thing that can soften a miffed book seal is a coating of snicker-snap saliva. So, I guess you're going to get one better than interacting with books and pictures today. You're going to get to confront a netherling creature, live and up close."

Though reluctant and scared, I let Morpheus take me from the library and fly me here to the darkest caves of Wonderland. The neon blue trees, orange shrubbery, yellow thistles, and pink moss in the distance look bright from my shadowy perch on the fernlike leaf that hangs over a hungry plant. The snicker-snap species grows only in gloomy places like this, floating on the surface of lakes like toothy water lilies.

I shiver and trace the edge of my wet, fleecy pajamas. I got them for my fifth birthday, two days ago. They have pink and purple superhero girls in the print and should make me feel strong. But I don't.

I'm as small as a cricket, wondering why I drank the shrinking potion. Kind of because it tasted like butterscotch. But more because my playmate drank it first, and I can't let him be braver than me. In my world, he's a moth, and I'm bigger and stronger. But here, he always beats me at everything.

I look again at the drooling plant below. It matches the Venus flytraps at home in Mommy's photo books even more than it does a water lily. But flytraps aren't like snicker-snaps. They don't have jaws lined with wriggling, hungry worms covered with glowing droplets of spit. The light attracts tiny Wonderland creatures into their mouths, and then the jaws snap shut to capture them.

Minutes ago, Luna—a grumpy sprite who had joined our trip to the cave uninvited—was teasing me for my lack of sparkly scales while pointing out the silvery ones covering her like a swimsuit. Morpheus told her to get lost, but she ignored him and chased us as we played follow-the-leader on our hunt for saliva. She was stupid and fell prey to the "glowworms" hanging in the snicker-snap's mouth.

I hear her whimpering now, even though the hungry plant has snapped its jaws tight and sunk lower into the water. She might be a nasty sprite, but we still have to save her. Because it's my fault we're here.

Struggling not to cry, I stare at the turtles bobbing in the stinky lake. I tried to jump across them to reach the plant, but fell in. Morpheus had to drag me out, dripping wet. He's been bragging ever since.

"You just hop from one to another until you're across," he interrupts my thoughts as he shows me the right way to do it—for the hundredth time. He bounces along, never once sinking, as if it's the easiest thing he's ever done. He doesn't even get the hem of his velvet pants wet. Just once, I wish I could be better than him at something in Wonderland. I wish I could win.

"You have wings to help," I grump and wriggle my nose. "Why don't you carry me?"

"You'll have your own wings one day. Until then, you need to learn other ways. Sometimes you'll wish to explore the wilds on your own. I can't always be there to fly you about."

"*You* should save Luna," I mumble. "You're faster than me."

"First off, *you're* still the leader. Second, we wouldn't be here if you hadn't offended the creature tome. And third, I have a pact with snicker-snaps. They leave my moths alone, so long as I let them eat whatever else they deem tasty. Now watch and learn." He bounds across the turtles once more. "Like stepping across rocks in a creek. Simple as that."

I look at my footed pajamas. "They'll bite my toes again."

"They don't want to bite you. They'll only turn on you if you turn on them. You need to get on their good side. Give it a try."

I bury my face deeper into the wet fabric covering my knees.

The leaf I'm on bends slightly as Morpheus settles beside me. I peek with one eye to find him studying me like he often does, his expression serious and full of wonder. His left wing comes to rest on my back, soft and rustling, warming my chilly bones.

"You almost did it," he says, gentle this time. "You just lost your footing . . . lost your faith. You have to have faith in yourself if you wish to help anyone else. It's the only way to be a good leader."

"The turtles keep moving. I don't trust them. They don't play fair."

"You're right not to trust them. And little in life is fair."

"Games should be," I argue. "They should have rules."

Morpheus snorts. "Not in Wonderland. And by the by, those aren't turtles, really. They're playing at being turtles . . . mock turtles, one might say. They're evolved from what's left of the snicker-snap's undigested food. *Mostly dead* body pieces and such."

I shudder to think that Luna might be one of the floating mostly deads if I can't rescue her. "They're icky. Icky and rotten as snot." I sniffle and the action sucks the lake scum from my dripping pants into my nose. I swallow it down, coughing. "I don't want to be the leader anymore. It's hard."

"Aw, c'mon. There are so many perks for the leader. First shot with the mallet at dinner . . . a fancy crown of jewels . . . oh, and the only one in Wonderland who can tame a bandersnatch with a secret password. Give it one more try."

I shake my head. The taste of lake water mixed with fabric softener has settled in the back of my throat. I shiver and think of Mommy and my warm bed. "I want to go home now."

"So, you will leave Luna to be eaten?"

Tears burn my eyes. "I don't want to. But what if it's too late already?"

Luna's tiny voice pleads from inside the snicker-snap as if in answer.

Morpheus and I meet gazes and I scramble to my feet, though I'm too scared to move.

"What if I lend a bit of magic to help you along?" he asks. "Will you try once more then?"

As always, the offer of magic is too intriguing to ignore. I nod my head and wipe snot from my nose.

Morpheus offers a hanky along with a sideways grin.

After I clean my face and hands, he tugs me to the edge of the leaf. "Mostly deads are close enough to *being* dead that they're very grim. And to get on death's good side, we must share a taste of life."

"Huh?"

"I'll show you." Gripping under my arms, he flies us back to the rock that was my starting point earlier.

I perch at the slippery edge, studying the mock turtles in the stagnant liquid. Now that I know what they really are, I'm even less eager to touch them.

Morpheus settles beside me and lights up a fiery orb in his small hand, blue and electric. It sizzles and smokes. He tosses the ball down and it ignites the lake. Within seconds, moans erupt from the blue flames now spreading to the turtles' shells.

"Why did you do that?" I ask, backing away from the heat scorching my cheeks.

"Fire is *life*," Morpheus says beneath his breath, his porcelain skin lit up with the blaze. His jeweled eye patches glitter a feverish orange.

Hisses and pops rise from the mock turtles, turning into whispers. It's hard to hear what they're saying, though Morpheus seems to know. He answers them: "Turn over a new leaf . . . show us your good side."

The blobs rotate in the water and snuff out the flames on their backs. Only their bellies stick up—too wet to catch fire.

"Now, Alyssa!" Morpheus shouts and pushes me into motion.

Yelping, I leap from one bobbing post to the other, clearing the embers still afloat on the water and making it to the snicker-snap's mouth without getting any turtle bites. Upon arrival, I pause on my landing spot, unsure how to open the plant's jaws.

I'm about to pry them apart when the mouth pops open in a hysterical laugh—guffawing and snorting so loud it ripples the water and unbalances my perch. I slip, almost toppling into the snicker-snap's open jaws. Luna, propelled from the plant's throat on a loud chortle, catches me and lifts me into the air before I can fall.

Morpheus joins us in flight. "Good show, Luna!" He offers her a carefree, beaming smile that seems to suck out the light from inside me. Why doesn't he ever smile at me like that?

Luna blushes and nearly drops from midair, but catches herself. I notice she's covered in glowing goo.

"Should've seen your eyes," she says to me at last as she lands us atop the safety of the fern. "They were almost the size of mine!"

"Wait . . ." I watch as Morpheus helps her scrape thick drool from her green skin and scoop it into a jar. "This was a game? To get the saliva?"

"There's a trick to snicker-snaps," Morpheus answers. "If you'd been patient in your lessons today, you would've learned it by the eighth lecture. Their throats are ticklish. Luna merely had to play victim long enough to be pulled into its esophagus. Then, it coughed her back out on an irrepressible snicker attack."

Luna holds up a goop-slicked feather, her giggles tinkling.

"Once you learn the weaknesses of the creatures in this world,"

Morpheus says, plugging the jar with a cork lid, "you can trump each and every one, face any danger, and always have a way out. That's why it's important for you to pay attention to the droning books. So . . . are you ready to go back to your boring studies, or did you want to give the feather a try and learn things the hard way?"

Without another word, I allow Morpheus to fly us back to the library, watching the landscapes pass below us. Wonderland is fun, but dangerous. For some reason, instead of scaring me, that makes me hungrier to know more.

More about the world and its creatures. More about its landscapes and lore. And most of all, more about my strange playmate. Because one day, I'm going to beat him at his own game. And then he'll smile at me, just like he did at Luna today.

❋ · I · ❋

MEMORY TWO: IN WHICH
I BROKE WONDERLAND

Morpheus and I sit inside his flying carriage on seats of red velvet. Fluorescent swirls move along the walls, creating a spinning effect. They glide up and around the roof, stopping only where purple curtains drape either side of the window.

Seated opposite him, I clutch my lace gloves around the rose he gave me earlier when he picked me up from Ivory's ball. The flower's perfume entwines with his hookah smoke, stirring a sensual warmth in my lungs. There are eight hours left of my vow to spend the night with him, and we're heading back to his manor now.

"*Every part and parcel of your kingdom will be laid at your feet tonight,*" he told me a few hours ago, before we embarked on this tour. We've already seen so much of Wonderland, my mind is spinning in resplendent ultraviolet hues and bizarre terrains.

He places his hat and gloves on the seat next to him. I feel him watching me as he smokes, but pretend not to notice. Instead, I concentrate on Wonderland's landscapes through the window. The neon colors pass in smears, lit up by the magical blue harnesses attached to the moths propelling us forward.

During my seventeen years of life, I've seen the Red domain enough times—in dreams and in reality—that I know it by memory. But tonight's tour is different, more precious.

Everything in Wonderland was reborn today, painted alive at Jeb's hand. Even my heart is new, held intact by Jeb and Morpheus's combined magic.

As I'm seated with Morpheus in such tight proximity, my heart glows and draws toward his, almost magnetized. It's a breathless, exhilarating sensation—as if starbursts of energy pulse within the muscle.

I have to wonder if Morpheus senses the reaction. If he knows that because of the magical sutures he and Jeb provided, I'm tied to them both on the most profound level. That they feed my every breath.

I suspect he does, and can only hope he isn't going to use it as leverage, because I recognize his quiet meditative state from our childhood. He has a plan simmering in his mind . . . I can feel his wheels turning.

At our last stop, we visited the flower garden outside the rabbit hole's teensy door. With Morpheus's patient coaching, I commanded the wraiths in the soil to reverse their damage. Their wails shattered through me. Their black, inky cyclones raced through my blood before whipping around my clothes. They were obstinate, but obeyed, sensing my royal heritage. They put everything back as Wonderland's gateway was in the beginning, little-boy sundial statue and all. And now the portals into the human realm are fixed, too. Everything is back as it should be.

I'm still half-manic after the experience. One can't dance with nightmares and not be affected. My skin prickles—as if charged with electricity.

"How are you feeling, luv?" Morpheus asks. I turn to meet his gaze, only to catch him studying the purple light behind my sternum. My heart shines bright enough that even when muted by the white satin and miniature crimson rosebuds sewn into the bodice of my dress, it's still visible. His eyes level to mine. "Commanding the wraiths leaves a din that rings in the blood. Is that what has you so quiet?"

I nod. My fingertips stroke the rose's silky petals in a nervous rhythm. Better to let him think he's figured me out. I can't tell him what's really taunting me: the fear that he won't let me live out my days in the human realm with Jeb without a fight.

He can't be happy about it. We'll only have my dreams after this. Tonight will be our first and last night together in reality for many years to come. And that's *if* he decides to wait for me at all. But if he doesn't, I will spend my eternal future trying to win him back.

I swallow the lump of emotion in my throat, struggling to think of something else. Anything else. My need for distraction is answered when I notice we're not headed back to his manor like he said we were.

"Where are you taking me?" I ask. "I thought the tour was over."

Two hurricane-style candelabras are mounted on either side of the window, filled with ultraviolet fireflies. Morpheus's white suit and porcelain skin look almost blue in the light they radiate.

"You keep insisting that you wish to experience all the things Alice didn't in the human realm." Several puffs of smoke float toward me, some shaped like hearts, others like chains. "However, it's just as important that you experience what she *did* whilst she was here."

It's a veiled answer, as clouded as the smoky air between us. I narrow my eyes and an uneasy crimp winds through my stomach that has nothing to do with the candied spider and dandelion wine I indulged in earlier.

"You look pale, blossom." Morpheus waves some smoke away and bends over the picnic basket at my feet. After sifting through its contents, he tucks an amplifying pastry into his front jacket pocket. Then, taking out a clear glass thermos, he fills a teacup for each of us. "Let's have some tea to cleanse the wraiths' residue from your blood. It will be a while yet, till we reach our destination."

The steam smells familiar and comforting, but I've learned to be cautious with what I eat or drink in Wonderland. "What's in it?"

He smirks, that proud glimmer behind his eyes. "You are wise to ask. 'Tis mushroom tea. To truly empathize with Alice's predicament, you must be the size she was."

I study the pocket where he placed the amplifying pastry. "So . . . we're going to shrink?"

"Do you know of a better way to fill her shoes?" He clinks his cup to mine, then puts the rim to his lips.

I take several sips before noticing he's lowered the cup from his mouth without drinking. He watches me, studiously.

I've been duped.

"*Morpheus*," I warn.

He grins.

I'm angry, but not helpless. Even though my muscles jerk and my bones click. Even though every inch of my skin warms and tightens as I grow smaller while Morpheus and the carriage tower around me. I might be the size of a sprite, but after everything I've been through this past year, my netherling side is as strong as my human one.

My wings erupt on instinct. I dart for the amplifying pastry in his pocket so I can return to normal size and clobber him, but Morpheus raises a hand and catches me in a handkerchief, wrapping me inside. I'm blinded and didn't pay close enough attention to my surroundings earlier. I can't remember what's available to use as weapons.

Cheater.

"Reminiscent of when you trapped me in a jar in the human realm, yes?" Morpheus whispers, as if hearing my silent accusation.

Anger boils my neck, face, and ears.

"Sorry, luv." My captor's breath warms the cloth cocooning my body, heating my already simmering nerves. "Can't let you unleash all that beautiful wrath . . . not just yet."

I demand release, struggling to escape the soft folds of licorice-scented fabric, but of course he doesn't listen. Any more than I did when I'd trapped him.

"Turnabout's fair play. Isn't that a saying in your *precious* human realm?" he baits.

Clenching my teeth, I resign myself to wait for an opportunity to escape. My surroundings become snug. That magical magnetic pull calls to my heart and his answering pulse pounds through me like a giant snare drum, confirming he's placed me inside his jacket pocket.

Minutes later, I feel the sway of his body as he disembarks from the carriage. His boot soles shuffle against gritty stone.

He fishes me from his pocket, still wrapped like a mummy. Once the handkerchief loosens, I'm unceremoniously dropped onto something wooden and cool. A stagnant, damp scent surrounds me. I scramble to stand, blinking in the soft blue light given off by the firefly lantern Morpheus brought from the carriage. Hinges squeak but I'm not fast enough, and the cage's door locks before I can flutter through.

I buzz about the tightly barred enclosure, cursing Morpheus and his manipulative mind. The sound of ticking clocks accompanies his subsequent laughter, their combined cacophony loud enough to shake my tiny bones. I plug my ears.

Morpheus's giant face looms close to the hanging cage, the gems beneath his eyes pink with affection. "Welcome to the highest cliffs of Wonderland's wilds, my blossom. Perhaps, if you prove cooperative, you might see them from the outside sometime before the next few decades go by."

I snarl.

He mentioned earlier that he had Jebediah paint scenes from the past that are part of the history we share: the cave Alice was held in, birdcage and all . . . and the cocoon from which he was born anew.

I recognize the dodo's hideaway by the roughly sketched calendar sheets papering the stone walls. Queen Red, upon imprisoning him here as Alice's keeper, warned him if he tried to escape, his days were numbered. As a result, the dodo collected days on paper, so he'd have an ample supply. Ticking clocks hang from dripstones upon the ceilings, in an effort to hoard every minute of every hour.

Which is exactly what Morpheus is planning for me. To hoard

me here for all time against my will, unless I give in to his demands. He's going to bargain another life-magic vow out of me. Something to force me to leave Jeb—so I'll age alone in the mortal realm, without him.

If anyone can manage the perfect wording, Morpheus can.

Growling, I shove a fist through the bars, clipping his nose. "Jerk!"

He laughs and draws back, tapping his nose with his forefinger as if I were nothing but a gnat. "Tsk. Naughty majesty. That's no way to win my favor. I'm the one with the upper hand now, aye? Play nice. You wouldn't wish to repeat the fate of little Alice."

My throat tightens as I envision her as a child at the shadowy bottom of the cage. A few stray apple seeds lie abandoned there, the size of ottomans in proportion to me. A bed made out of a matchbox and bits of fabric huddles in the center. How did Alice survive in these conditions for so many decades? Actually growing old in this dark place? It's no wonder she went mad.

Claustrophobia niggles at me, but I shut it down. "You can't keep me here."

Morpheus slips off his jacket, arranges it across a wooden chair, and nudges the cage so it swings softly. "I can, and I will."

It's too difficult to hover in place while my surroundings pendulate, so I drop to the tiny bed to ride the rocking sway. My heart glows brighter, a reminder of my one bargaining chip. "I have to divide my time between the human realm and here. To live fulfilled lives in both places. For my heart to mend. Ivory said—"

"I'm well aware of your physical limitations, plum," Morpheus interjects. "And I would ne'er risk harming you." He skims a dusty satin drape from a table nearby and shakes it out. "I believe I've proven that tenfold by now. I will sneak you into your other world each and every day. 'Twill be easy to slip past the guards. They're accustomed to my sojourns in and out of the mortal realm. I often carry pet moths with me, in terrariums cloaked with cloth. They prefer to be covered, you see. They're nervous travelers otherwise." I yelp as he drapes the sheet over the cage and ties it around the bottom, sealing me in and cutting off my view of everything.

"We'll live out our days somewhere private," he murmurs. The silhouette of his hand glides across the bars on the other side of the satin. "Somewhere magi-kind friendly. And I guarantee to keep you fulfilled in all the ways that matter."

The sensual implication behind his promise heats my skin to a hot blush. So this is why he waited to bring me here until after I fixed the portals. He's always one step ahead. But not this time.

I've used my powers while blind . . . over a month ago, in a pitch-black gymnasium at school, and again, yesterday, when I was masked with a bloody bag and attacked by a thousand murderous prisoners in AnyElsewhere. It can be done, if I concentrate.

I temper my erratic pulse, trying to remember how everything looked along the cave's ceiling and walls before he covered me.

"You're wrong." I attempt to reason with him, buying time so I can feel things out in my mind. "What's required to fulfill my human heart goes deeper than physical needs. PTA meetings. Cheering for runny-nosed toddlers at soccer games. Helping my kids with homework after school, attending their plays and graduations. Taking care of my parents as they grow old, the way they cared for me when I was young. I'm the only child they have. The only one to step in when they're feeble. Then there's welcoming grandchildren of my own, getting age spots . . . and wrinkles. These are the things cherished human memories are made of."

Morpheus huffs, as if the notions are ridiculous. "You're netherling royalty. In little time, I could make you forget those asinine and boring aspirations."

"Right, by holding me prisoner." I grind my teeth. "There's no such place, you know," I change tactics. "No other sanctuary where netherlings can hole up in the human realm . . . other than Humphrey's Inn. And my parents and Jeb will be looking there for me. They'll never give up."

Morpheus laughs, causing the covering on the cage to flutter. "Do you really think Humphrey's is the only halfway house for netherlings in the mortal realm? There are hideaways only the solitary of our kind know about. Shady and furtive places. There, we can vanish throughout the day and never be found. Then we'll return here to spend our nights." His shadowy outline leans across the cage, arms encircling the bars in a malicious embrace. "And, if you behave, I'll shrink to your size and we can catch that little matchbox bed of yours on fire. *Sans any matches.*" His voice hugs my ears like dark velvet—intimate and carnal. It muffles the clocks that are ticking like time bombs along the ceiling.

Instead of letting his seduction tactics disarm me like they once would've, I use them to my advantage. I allow the suggestive, mellifluous cadence of his words to relax me. And that's all I need to tame my magic.

In my mind's eye, I picture the clocks and their skinny metal hands—tick, tock, turning—left to right, left to right. I imagine their arms bending perpendicular from their flat faces—and the clicking stops short.

Morpheus's surprised gasp indents the sheet. Before he can surmise my plan, I envision the calendar pages peeling from the walls, tearing into quarters, and winding themselves into paper chains—much like the ones I made as a child in preschool crafts. Only these are alive and strong as steel.

I can't see them, but I hear them: dragging along the floor. I animate them to follow the sound of Morpheus's footsteps and his flashes of blue magic as he scrambles around the gritty cave in hopes of escape.

"Dammit, Alyssa!"

"Bind him tight," I command my chains.

Morpheus's snarls and groans confirm their success.

While he's preoccupied, I concentrate on the clocks' hands once more: bending them back and forth, back and forth, until finally they snap off in a metallic rain to the floor. I coax them up, high enough their skinny shadows line the sheet, lit up by the lantern. In my mind, they're a swarm of metallic bees. I focus on them, using their pointy ends like knives, to slice through the cloth and pry open the door.

By the time I flutter out of the cage, Morpheus is pinned to the wall in paper binds, struggling to break free—the proverbial moth in a web. *My web.*

As beautiful as he is when he's alight with power, poise, and potency, there's something undeniably alluring about him captured and at my mercy.

The queen in me purrs.

Leisurely, I fly to the chair where he laid his jacket and search his pocket for the amplifying pastry. After several bites, I return to my natural size and alight on the floor to face him.

At my command, the chains tighten around his chest and arms.

Yes, this scene is familiar. Except last time, I coaxed Red's vines from within me to hold him prisoner.

"You said you liked to play rough," I taunt.

"I can give as good as I get." He stares at me, unflinching. "Should I so choose," he adds, and ignites his magic enough to slice through the chains on one wrist—sure proof that he could cut them all loose if he wanted. Yet he doesn't. His eye patches glitter in prismatic disarray, hiding whatever it is he's feeling.

"Well, I'm in no mood to play anyway," I answer, angry I can't read him. Or maybe I'm flustered that he doesn't break free and fight back . . . that there's no teasing twitch at his lips or yellow flash through his jeweled markings. "Tell me why I shouldn't drag you to court. Holding the queen hostage is treason."

He growls. Long strands of unruly enchanted blue hair slap across his chin and tease out a grimace. "You're under a vow to spend twelve hours with me. Back out now, and lose all those pretty powers you so love to flaunt."

I force a smile. "Oh, I'm not abandoning my vow. I'll sit with you in the dungeon for our remaining eight hours while you wait to be sentenced."

He grunts. "For your information, I wasn't hungry . . . nor was I small."

I tilt my head. "What are you babbling about?"

Sighing, he looks down at the chains clamped around his chest. "If I hadn't wanted you to triumph, I would ne'er have put the pastry in my pocket and brought it in. It certainly wasn't for *me*."

His logic rings true. I command the chains to release him. They gather in a limp, snaky pile at his feet.

He stays pressed against the wall as if held in place by the imprints left upon his skin. His wings splay out behind him—majestic and proud—his only cushion against the stone.

I step up to him. "You've always claimed to have faith in me," I press, sympathy and frustration twisting my insides to a perplexed pretzel. "So why do I have to keep walking over coals for you?"

He frowns, managing to look both apologetic and haughty at the same time. "I *had* to trap you. To remind you of your better half. You want so much to be Alice . . . the Alice *that could've been*. I fear you'll become her in every way. Helpless. Human. Unless you keep your guard up. You must never be a victim like she was. I saw you almost die yesterday. Your heart splitting in twain." His chin trembles. "I can ne'er face that again. So I will let you go for your own sake, to fulfill your mundane human expectations. At least, since you're visiting me in dreams each night, I'm fairly certain you won't forget us like you did as a child."

His accusation scores through me. "I didn't mean to. I was so little . . ."

"I'm not *blaming* you, Alyssa. It was unavoidable. You would not have been the same person, capable of compassion and imagination, without those uninterrupted human experiences. You couldn't have functioned in the mortal world and learned what you needed to if you were constantly yearning to stir up trouble with me in Wonderland. After seeing the destruction that Red's single-minded cruelty and lack of compassion had wrought, I knew something had to change in the royal bloodline."

"Even if it took you stepping back to make it happen." Once again, I'm floored by the scope of his machinations. By his love for our world. I slide my hand along the buttons of his shirt. "All you need to know now is that I will never forget you again, or my feelings for you. *Never.* Even if I weren't spending my dreams in Wonderland." My fingers stop at the satiny fabric over his heartbeat.

His lashes flutter closed. He presses his hand over mine. "I need to know more than that. You must survive each day we aren't together, so you can come back—come back to take your place upon the Red throne in reality, forever. I need that assurance, or I can't . . . *won't* . . . let you out of my sight."

"I'm immortal. I have crown magic in my blood."

His lashes lift and he meets my gaze. "As indicated by your vulnerable heart, your body is not indestructible. Especially in the mortal realm. You will age there. And if your shell is destroyed or dies, your eternal spirit will be left an orphan. Unless you can find a new vessel, it will wither away. A netherling spirit cannot exist for more than a few hours without being housed within a body, or tucked safely within the cemetery, tended by Sister One or Sister Two's magic. So do not make me find a new home for your life essence. You must come back to this world, *whole.* Yourself, in every way."

Even without his gems revealing his moods, I see it so clearly: the raw vulnerability he's been hiding behind smoke and illusion all night. There's so much more he's afraid of losing than Wonderland's Red Queen. His childhood friend, his future bride . . . their dream-child. These are the fears that cast shadows behind his plea.

"I promised you once that I would come back to you," I assure him. "Trust in that. In my strength. You've taught me well. Will you ever be convinced I'm worthy of your faith? Worthy enough to stop testing me?"

"I've always had faith in you, blossom. It's putting the *future* in someone's hands other than my own that I'm having difficulty with.

But I will try." He draws me into a hug, his fingers bunching inside the long strands of hair at my nape. "No more tricks tonight."

I snuggle against his chest, dragging in a breath to saturate myself in his scent. My heart tugs toward him, a powerful, invigorating hum behind my sternum.

"You win." His muffled admission stirs the hair at the top of my head, so quiet I almost don't hear it.

My pulse jumps. *I win.* After all these years, I finally bettered my playmate on his own turf. But any gratification eludes me, because I also left him a little broken.

There's no satisfaction in tonight's victory. It's never been about my being stronger or more manipulative than him . . . it was about making him happy and proud by proving I was his equal. It was about wanting to see him smile. The way he did when we were children—carefree, and unkempt.

Only I'd forgotten that, until just now.

❧ · I · ❦

MEMORY THREE: IN WHICH I HEALED WONDERLAND

The damp incense of fungus mingles with an earthy, grassy scent. Mushrooms loom overhead, their caps the size of truck tires. I half flutter, half run behind Morpheus through the tall, fluorescent grass. My dress's long skirt snags on the grass in intervals, eliciting tiny popping sounds. But that's the only thing I hear. Wonderland is quiet tonight, due to almost all the citizens attending the ball at Ivory's.

Morpheus is pensive and quiet. His wings drape from his

shoulders at the back of his jacket, his stride long and purposeful. I'm having trouble keeping up, even though I clear the ground every four steps or so. Other than assuring me the tricks were behind us, he's barely spoken since we left the dodo's cave. He didn't tell me where we were going, but I already knew.

Since we'd visited Alice's prison, we had to visit his next. Our tour wouldn't be complete without stopping here. This is the last place he saw young Alice, the last place she was free before the card guards captured her. The place where the Caterpillar once sat to offer advice and friendship, and where Chessie's decapitated head floated by, just as Alice found the Caterpillar mummified in a cocoon, unable to help her as he transformed into a beautiful, alluring humanoid fae.

That particular winged man would not be fully formed and free to help her until seventy-five years later, after she'd already lost her mind to age and madness. He's never forgiven himself for being absent when Alice needed him most.

"You know now . . . that it wasn't your fault. Right?" My question carries over the swish of grass under his feet.

He doesn't answer, but I'm not giving up. He needs to let go of the guilt.

"It was Red's plan all along. She was in my body, in my head. I saw what she kept hidden. She had a vision, back when she still wore the crown. It told her that Alice was the key to everything. That an immortal dream-child would be born through Red's lineage if she trapped Alice Liddell and lived her human life. Red would've made it happen—even if you'd been free to offer Alice help. She was so determined, she made herself forget how to be merciful. That's something you can't be responsible for. I won't have you blaming yourself. Not another day."

Morpheus's steps grow slower. "Thank you, blossom. I needed to hear that. But you are mistaken. That isn't the guilt I'm battling."

He stops, his back to me, wings drooping.

"I don't understand," I say, stalled a few feet behind. I give him space even though I want to touch him, to turn him so I can read his face.

"I brought you into this, just like your mum accused. I never gave you a choice. I put everything into motion—causing you to release Red from the cemetery to save *my* spirit from being imprisoned. Wonderland fell to rot and you nearly died. And I let you take the blame for it all, whilst knowing that I was the catalyst."

My jaw drops. I did *not* just hear an actual confession. Not from him. Did I?

Stepping up between his wings, I wrap my arms around his torso and press my cheek to his back, seeking the echo of his heartbeat with my palms. "You weren't the catalyst. Red was. And I made mistakes, too. I failed to follow your instructions for my wish."

"But you were driven by compassion, and a desire to save another. It's innate in you."

"It's innate in you, too. You saved my dad's life. Twice. Kept Jeb out of the hands of the prisoners for a month. And chose not to crown me and strip away my humanity. All those things took compassion. You forgave my mistakes, so I forgive yours. We start fresh from here."

"How?" he asks, and I'm touched by the sincere bewilderment in his voice.

I hold him closer. "An old childhood playmate once told me: 'Second-guessing every step prevents any forward momentum. Trust yourself, forgive yourself, and move on.'"

His wings lift on either side of me, as if they weigh less. His hands find mine where they're laced at his chest. "Your playmate sounds wise. And handsome, too." There's a smile in the statement.

I muffle a laugh against the back muscles twitching under his jacket. "Oh, he is. And humble. Humility is his *best* quality."

He snorts softly, then breaks our embrace and secures my gloved palm in his as he leads me just a few more steps, where the mushrooms' dense growth patterns form a dead end. I know what to expect even before we step inside. Still, I gasp when I see it in the phosphorescent moonlight: a mushroom bigger than a garden shed, half-cloaked in a webby cocoon.

Morpheus watches my reaction. Nostalgia flashes through his expressive gems—along with regret and then tranquility.

I'm hoping I had a hand in that last emotion.

We step up to the mushroom together. The air chills as the shadow envelops us, cutting off the starlight overhead.

"Why did it happen?" I ask, looking at the giant cap. "What made you change from the Caterpillar?"

"It was simply time. Time for me to take my most immaculate form. The one I would wear for all eternity. There were things I needed to do that couldn't be accomplished in my inferior form. We each have a gradual metamorphosis. You've been going through yours your entire life thus far. You're still not quite there. But one day, you will be complete at last. You will shed your mortality to be the queen Wonderland needs. And then you will have nowhere left to belong but *here*."

I swallow hard, because the thought is both inspiring and wondrous. "What was it like for you? Being trapped inside a cocoon for seventy-five years? Was it lonely?"

His profile smiles. "Surely you jest. I had Wonderland's most fascinating and charming netherling to keep me company."

I laugh. "Like I said, humble."

The amused expression on his face grows grim. "It wasn't company I missed. It was my magic and Wonderland's landscapes. Being without them. It was torment . . ."

His voice trails. Of course. He's a solitary fae. Their one true companion—their passion—is Wonderland itself. I think of how he acted after we escaped AnyElsewhere and finally found our way back here. How he stood in the middle of the frozen tulgey wood, wings arced high, and used his blue lightning to shake down tufts of snow from the branches. How he laughed and danced in the downpour. He was carefree and playful, drunk on magic after having been without it so long. And that was after only a month. I can't imagine how it would be after decades.

"I wonder if it was different for Red," I conjecture aloud. "She did the same thing, in a way. Gave up her magic for Alice's imprint. Lived years and years in the human realm without her powers . . . grew old—" I cut my words short, seeing how intently he's watching me in the moonlight. "Would you be happy?" I ask before he can admit what he's thinking. It's incredible how I can read him now. "Living out your life with Finley's imprint. Aging under his visage in the human realm. Because you wouldn't be able to use your magic if you wore an imprint."

Morpheus's jaw twitches. "Perhaps I could learn to tolerate it."

"*Tolerating* a future with me. There is nothing romantic or fulfilling about that scenario." I place a hand on his arm. "Remember what I told you earlier in the dodo's cave . . . about the experiences mortality has to offer?"

His eyes meet mine, but hard as he tries, he can't hide the sickly green flash to his jeweled markings. He looks away, nose crinkled. "Ugh. I remember how pathetically pedestrian they are."

I nod. "To you, yes. You're not made for that life. You're meant to be eternally young . . . free to soar in the skies here in Wonderland. To watch over the world you love. I don't want you faking it every day for me. It would be another prison, just like your cocoon. Another span of decades without the madness and magic that make you know you're alive. But me? Ever since I was a child, I've aspired to have those *pedestrian* experiences. It's hardwired to my genetic makeup. And Jeb's—"

Morpheus's snarl cuts me off. "Of course. *Jebediah*. He would certainly appreciate such a life, being a simpleton."

"Being a *human*," I correct, moving my hand from the bicep that's now stiff with tension. "For mortals, those things are sacred. It's innate in us, the desire to grow old with someone we love. To share the simple things along the journey, to cherish each one as the treasure it is. My mom missed out on so much of that with my dad. But they have a second chance now. They can still have some of it. Poor Alice didn't have *any* chances. No one to love and grow old with. She aged alone in a cage with a dodo bird as her only companion. That was a tragedy. A wasted human life. All she had were sad fantasies of what might've been. Jeb deserves better than that. He deserves something real. So do *you*. And I do, too. No more pretending. Not between the three of us."

There's a moment of silence. Then Morpheus sighs. "When did you get so wise, little truffle?"

I fight the sting of tears in my eyes. "You already know. You had a hand in that journey."

He shakes his head. "My offer still stands to hide you somewhere.

I can protect you from the mortals. They are destined to break your heart in ways I never could." The words are sincere, his voice deep and gruff, as if it's already happened and he's hurting for me.

"Jeb would never—"

"When he dies one day, he will. Your parents will, too. And anyone else you might outlive."

My throat swells. If I'm not careful, I'll lose the battle against crying. "Yes, it's going to be painful."

"I don't think you realize how much."

I stand firm. "The experience will make me stronger . . . a better queen." I've already faced this fear in my mind. I've accepted that it's the tragic trade-off for living a full human life. "My heart's unbreakable now," I add, just loud enough for Morpheus to hear. I hold my hand over the glow behind my sternum. "You and Jeb saw to that."

"I suppose we did," Morpheus answers. "He and I outsmarted magic."

Though his statement is soft and smooth as silk, the unspoken echo—"*And now there's a price to be paid*"—razes through me like a serrated knife.

Jeb paid his price, losing his dreams and artistic muse forever. And now Morpheus is paying his.

Silent once more, he wraps his fingers around my free hand. Together, we fly up to the mushroom's cap and perch on the half that isn't cloaked in gauzy threads.

Considering he sliced his way out of the cocoon decades earlier, I'm shocked to see the gauzy blanket move like a living, breathing thing. There's something the size of a rottweiler inside making snoring sounds.

I flap my wings nervously, but Morpheus holds me in place.

Frowning, I turn to him. "You said no more tricks tonight," I accuse.

"This isn't a trick. 'Tis a gift. Although it is a bit *tricky*, in that it's dangerous in the wrong hands."

The hairs on my neck stand up. "Dangerous?"

"*Feral.* That's a better description."

I inch toward the mushroom's edge to escape.

He catches my wrist and stops me. "Tut, be brave. You are a Red Queen. You've nothing to fear of the creatures of this world. In fact, this particular creature will be loyal and devoted only to you. We're going to see to that right now. It is the rest of Wonderland who needs to be wary after tonight. So . . ."

"So?"

"This gift was no easy feat to wrap. At least give me the pleasure of watching you open it." He draws a shimmery silver blade as small as a fillet knife from his jacket and offers it on his outstretched palm.

The vorpal sword. The most magical weapon in all of Wonderland.

I pause. "This is mine now?"

He laughs. "Absolutely not. The vorpal sword will always belong to me. I worked hard for it."

I scowl at him.

Grinning sheepishly, he clears his throat. "Well, with some help from you, of course. 'Tis why I'm willing to let you borrow it on special occasions."

"That's grand of you." I wrinkle my nose at him playfully, then take the sword. Just as I remember, the handle feels warm even through my gloves. Everywhere I touch, glowing blue prints appear on the silver metal. I prepare to slice through the thick white web.

Morpheus stalls me with a fingertip at my elbow. "Be sure to step back the moment it's free, luv."

I squint. "Seriously?"

"It will be fine. Their kind awakens rather slowly."

Their kind. My stomach knots. Fingers trembling, I slice through the sticky webbing. A sparkle of magic chases the cutting motions as the cocoon peels open. A stench, ten times worse than rotten cabbage, drifts out. Covering my nose, I step back and return the vorpal sword to Morpheus's waiting hand.

Both sides of the cocoon fall apart to reveal a snoozing dog-size creature with a rhino's gray hide. Its triangular, feline head snuggles between scaled forepaws. I recognize what it is, although I've never seen one smaller than a freight car. It must be a baby. A really *big* baby. I gulp.

"Queen Alyssa," Morpheus says in a low voice. "Meet your royal pet, the bandersnatch."

I stare, gaping.

"Remember," Morpheus continues, "I once told you Grenadine had the word the original bandersnatch was trained to obey. It was a command passed down in the Red Kingdom from queen to queen. But she couldn't remember it, and lost the ribbon that held that secret. It's moot now anyway, since the royal bandersnatch died at my hand. So tonight, it is up to you to start a new legacy."

I don't even have time to respond before the creature's milky white eyes snap open. It snarls, exposing fangs like a reptilian saber-toothed tiger. In one blink, three tongues lash out. At the ends of each appendage, a snakelike face opens toothless jaws and hisses, like eels.

I dart toward the mushroom's edge, too late. One tongue captures my ankle and I'm left dangling upside down, some ten feet from the ground, my skirt ballooning around my head and all the blood rushing into my skull. The creature's drool oozes from my shin to my thigh.

"Morpheus!" I screech, furious he's already beneath me standing on the grass, safely out of reach of the creature.

The noose on my ankle tightens and I feel my body being dragged upward toward the snarling bandersnatch pup. I wriggle.

"Morpheus, get me out of this!"

"Get yourself out. It's imperative *you* do it. Cut yourself free." He uses his blue magic to guide the vorpal sword up to me.

I snag the blade's handle but pause. The second I'm loose, I'll descend headfirst to the ground. There's not enough distance for my wings to slow the fall.

"Oh, get on with it," Morpheus scolds, impatient. "You bloody well know I'll catch you. Why else would I be standing down here?"

"Well," I grump, "my first guess is so you can see up my dress."

"I'll admit, the view is spectacular. But that's merely a happy coincidence."

"As if anything with you is ever a coincidence."

His smug chuckle grinds through me.

Snarling, I sever the tongue with one clean cut. The bandersnatch yelps and I regret having to hurt him.

My stomach flips as I fall, but Morpheus catches me, just as promised.

"Well done," he says like he has so many times throughout my life. He cradles me close.

I tighten my arms around the nape of his neck, my head snuggled under his chin, reluctant to let him go. He squeezes me against his warm chest, as if he shares my hesitation. Then he sets me down. Without explanation, he flies up to the cap where the bandersnatch warm chest, as if he shares my hesitation. Then he sets me down. Without explanation, he flies up to the cap where the bandersnatch is bellowing. Soon, the creature grows quiet.

I stare at the beast's severed tongue. It flops on the ground beside me as if alive, hissing—strange sounds like whispers—as it slithers ever closer. I back up a few steps.

Morpheus returns from atop the mushroom, picks up the vorpal sword I dropped, and wipes blood and sparkling magic from the blade before slipping it into his jacket pocket.

"What did you do with the bandersnatch?" I ask.

"I put him back to sleep for the journey to your castle. When he wakes, he'll be healing and ill-tempered, so we will need to have him confined."

"Healing? How? The bandersnatch's hide is indestructible, not its tongues."

"True. However, they're regenerative if they're cut with the vorpal sword. It will grow back. And the severed tongue"—he glances down at the bloody detached piece, which has found its way to the tip of my boot—"becomes an extension of the beast's spirit."

The oozing, slimy appendage pats my toe, making sucking sounds, like a plant searching for a place to root. The whispers it emits become louder, but still impossible to decipher. I shudder and prepare to kick it away.

"No. Pick it up," Morpheus insists.

I shudder again.

"Since when have you been squeamish, my fair assassin of bugs, flowers, and mutated prisoners?" Morpheus teases.

"Since I saw the damage those tongues can do. When they

carried you away to what I thought was your death." Remembering how horrible it was to watch him be swallowed alive stings my chest and my eyes.

Morpheus smiles gently, obviously pleased I'm still affected by his sacrifice over a year ago. "You want I should have faith in you. Then show me the same courtesy. That tongue retains the most integral part of the bandersnatch. Each of these creatures has something unique to them alone. Something that soothes them. They're born with it. Take off your gloves and hold the tongue in your hand—flesh to flesh. Let it impart the wisdom. Thus, you'll know the word which will tame it, in its own language. It's a form of Deathspeak, but because you spared the beast's life and took only its tongue, it doesn't bind you to the bandersnatch's command. Instead, it binds the beast to *yours*."

Pressing my lips together, I do as he says. The moment my bare skin touches the squishy, warm tongue, the whispers rush through me, lighting my skin for an instant, then fading. The tongue withers to a black, dried thing, and I toss it down.

The word spins inside me . . . in a language I've never heard. Yet I know exactly how to articulate it.

I start to speak it aloud but Morpheus touches a finger to my lips. "Never tell anyone the word. You'll only pass it down to another Red Queen, should one succeed you some day. Not even your king can know it."

He crouches to pick up my gloves. I seek the courage to ask him if that king will be him. If he's going to wait for me. But I have no right to expect him to make such a sacrifice, so I bite my lip instead.

"We need to go," he says. "We'll drop the bandersnatch at the

Red castle. You should set things to rights there before spending the night at my manor. Starting tomorrow, when you visit in your dreamscapes, I'll show you how to train the beastly pup to obey your secret word. As he grows, he will learn to respond to your call."

Morpheus binds the bandersnatch in a net of blue magic and levitates it down from the mushroom, then drags it behind us as we head back to the carriage.

"One last thing, Alyssa." The words drift from over his shoulder. "I brought you to Alice's haunts because Jebediah didn't share them with you. They belong to me and you alone. Part of our history, part of how we came together. And they will be here waiting, when you return to live reality here in Wonderland. *When*. I'm taking you at your word. Be the one soul who doesn't let me down. That is all I ask. For now."

JUBILATION

The memories worked like a charm. There aren't any clocks in the royal bedroom. It doesn't matter, since time is irrelevant in Wonderland. But it feels like it's been hours since the baby was born.

The moment I heard his melodious cry and held his tiny, warm body, all of the pain, all of the fears, all of the sadness I'd been battling melted away. And Morpheus wasted no time ushering our helpful but noisy entourage out the door so we could be alone, just the three of us.

After I nursed the baby, I showed my king how to swaddle him in a blanket and hold him. At first, Morpheus held his arms rigid like a shelf, as if he feared our child was breakable. To see someone as powerful and confident as Morpheus leveled to helplessness by a wriggling bundle of wings, arms, and legs was both endearing and poignant. But with a little gentle coaching, he was soon nuzzling and cooing to his son like a pro. Once the baby had relaxed in Morpheus's arms, he started to leave him in the cradle, but changed his mind and laid the prince gently next to me in the bed, settling himself on the other side with our son safely penned between us.

Talking to our prince in sweet and honeyed tones, Morpheus drizzled strands of blue light from his fingertips and called upon the moths in some opened terrariums across the room. The moment the bugs fluttered around us, Morpheus connected them to his magic. Guided by their enchanted harnesses, the moths flew in a circle, like a baby mobile.

Morpheus's expression became dreamy, his face and the baby's both glowing from the magical mobile lights. Our prince watched, his bright blue eyes dancing and his teensy wings trying to flutter inside the blanket that swaddled him. One day, he would have his father's jeweled markings around his lower lashes and along his cheeks. For now, the intricate tracery of lines appeared more faded—like veins beneath the skin. He did have one patch of color on his left wrist, though, where his netherling birthmark coiled, visible and prominent.

"Do you see that?" Morpheus asked me, catching the baby's tiny hand in one of his as our prince tried to reach for a moth with his own blue magic while cooing contentedly. "His pinky . . . it's the size of my thumbnail." Morpheus focused on me—those unfathomable eyes filled with enough love and wonder to breach the depths of my being. "And he has your nose. Look, see how it's crinkled? He's frustrated because I won't let him catch the moth. You do that when I'm challenging you."

I laughed. "No I don't!"

Morpheus grinned. "You've done it ever since we were children together. You're doing it now."

I wriggled my nose. He was right, as per usual. I sighed, but as much as I wanted the puff of air to sound irritable, it came out as a purr of pure contentment.

"How is it possible?" my king asked. "That he's so little, yet so profoundly, perfectly formed?"

"Because he's a part of you," I responded without even thinking.

Morpheus held my gaze. "And the other part you. You're right. How could he be anything *but* perfect?"

Teary, I smiled and counted the baby's fingers for the hundredth time, entranced by the blue sparks already brewing at their tips. "I never expected his magic to have a color," I conjectured aloud. "Mine doesn't. And he's a half-blood, like me."

Morpheus rested his cheek on his pillow, eyelids growing heavy. "Not like you, blossom. Both of his parents have magic."

I quietly studied the baby's hands, curious if he'd ever be able to take another form like his father, and wondering over the chaos he'd soon wreak upon this castle and its occupants. Raising a fairy child blessed with imagination was going to keep us all busy, to say the least.

As soon as our son fell asleep, so did Morpheus and I—exhausted from the night's events.

Now I'm awake, and in the soft amber glow of the candlelight, I study them: my prince, and my king, lying side by side next to me. My throat catches at their beauty, and my heart brims with love. They have the same pout when they sleep . . . that mischievous turn to their lips softened to an angelic expression and shaped by fragile tremors of breath.

As if sensing me watching him, Morpheus's fathomless eyes open. I brush back a strand of hair from his face. He catches my palm and kisses it.

"It took a while to get here," he murmurs against my scars, his voice rough with sleep.

By *here*, I'm not sure if he means the birth, or the two of us.

"Thank you for your unfathomable patience," I respond, because either way, it's the answer he deserves. I caress our prince's plump elbow with my free hand, memorizing his cherubic face. Though his eyes are shaped like his father's, they're colored like mine. And I can see myself in other places . . . in the dimple on his chin, his button nose, and the platinum blond tips frosting the ends of his long, dark lashes. "Good things come to those who wait."

Morpheus releases me and stretches, his powerful wings fluttering on the other side of him. "The *best* things. Impossible things. Most impossible of all is a lone creature, who never once needed another living soul, having a family he would die and kill for."

Still studying the baby, my face flushes. The possessive resolve in Morpheus's confession comes from a place so deep inside, it must've gored his heart to say it. It's obvious he's awed by being capable of such a love.

"We haven't decided on a name yet," I whisper to hide how touched I am by this rare glimpse of his frailties. I refuse to embarrass him. Tomorrow we'll be presenting our son to the kingdom, which makes for the perfect segue. "I don't think *Trouble* is a name befitting the prince who's going to make our world a better place."

Morpheus nods sagely, but there's a wicked glint in his eyes. "Yes, we wouldn't wish to risk a self-fulfilling prophecy. Can't have him too much like his old man."

I smirk, although I'm going do everything I can to assure our son *will* be like Morpheus—as fierce and unpredictable and chaotic as all the varied landscapes of Wonderland that we'll one day share with him. "Should we look through your list again?"

We spent the afternoon yesterday sorting through the options as we had so often before: Argon, Durian, Iseld, Rhyanon . . . and so many more I can't even recall. Each one was lyrical and powerful, and ideal for a fairy prince, yet nothing seemed to capture all that he would someday be.

"Only one will do, now that I've seen him." Morpheus strokes the blue, downy tufts on our son's head. In time, he'll have a full head of luminous hair like his daddy's. "*Muse*."

I consider the name. It wasn't on the list, but as I study the baby's flawless features, I can't deny it fits. My muse led me into this world in the first place, then gave me the power to rule it; Jeb's muse repainted Wonderland so many years ago, then stayed here to bring peace between two realms. Even though Morpheus would never admit it aloud, this is his way of honoring Jeb's contribution, my other side, and human flights of fancy. The sentiment affects me deeply, warms me all the way from my wing tips to my toes, and I'm grateful beyond words.

But there's one more thing that makes this name fitting above all else: This baby is our dream-child, destined to inspire the imagination of the creatures in the nether-realm, a gift that will bring eternal balance to our kingdom.

I smile, big enough it strains my face. "*Muse*, first prince of the Red Court. I love it." I tear my gaze from the baby—as difficult as it is to look away—because I want to see my king's expression.

My effort is rewarded. He's happy and proud; carefree and

unkempt; most of all, smiling. A beaming smile, just like he used to flash as a child. After all this time, he's young at heart again.

I can't resist, and catch him by his nightshirt to pull his face close for a kiss. "Do you realize?" I ask against his savory lips, overwhelmed by so many emotions I have to struggle to stay afloat. "He'll have the same initial as you: *M*." The teasing statement barely leaves my tongue before I'm giggling.

Morpheus laughs, too, deep and soft. He clamps a hand over his mouth when our son begins to squirm, long-lashed eyes struggling to open.

"*Shhhh*, go back to your dreams, little one." Still smiling, I cuddle Muse's body to mine, nuzzle his head, and inhale his baby scent. Triggered by my senses, I'm reminded of other babies I once welcomed into my arms—each precious birth preserved like a fossil within the amber tinge of distant memory. It makes me happy just to glance upon them now, knowing that I had a hand in their lives, if only for a fleeting moment. Knowing that in this world, I'll never be separated by death from Muse or Morpheus, or the netherling creatures that I've come to love like family.

"Where are you, Alyssa?" Morpheus asks in a breathy voice, stroking my braided hair. "Reminiscing?"

I lean my cheek into his palm. "I'm here with you. Always with you. And our prince." Tilting my face, I whisper into the baby's tiny ear. "I intend to see that you never have to learn the word *good-bye*." He snuggles close, and my heart fills with so much adoration I could burst. I turn my teary eyes to Morpheus, who's watching us both reverently. "I think your son wants you to sing to him."

My king trails the skin around my eyes with a fingertip. "I think *you* do. You're spoiled to my lullabies."

"I am," I say, and wriggle my nose for emphasis.

He beams once more, his jeweled markings sparkling pink and purple. "Good. I can't be the only diva in this relationship. It is far too exhausting."

And with that, he drapes a long, satiny wing over me and Muse, sheltering our family from the world as he sings a new song with new words—a tribute to all things mad, wild, and beautiful.

An anthem to our beloved and eternal Wonderland.

ACKNOWLEDGMENTS

As always, gratitude to my husband and kids for turning a blind eye to dusty furniture, mountains of laundry, and TV dinners when deadlines loom, and to my Agent Goddess, Jenny Bent, whose business savvy, diplomacy, and faith in her clients know no bounds.

Thank you to my Abrams family: Tamar Brazis, Nicole Sclama, Anne Heltzel, and countless copyeditors and proofreaders, for helping me polish each diamond in the rough until it sparkles. Also, gratitude to Jason Wells and Nicole Russo, my in-house publicists; the printing-press specialists who oversee the pages and special effects; and the marketing advisors and everyone who plays a part behind the scenes in the making of the books.

Appreciation to Maria Middleton, who always finds the perfect artistic themes for my books—both inside and out—and to Nathália Suellen, for providing the enchanted artistry that has brought my characters to life on the series covers.

Heartfelt thanks to every indie bookstore and bookseller, along with a fabulous community of online bloggers, who have put my books on countless readers' radar.

Cheers to my local crit group, the Divas: Linda Castillo, Jennifer Archer, Marcy McKay, and April Redmon, for lending keen eyes, sharp minds, and listening ears to my projects. Thank you for teaching me how to be humble yet fierce during edits.

Hugs to my online critters and beta readers: Rookie (aka Bethany Crandell), the White Chocolate to my Godiva Dark; POM (aka Jessica Nelson), who loves cookie dough and bad boys almost as much as me; Stacee (aka @book_junkee), for being a most EPIC cheerleader; Owly (aka Ashlee Supringer), for adding in-depth insights into my characters and plots; Marlene Ruggles, my unpaid copyeditor; and Chris Lapel, my number-one fan.

Affectionate head butts to my #Goatposse, who are wiser and funnier than the average domesticated ruminant animal. Also, a holla to the WrAHM girls.

High fives to the twitter Splintered RP players: @SplinteredCrew, @LongLiveTheMuse, @AlyssaPaints, @PunkPrincessJen, @seductive_fae, @MorphTheMoth, @NetherlingQueen, @splinteredivory, @tyedribbions, @RabbitNotBeMe, @taelor_tremont, and @Chevy LovingJock, for bringing my characters out to play in the real world, and keeping the madness alive.

My respect and awe to the talented fans who send artwork for my

Pinterest board and write incredible fan fiction, and to the readers who follow/chat with me via Goodreads, Tumblr, Pinterest, and Twitter.

A shout-out to all my Facebook supporters, with special thanks to Saleana Rae Carneiro, Katie Clifton, and Diane Marie Hinds (and a hat tip to Harley Liddell and P Cat Moonchild)—the frabjous administrators on my Facebook fan page, who keep the peace and step on fires so I don't have to get my hands dirty or singe my toes. And to Heather Love King (my Pinterest pal) and Elexis Darden, for talking up my books online every chance you get. Consider this an IOU for a hug when we meet one day in person.

Thanks to Jaime and Rachel at RockStar Book Tours for mastering the blog-tour ropes and being so supportive and generous with their time.

An eternal debt of gratitude to Lewis Carroll and Tim Burton for inspiring me to believe in the magic of Wonderland, and to sample it for myself.

And most importantly, gratefulness to the One who gives me the ability to write and the opportunity to do what I love every day.

ABOUT THE AUTHOR

New York Times bestselling novelist A. G. Howard started writing the Splintered series while working at a school library. She always wondered what would've happened had the subtle creepiness of *Alice's Adventures in Wonderland* taken center stage, and she hopes her darker and funkier tribute to Carroll will inspire readers to seek out the stories that won her heart as a child. She lives in Amarillo, Texas.